# TERRY AND
# THE PIRATES

# JULIAN F. THOMPSON

# TERRY AND THE PIRATES

**SIMON PULSE**

New York  London  Toronto  Sydney  Singapore

First Simon Pulse edition May 2002

Text copyright © 2000 by Julian F. Thompson
Photograph copyright © 2000 by Russell Gordon

SIMON PULSE
An imprint of Simon & Schuster
Children's Publishing Division
1230 Avenue of the Americas
New York, NY 10020

Also available in an Atheneum Books for Young Readers
hardcover edition.
Designed by Angela Carlino
The text of this book was set in Minion.

Printed in the United States of America
2  4  6  8  10  9  7  5  3  1

The Library of Congress has cataloged the hardcover edition
as follows:
Thompson, Julian F.
Terry and the pirates / by Julian F. Thompson
p. cm.
Summary: When sixteen-year-old Terry Talley stows away on a yacht,
she doesn't expect to encounter another runaway and end up
shipwrecked on a tiny island with a bunch of oddball pirates who are
looking for some buried treasure.
ISBN 0-689-83076-9 (hc)
[1. Pirates—Fiction.  2. Buried treasure—Fiction.  3. Islands—Fiction.]
I. Title.
PZ7.T371596 Te 2000
[Fic]—dc21 99-086218
ISBN 0-689-85085-9 (pbk)

*For Polly and for Reggie, raiders of my heart.*

# chapter 1

Teresa Fremont Talley, more often known as Tee or Terry, was sixteen years and eight months old the day she polished off her junior year at Cape Enid High School.

At about 8:15 P.M. nine days later, she pretty much decided that the time had come for her to change her life dramatically, to stow away aboard the *Cormorant*, a thirty-four-foot yawl, and by so doing to sample "life" as an adult, some distance from the town that she'd grown up in.

For more than two years, Terry Talley'd been in love with a man named Kirt Manwaring, who was a catcher on the San Francisco Giants baseball team.

Not being tolerant of ridicule, she'd never told a soul, however.

What drew her to him was his name, of course: *Kirt Manwaring*. She came upon it in the paper, underneath a photograph of two men, baseball players, colliding near home plate. Up until then, she'd never had much interest in the paper's sports section, but that photo caught her eye and held it.

One man, whose name had no effect on her whatever, was sailing through the air, about to do an awful belly flop, apparently. The caption said the other one was Kirt Manwaring. Crouching low, with the baseball in his hand, he'd caused the first man to go airborne by knocking his legs out from under him. You couldn't see his face, but Terry didn't have to, once she'd read his name. She knew he had to be good-looking. Also powerful, but gentle; a champion, yet humble; supersensitive, although robustly masculine.

Terry wasn't counting on the *Cormorant* to sail around the Cape, or through the Panama Canal, and up the other coast to San Francisco. Although she was in love with him, she didn't plan on ever meeting Kirt Manwaring. She didn't fantasize a life with him, or even an orgasmic, blush-all-over half an hour. She pitied girls who said they couldn't get their minds off Eddie-this, or Johnny-that, or Antonio-the-other-thing. No, Kirt Manwaring was different.

He filled a role she'd needed somebody to play: He set the standard. She would *never,* she decided, be the girlfriend of a boy who didn't measure up to him.

That didn't mean she didn't date—go out with many different boys—or check out the members of that other gender in the halls of ol' Cape Enid High. She did, she did. But no one she saw, or met, or chastely cuddled with seemed fit to even carry K. M.'s chest protector, shin guards, mask, or other catcherly deflectors.

In and of itself, that might have been sufficient reason for her to sneak on board the *Cormorant:* the total lack of Kirt Manwaringness in what her mother called "your age group." But there was more, much more.

Maitland St. Ansgar Crane was thirty-six years old and the owner of the *Cormorant,* as well as many other playthings. In the paper he was sometimes labeled "an adventurer." He was a mountain climber, race-car driver, and a single-handed sailor on a lot of different seas.

Out of his earliest adventures, at the age of twenty-one, was a marriage to a woman whose name he wished he could forget. It (or, as he often put it, "she") had caused him to become the father of a boy he didn't have much use for.

Though he'd surely noticed Terry Talley's bright red hair at the Cape Enid Club, he had no interest in the girl's existence.

Monica Fremont, Terry's mom, had taken back her maiden name soon after her divorce from Terry's father, David. But the two of them had stayed good friends. They talked, long distance on the telephone, once or twice a week, and met on neutral ground—in Minneapolis, New Orleans, or Chicago (even Kansas City, once)—for "weekend get-togethers," as they called their every-other-monthly assignations. David lived in Eugene, Oregon, these days.

It was, in fact, a phone chat that her parents had, nine days after school let out, that triggered Terry's big decision.

That year Monica—called "Mone" by friends, and sometimes by her daughter—had become an aromatherapist. What that involved was her prescribing different fragrances that would either counteract or heighten clients' moods—or sometimes "cure" what ailed them. Mone believed she was "a natural" at this.

"I'm supersensitive to *smell*," she said to Terry once. "It's a matter of nose-brain coordination." Another feature of aromatherapy she liked was that you didn't have to take a test to practice it.

There were basically two ways aroma did its therapeutic work, Tee Talley's mother told her. Essential oils (the source of the aromas) could go straight onto the client's body, ideally on his or her "thin membranes," Mone said. (Terry never asked where *they* were.) Or the oils could be "infused into the air" by heating carefully counted drops of them, added to some water in a small ceramic cup, that was then placed over one pure, steady candle flame. On the night in question, after dinner, Monica had set some lavender to heating. That got Terry's guard up right away. She remembered lavender was "calming."

"Your father rang me up this morning," Mone began, once her number two child, Richard, twelve, had gone up to his room. Probably to count his money, Terry thought. Richie was notoriously frugal. "He said we ought to talk about your . . . situation."

Monica, with demitasse in hand, was sitting on the sofa. Terry put one knee on a chair and turned to face her—not absolutely staying, but not going, either. "Situation," used by Daddy David, was not a word she liked to hear with "your" in front of it. It was not, for him, synonymous with "unbroken series of successes."

"And?" she answered, warily. She and her mother hardly ever had a conversation they regretted afterward. But it paid to be alert when her absent parent got some big idea, concerning her.

"He thought, and I agree," her mother said, "that possibly a change of school would be a good idea for you, next year."

"A change of *school*," repeated Terry solemnly, picking at one copper-colored eyebrow.

"Yes," continued Mone. "Not that there's anything *wrong* with the high school, or the way you've *handled* it . . . "

"I'm on the honor roll," said Tee. "I have a host of loyal friends. I'm active in school publications and *presidenta* of the Spanish Club. Next year I will be manager of the boys' varsity baseball team."

"Er, yes," her mother said. She couldn't for the life of her imagine why her daughter chose to be involved with *baseball*. It was, she felt, a game marked principally by *spitting*, and by boring, *boring* periods, called "innings," in which almost nothing happened.

"But what your father and I believe is that you ought to have the opportunity to *spread your wings* a little. To take off and *fly*."

"Away to *boarding* school," said Terry.

"Well, of course to boarding school," her mother said. "There aren't any first-class day schools near Cape Enid, as you know. And what's so bad about the 'boarding' part, pray tell? Almost everybody 'boards' at *college*."

Terry knew her mother knew that boarding school and college were quite different institutions, when it came to . . . well, *controls*. Her mother'd brought her up to be extremely self-sufficient, to take care of herself and make her own decisions. In a rare moment of anger three or four years before (when left alone again and told, "Just don't let your brother burn the house down"), she'd accused her mother of practicing the "cross your fingers for luck and sashay out the door" school of child-rearing. But now that she was almost seventeen, she was glad she'd learned resourcefulness so well so young— and had a taste for independence. Her mother must have known she wasn't "boarding school material." Her father, on the other hand, wouldn't have a clue. This whole thing had to be her dad's idea.

"So, have you two picked one out for me already?" she inquired, pleasantly enough. Because she really liked her mom, she saw no need to "make an issue" out of this, not yet. Perhaps the subject would expire in a day or two. She knew she wasn't going to go to any boarding school, but that didn't mean she couldn't *talk* about them for a little while. She took a big deep breath of lavender.

"No, not at all," her mother said, emphatically. "I'd never do a thing like that—you know I wouldn't. We talked about some possiblities, is all."

"For instance," Terry said.

"Well, Cramer was the one that came to *my* mind, right away," Mone said. "It's co-ed—naturally—and in Vermont, and quite—from what I've heard—*free-wheeling.*" She said that last word awkwardly, the same way she said, "rock and roll."

"Your father said he'd go along with Cramer—by which I'm pretty sure he meant he'd pay for it—but it wouldn't be his number one first choice."

"*He* thinks I'd be better off at . . . ?" said Tee, obligingly.

"Oh, possibly an older, more established school, like Newburn *Hall,*" her mother said. "A school with some traditions and more . . . structure."

"And ivy *on* its structures, I presume," said Terry.

"Another possibility would be a place like Ogden *Manor,*" Mone went on. "All girls, but absolutely gorgeous, I've been told. It'd be like living on a huge estate, surrounded by attractive friends—on *horseback!*"

Terry pawed the air in front of her with hands made into fists, and whinnied.

"But regardless of the school"—her mother was a masterful ignorer—"there is one little, *teensy-weensy* problem."

"Let me guess, Mone," Terry said. "If it isn't money, then let's see . . . Is it that I'm too—or maybe not sufficiently—*religious?*"

"*Time*," her mother said. "We're starting awfully late on this. Your dad and I are going to make some calls, and find out who has what connections where. But time is of the essence."

"And there's thinking that *I* have to do," said Tee.

"*Absolutely*," said her mother. "What I'd do right now, if I were you, is take a nice hot bath and think about your choices."

"Good idea," said Terry, standing up. "A *bath*. Of course, that means I'll have to make another choice, though. I hope you got more myrrh—we were almost out of it last time I looked. I'd hate to have to settle for wild ass's milk again."

"Good night, dear heart," said Monica. She thought her daughter had the most delightful sense of humor.

"Sleep tight," said Terry, starting up the stairs. It was exactly ten past eight. A young idea, another choice, was sprouting in her head, already.

At 8:16 Terry called up Connie Slavin on her private line and told her what her mother'd said, and what *she'd* just decided as a consequence. Connie was the loyalest of friends; she could keep her mouth shut, not let secrets dribble out of its corners.

"You don't know Maitland Crane, Tee," was Connie's first reaction. "Do you?"

"Of-course-I-don't-know-Maitland-Crane," said Terry, imitating Connie's rapid-fire pooched-up way of speaking. "But I've seen him, same as you have, at the club. I think he's cool. And I'm pretty sure I read he's off to somewhere pretty soon, again. Aboard the *Cormorant,* I mean. Alone."

"Right. But let's suppose you *can* sneak on it, and he doesn't know you're there for a while," said Connie. "Don't you think he'll turn around and come right back as soon as he lays eyes on you?"

Connie took a breath and kept on babbling. "You're a *minor,* Terry. Guys can't go off with minors on a sailboat to another country. Guys can't take minors to a Howard Johnson's Motor Lodge— or *Pennsylvania,* even."

"Maybe 'guys' can't," Terry said. "But Maitland Cranes sure can. Maitland Cranes can do most anything they want."

Connie sighed. "He could do most anything he wanted to with *me,*" she said. "Maitland Crane is possibly the cutest member of his age group in the world."

"To me," said Terry, calmly, "Maitland Crane is like a taxi driver. I need someone to get me out of here, to take me someplace else. What he looks like doesn't matter beans. As long as he can drive the cab."

"Yeah, but just suppose he asks you for the

*fare,*" said Connie. She made a little gurgle sound. "Taxis aren't free, you know."

"Put it this way," Terry said. "I'm prepared to do whatever is required by the . . . situation."

She was only making Connie-conversation when she said that, saying what would get a rise out of her friend. But then she wondered, *Am I? Would I?* The truth was that she wouldn't have a choice, way out at sea, somewhere. But Maitland Crane . . . *he* wouldn't. Would he? Way out at sea, with no one else around?

"Hoo-ee!" Con was laughing up a storm. "Will you listen to the girl?" She cupped a hand and spoke into the phone through it, as if it were a megaphone. "One of the most sought-after virgins at Cape Enid High now says she'll *work* her way across the ocean, on her back if need be. Story at eleven."

"You laugh," said Terry. "But I'm serious. I'm not going to go to any boarding school, but Mom's quite right. It's time for me to spread my wings. And leave my little nestie-pie."

"Well, if you're really serious," said Connie, "I'll do anything I can to help. How about I meet you at the club tomorrow morning? I could be there by eleven."

"Great," said Terry. "You can help me make a perfect plan."

She hung up the phone and rose from her bed.

*11*

She felt terrific. She wished it were tomorrow, or next month, already. She was going to be a "woman on her own." That sounded so . . . exclusive.

She decided she would take a hot bath after all. A celebratory one. She undressed quickly, tossing most of her clothes in the direction of her chaise longue, but kicking her underpants into the closet. Before she went into the bathroom, though, she got a lengthy string of beads from off her dresser and looped them twice around her neck. They were black beads, shiny onyx ones.

She checked herself out in the full-length mirror on her bathroom door. Visible, already, were this summer's sun lines—she did not exactly *tan*—faint but definitely there. The winter's treats had metamorphosed into just a little flab, but sweating in the tropics would take care of that, she thought. She believed she looked like an adventuress, with heavy brows (one with a devilish slant to it), big light eyes, a small but definitely determined chin, and that jaunty sprinkling of freckles. She was afraid she might also look a little *young* for almost seventeen—but at the moment, anyway, she found herself quite striking, with her tousled mop of bright red hair and wearing only coal black beads that dropped between a pair of breasts that seemed, well, really perfect for the way she was: positive, and clearly there, but never ostentatious.

Terry slipped the beads back off her head. She'd get a haircut, she decided, maybe more than just a trim. Something easy-care but stylish.

The beads sailed through the air and landed on her bed, and Terry walked directly at her own reflection and the bathroom just beyond it, taking graceful, rhythmic, straight-line steps, the way a model would.

# chapter 2

They were sitting in a dinghy that was the property
of the Cape Enid Club, about two hundred feet
from shore and far from any mooring.

"Getting *on* the *Cormorant* should be no
sweat," said Terry, once Connie and she'd reached
some open water. "He'll move it from its mooring
to beside his dock, so he can load it up with all of
the provisions that he has to take. He'll probably
do that tomorrow or the next day."

She let her eyes go up the shore, a half mile or
so. Crane's beach and dock were there, down a slop-
ing lawn from what was generally called his "compound" (although sometimes "Capo Grosso"). On
one of his "adventures" up the Amazon River, Mait-

land Crane had come upon the remains of what once had been a populous and thriving town during the Brazilian rubber boom of the late nineteenth century, but now was almost uninhabited. In its center was a magnificent, ornate old opera house, surrounded by the city mansions of the rubber barons; the jungle hadn't quite reclaimed them yet. Crane traded the locals an aisle's worth of Wal-Mart merchandise for the lot, then had the buildings taken apart, and shipped and reerected in Cape Enid. It was said that he'd installed the largest TV screen in the world in the opera house, but that when he'd brought the Met up from New York to do *Aida* there, the acoustics hadn't been so hot.

"You'll sneak on board the night before he leaves 'on the rising tide,' I guess," said Connie.

"Yup," said Tee. "That'll be next Monday, I believe. So I thought that Sunday night I'd tiptoe over from the club, here; just walk along the shoreline."

"What you could do is borrow my bike and ride *it* from your house to the club and just leave it there," said Connie. "I'd pick it up the following day, after you're long gone. The only trouble is . . ." She stopped and wrinkled up her brow.

"What?" said Terry.

"Well, that doesn't take your *trunk* into consideration, or all your other luggage," said her friend. "Even if you *walk* the bike."

Terry reached over the side of the dinghy and cupped some throwing water in one hand.

"Get *out!*" she said. She flipped the water high, and it came down like heavy summer raindrops on the two of them. "I'm only going to take one little nylon duffel bag, probably half full."

"Tee, be real," said Connie. "You take more stuff than that for an overnight at *my* house."

Terry waved a hand. *"Used to,"* she insisted. "I *used to,* in the days when I was still a kid, all frivolous and flighty. I'm putting childish things behind me, Con. The older you are, the smarter you pack. My mom can get a weekend's worth of duds in one small shoulder bag."

"Oh, I *see,*" said Connie. "You're going to turn into your *mother.*" And she started laughing. "Or how about *my* mother? That'd make this trip a perfect blast for Maitland Crane!"

Terry started laughing too. "Is it too much to ask for you to hang up your wet *towels?*" she whined. She could do a drop-dead Mrs. Slavin imitation. "I told the cleaning lady not to even *bother* with your cabin, Maitland, if she had to wade through clothes six inches deep, just getting to your bed—or *berth,* I guess you say on shipboard. . . ."

Connie clapped her hands in glee, it *was* her mother, to a T. "But seriously, though," she said. "What *are* you going to take?"

"Money," Terry said. "Grammy's given me a savings bond my last seven birthdays—ever since I got to double digits; I'm going to cash them in. And I'll take whatever I can find in Richard's room; Mom'll pay him back. I bet he has at least two hundred dollars stashed away in there. He never spends a dime, the little miser."

"But *clothes*," said Connie. "You're going to just take jeans and stuff?"

"I don't think," said Terry. "You can tell me if I'm right on this or not. I thought I'd mostly take *nice* things. Resorty sort of dresses—easy-care, of course, but nice. That's because I'll have to look real good—and older."

Connie nodded. "Maybe you could get off at Montego Bay, Jamaica," she said. "Where *we* stayed, spring vacation? There's lots of yummy stores down there." But then she thought of something altogether different. "But listen—are you going to leave your mom a note?"

"Yeah, I've got to," Terry said. "Though I'm not sure what to put in it."

"Why don't you say you're going to work your way across the country? That you got an urge to see the U. S. A.? You could say you plan to end up where your father lives. Seattle, is it?"

"Eugene," Terry said. She thought that over. "You may have a great idea there, girlfriend. I think

17

my mom might even *understand* my doing that. It's kind of like a thing she'd do. Or want to do—*have* wanted to do, when she was my age."

"Then, when you get to wherever it is, and get yourself all settled," Connie said, having forgotten she was sure that Maitland Crane would turn around the moment he saw Terry, "you could write *me* a letter and include a note I could mail to your mom from someplace when we take our family trip this summer. Your mom would learn you were okay, but she couldn't possibly pick up your trail, seeing as you'd never been to wherever it was."

"And by the time they find me, or more likely, I decide to pop back home, I'll be totally transformed into a woman of the world," said Terry. "What will have happened is . . . " She looked off into space. "Let's see, maybe I came upon the wreckage of a Spanish treasure ship, while snorkeling one day . . . " She paused, a half smile on her face.

"And quickly forming a salvage company with a former high school classmate from the States," suggested Connie, rapid-fire, "you chartered an old coastal steamer cocaptained by Tom Cruise and Sean Connery, and started bringing up jeweled chamber pots and gold doubloons by the bucketful."

"Hey, why not?" said Terry, although in *her* fantasy there hadn't been any classmate, or coastal steamer, or Connerys or Cruises. The way she had it, *she'd* brought up doubloons and other artifacts with the help of a beautiful but mysterious boy she'd found washed up on the beach one morning, naked and tied to the wreckage of a balsa-wood raft. She'd nursed him back to life and then to flourishing good health in the beachfront cottage that was one of the perks of her jobs as manager of the Banana Republic on this particular island, and although he'd never said a word so far, he seemed to understand the words *she* said. She guessed he was about her age, going by his lack of beard or evidence of any wear on his teeth. He was strong enough to lift a cannon from the wreck, but he also handled delicate things carefully—which made him about as much like Kirt Manwaring as any boy she'd met so far. But for the time being, she had his robust masculinity sleeping on a cot out in the beachfront cottage's airy living room.

# chapter 3

The night she was to sneak on board the *Cormorant*, Terry didn't go to bed at all. There wasn't any point; She was too buzzed by the excitement, and besides, she wanted to be really, really tired when she got there. Her plan was to postpone her coming-out party until the second day at sea—and to sleep most of the time till then.

"But won't you have to pee?" asked Connie, practically, when Terry told her what the plan was. "I know *I* would. Of course, I'm probably deformed. I ought to leave my body to the Harvard Medical School, so some students of anatomy can get their jollies taking me apart. 'Is that her bladder?' they'd all say. 'That tiny little thing?'"

"Well, I'm the opposite of you," said Tee. "I'm like a hibernating bear. I saw this special on TV. D'you know bears don't do *anything* for months and months? The day I go aboard I'm going to almost fast and only drink a little bit. And I'll have a jar of water with me, in case I start to die of thirst. So if I have to, later, I can use the jar—*you* know."

Once she'd heard her mother come upstairs, she put some music on, and headphones, and lay down on her bed. Time passed; she thought about Kirt Manwaring and what he might be doing at that exact moment. He probably wasn't out on a date. Night games on the West Coast didn't start until after ten, eastern time, so he was probably crouching down behind home plate, she thought, and giving the sign to his pitcher. At Cape Enid High, she'd found out, the catcher put down one finger for a fast ball and two fingers for a curve. Would it be the same in the big leagues? she'd wondered. You'd think the signs would be more complicated, seeing that the players were so advanced. But it wouldn't be possible for the catcher to signal "the square root of three" for a fast ball, and $\pi\partial^2$ for a curve, would it? She decided not and then switched to imagining the kind of sculpted thigh and fanny muscles Kirt must have from all that crouching and jumping up he had to do.

When her watch said a quarter after one, she got

up and began to pack. She'd never made a list of what she planned to take, for fear it might "fall into the wrong hands." And anyway, she planned to take so little stuff she didn't really need one.

The clothes that she'd decided on went in the duffel first, followed by her address book, her small jewelry box, a plastic Ziploc bag with her "survival rations" (nuts and chocolate) in it, a little flashlight, a small zipper bag that held her hairbrush, nail-care equipment, and cosmetics, and a rubber-lined drawstring bag containing all the necessaries from the medicine cabinet. Her money—five hundred and some dollars, which she'd asked the bank to give her in well-used, noncrispy bills—was distributed in many different hiding places: in the address book under *F* (for "filthy lucre"), folded up in the toes of her spectator pumps, slid into an unopened box of Tampax that she then glued shut again, etc. None of it was part of Richard's cash stash. She was afraid that he might count it (pat it, cuddle it, and kiss it) every night and, if a single bill was missing, he'd want the whole house searched at once. And he'd probably written down all the serial numbers someplace.

She looked around the room. Oh, yeah. With a sigh she walked over to her bulletin board, where there were photos of her parents, and of Richard, and of Connie and a bunch of other friends. She snatched off an assortment and quickly slid them into her bag.

"You're such a baby, Talley," she informed herself, but smiling as she did so.

Then something on the bedside table caught her eye. It was a key ring with a little can of Mace attached to it. Her mother'd stuck it in her stocking this past Christmas.

"Walking in the city," Mone had said, "you never know. . . ."

Terry'd made a little fun of her and called the thing "a postman's toy." But it had ended up beside her bed, in civilized Cape Enid. Now she picked it up and seemed to weigh it in her hand as she just stared off into space, her eyes unfocused. Then, moving quickly again, she jammed it in the duffel bag, all the way down at one end of it. And after that she got her Swiss army knife out of a desk drawer and put it in there too.

She'd promised Connie that she'd ring her up when she was almost ready to go, so she decided to get that over with. She flopped down on her bed and started dialing.

"Tee." Connie'd picked up fast, on the first ring.

"Hi," said Terry, light. "I guess it's just about that time."

"I know," said Connie. "I've been sitting here, imagining."

"Imagining?" said Terry. "What?"

"How I'd be feeling," Connie said, "if it was me, going."

"And?" said Terry.

Connie didn't answer right away. Then, in a typical torrent: "Oh-Terry-honey-please-don't-go. You can talk your mother out of boarding school. They'll let you stay; I know they will." It sounded as if she'd begun to cry. "You can't tell what all you might be getting into. . . ."

"*Con*-nee," Terry said. "You cut that out, all right? You're a fine one to talk."

Unlike most Cape Enid kids, who went sailing in the summer and skiing in the winter, Connie liked to go hang gliding and skydiving and bungee-jumping. "She seems to need to have both feet way off the ground a certain percentage of the time," her father liked to say. "Maybe she got hanged, in some past life or other." And he'd shake his head and chuckle. Terry was pretty sure Mr. Slavin *liked* having a daredevil for a daughter.

"Well, just be careful," Connie said now, in a perfectly normal tone of voice again.

"Sure," said Terry. "And I won't forget to floss. Maybe, when everything gets all worked out, you can come and visit me, okay?" Suddenly she wanted to get off the phone, to have this conversation over with.

"Okay, but you take care, you hear? I'll be thinking of you all the time."

"Okay then, Con. So long, be good, and thanks for everything. I'll leave your bike there at the club."

"Bye, Terry, dear. I love you."

"Love you too, Con. 'Bye." She took a big deep breath as she hung up the phone.

Terry wandered into the bathroom, stopped. Aha—she'd forgotten to pack a towel. No wonder she'd been drawn there. Or, come to think of it, a swimsuit. And shouldn't she take a shower now, before she left? Absolutely, yes. She had a raging case of whatchacallit . . . flop sweat.

When she'd showered and dried off, she didn't spare the antiperspirant (oops, forgot to pack *it*, too). As her mother often said, first impressions were important. And she wanted Maitland Crane to see her long before he smelled her.

That brought "essential oils" into her mind, and she decided she really should snag a few of the more potent ones on her way out. Her mother kept her whole collection in a cabinet in the pantry, and she had a lot of spares. *You never know,* she thought. *A whiff of jasmine might be just the thing to turn a pissed-off millionaire into a pussycat.*

Once she'd packed two swimsuits, actually, and a clean towel and her deodorant, the duffel bag was well over half full, but except for the jar of water and those little vials of essential oils, she was pretty sure she had everything in it that she needed. All she had to do was dress, scribble a quick note to Mone, and go.

The dressing part was quickly done: T-shirt, jeans and a sweatshirt, white wool socks and Top-siders, a Boston Red Sox baseball cap over her most becoming, almost *no*-care cut. The note didn't take much longer.

> *Dear Mom,*
>
> *Sorry about this, but I simply gotta go. This isn't about you, or Dad, or little bro—you're all the greatest—it's about "spreading my wings," just like you said. I'm going to work my way across the country, ending up at Daddy's. Please don't worry; I'll be fine. I've got money for emergencies.*
>
> Love you madly,<br>Terry

When she'd propped that on the pillow of her obviously unslept-in bed, she slung the duffel bag over her shoulder, took a last long look around the room, and hit the light switch by the door.

Terry'd done her homework. When she first set foot on the *Cormorant* with her flashlight in her hand, she already knew, thanks to an article and a picture in the paper, quite a few things about the boat.

It (she couldn't make herself think "she") was a yawl, which meant it had two masts, the smaller one behind the cockpit, which was where you steered the thing. It had been built somewhere in England in the 1920s out of old-fashioned wood (not Plexiglas, recycled milk jugs, or space-age metal), and lacked a lot of modern inventions that would have made single-handed sailing a whole lot easier. (Crane called the boat "a dear old girl.") It was thirty-something feet in length by ten feet at its widest.

As she hopped down off the rail into the cockpit, Terry bit her lower lip (which was, she thought, the thing to do). She'd come to the first really critical moment in all this—not counting that decision at the haircut place—when she had to open the little door to the main hatch and "go below." It was always possible that Maitland Crane was also on board, asleep, or making something "shipshape."

She decided she would knock—good manners never got a person into trouble, she'd been taught—and did, three times. There was no answer, so she tried the door and opened it and knocked again, this time on the wall of the companionway, inside.

Nothing—just the lapping of small waves against the hull.

"Mr. Crane?" she called, but softly, now one step down the little stair. She knocked a third time, with the flashlight. He'd have to have heard that if he was anywhere on board, she thought.

So when there was still no answer, she took a deep, deep breath, closed the little door behind her, and turned the flashlight on. She could almost feel her sweat glands send out little kamikaze squads of wet against the filmy barrier of chemicals and scent that she'd smeared on to stop them.

Two steps more and she was in the after cabin—or compartment, really—a room no more than eight feet long by more or less that wide. On her left, built in against the wall, there was a single bunk, made up, and on her right a sink and stove, along with lockers up and down. No bear, however, and not even any porridge. Perfect.

Straight in front of her there was another door. She knocked on it, more boldly now, and opened it right after doing that. The next room was a little smaller, even, and had a table in the middle, bolted down, and built-in couches on each side with storage lockers above them and what looked like water tanks below. Another door at the end of this room led even farther forward.

But the boat was getting narrower by then. It seemed that she was running out of space. So far she hadn't seen a place where you could hide a Norway rat (if that was the kind that left a sinking ship), let alone a passenger with luggage.

Behind that second door she found—and she was not surprised by this—the bathroom, which, she knew, was called the "head" on boats, for reasons she could not imagine. This head contained the minimum: a toilet with a handle tht you pumped to flush it—period. No shower and no sink. But the toilet was partitioned off, at least, and past *it* was the sort of space that she'd been hoping for.

It was a small dark room that came almost to a point. And on its left side was a canvas cot, fastened to the wall, that could fold up or down depending on the need for either it or extra floor space. At the moment it was partway up (or down) and had what looked to be some folded sails in it.

Terry realized she could move the sails around a bit and make a space that she could wiggle into, with her duffel. One folded sail could be her pillow, and any time she heard Crane coming she could duck her head right under it, so if he glanced inside the room, all he'd see was a lumpy mess of sails inside a partway open cot. Perfect, Terry told herself again, just perfect.

Fifteen minutes later, the duffel bag, the sails, and she herself were all in place; she'd even gotten out her "food" and water, and had them close at hand. The image of the hibernating bear came back to her. Here she was, safe inside her little den.

She then allowed herself one question: Did she really, *really* want to be there?

It was stuffy in the little room already, and it'd probably get worse. And probably when Crane found her, he *would* turn right around and take her back to Cape Enid, even if he had to "waste" a few days doing that. *Of course* he would, no "probably" about it.

But even if (or when) that happened, Connie (and a lot of other kids) would have to give her credit. She'd be the one who'd actually *done* what lots of other people had talked about: busting out (of stuffy old Cape Enid). And on top of that she would have shared a small adventure with none other than *the* Maitland Crane.

It seemed as if this *was* a no-lose situation.

Shortly after thinking that, she, unexpectedly, fell fast asleep.

# chapter 4

In the dream that she was having, Terry had a long black skirt on, and she was dancing. She kept wishing that her skirt were full and flowing, but it wasn't. Instead, it was the kind of skirt she'd only seen in pictures; it was tight around her butt and kept on being pretty tight all the way down to her knees, before it flared and made it just possible for her to take small steps, instead of hobble.

To make things even worse, the person she was dancing with had hold of her in such a way that both her chest and face were being squished against his body. Even when she craned her neck, she couldn't see his face. He just kept on squishing her and rocking back and forth, in place, and come to think of it, she couldn't even hear the music. One thing was for sure: She knew who this guy *wasn't*. He was rough, insensitive, and not even noticeably masculine.

And then . . . she was awake and staring into stuffy darkness, rocking up and down. Oh, yes—remembering—she was on the *Cormorant,* lying in a narrow space inside a folded cot, with sails. She had a little headache and felt dazed, but hey, the boat was moving, under way; they'd started.

The motion really wasn't bad at all. And the different kinds of creaks and rushing sounds she heard were natural, all natural. She was on a sailboat and it was running fast, its black hull slicing through the water, perhaps with happy porpoises frolicking along on either side. Cape Enid, she assumed, was disappearing in their wake. They were *at sea.*

She could imagine Maitland Crane, topside in the cockpit. In fact, the picture in the paper had been taken with him there. In it, his dark blond hair was wet and slicked straight back, and you could tell his eyes would be the nice soft blue of washed-out jeans. She thought that maybe "roman" described his nose and jawline—that is, if it meant straight and pretty much Greek-godish. (Terry wasn't always great at what words mean.) Around his head he'd tied a rolled bandanna (a dark blue one, probably) to keep his hair in place, and he also wore a polo shirt (dark blue again?) and pure white tennis shorts. His arms and legs looked muscular, mature, but not too hairy.

She'd seen him dressed almost the exact same way when he was playing tennis at the club. He only played with another guy, and they were both extremely good. Crane hardly ever came to the net; he'd glide around the court hitting picture-perfect ground strokes, one after another. He didn't seem to sweat. "Lovely!" he would sometimes shout, if his opponent put a ball away with special flair, or "Yes!" but mostly he just stroked the ball, showing no emotion when he won or lost a point.

Terry turned her little flashlight on to check her wristwatch. It said 12:16, which meant she'd slept a good nine hours. She was pretty sure that she could sleep a little more, and pretty soon she did.

When she woke up next, her heart was pounding in her chest, and she just lay there for a moment, terrified, but not knowing by exactly what.

Then she regained full consciousness and knew. Someone—Maitland Crane, who else?—was in the "head," and using it. She hadn't heard him coming, and now he was ensconced no more than three feet from *her* head. Great, just great. Thank God for that partition, insubstantial though it was. He was so close—oh, yuk!—she didn't even dare to lift her pillow up so it could hide her head.

Almost at once, she heard him pump the toilet quickly, flushing it, and then his footsteps, leaving—heading back to the cockpit, of course. At least these single-handed sailors didn't dawdle, carry magazines in there with them or anything. She checked her watch and saw that it was 2:08.

Terry'd rolled onto her back, and now she had to face the fact that she was wide-awake. She felt totally slept out. And something else: She wanted to get it over with, the moment she revealed herself and made her pitch to Maitland Crane, and found out how far those newly widespread wings of hers were going to carry her. It was conceivable she'd be back home before her mother knew she'd left; during school vacations, Mone told Tee that she could live on her own schedule.

So, motivated, Terry wiggled out of her tight-fitting den. She wasn't going to wait for the second day, after all; it was "coming ready or not" time. She got her baseball cap back on and, treading softly, walked back toward the cockpit.

The first, most screamingly obvious thing she noticed when she stuck her head out of the hatch was this: The person sprawled there on the bench seat with his whole arm resting on the tiller, steering, was stark naked—or the next thing to it. Somehow, Terry kept from screaming. Perhaps that was because he *did* have on a yachting cap that looked to be at least one size too big for him, and therefore slightly comical.

After one shocked eye-blink, she was forced to come to terms with something else: He—this person—wasn't Maitland Crane. For one thing, he was skinnier; he lacked Crane's *heft*, and muscle definition; clearly, he was much, much younger, less mature. His skin was also different, smooth and tan. And she would have bet that underneath the yachting cap, his hair, instead of honey blond, was black.

His first reaction to her presence was surprise, amazement. Clearly he'd believed he was alone on board, so he was not expecting company. He'd thought he could enjoy a "clothing optional" occasion.

Then his glance dropped down a notch, from more or less the *B* on this unwelcome stranger's baseball cap to squarely on her chest. What he saw there caused his face to turn a redder shade of tan and sent him into frantic action. With a gurgle, he grabbed wildly at the faded, multicolored surfer shorts that lay there on the floorboards. Letting go the tiller, he lurched to his feet and tried to get them on, doing a kind of crazy dance, hopping on one foot and then the other, reeling right across the cockpit. The oversize cap went flying off in the process, and Terry saw that she'd been right: His head, too, featured coal black hair, lank and sort of greasy-looking.

When he finally got his pants pulled up and fastened at the waist, he turned and faced her. His mouth opened, but at first no sound came out of it.

"Huh-huh-huh-who the huh-huh-hell are . . . *you?*" he finally stammered. For a moment Terry simply stared at him as she tried to get her thoughts together. She'd been expecting Maitland Crane; she'd known he was the only one who sailed the *Cormorant,* and that he always sailed alone. But now, instead of Maitland Crane, she had some kid to deal with. Someone not even her age. Some younger . . . exhibitionist. Hmm; *ugh.*

"I could ask you the same question," she finally said to him. She was damned if she was going to be interrogated by some weeny ninth or tenth grader. "Who the hell are *you?* Where's Maitland?"

His whole expression changed again, after he heard that. She infinitely preferred his earlier ones: his shocked/amazed/embarrassed/outraged looks. Now he actually was smirking at her. He was sending out "amused," "superior"—even a little bit of "disgusted." Her brother, Richard, sometimes looked like that when she was trying to borrow money from him.

"Muh-Maitland, is it?" he got out. "D-Daddy's into . . . young stuff now—I guh-guhguess." Then definitely disgustedly, "Juh-Jesus!"

"What?" He'd given Terry two things that she had to process. First, the little punk—actually, some six feet tall—had called her "young stuff"; didn't that imply he thought she was Crane's . . . girl-friend/bimbo/concubine? And he'd also called Crane "Daddy." She struggled momentarily to decide if she was more interested in that second thing than she was insulted by the first. That turned out to be no contest, really. No one had ever called her easy or experienced before; in a way, she rather liked that she could come across that way. It meant she didn't look too young.

"Maitland Crane's your father? I never heard he had a son," she said.

"W-well, now you have," he said, and smirked some more. "I duh-duh-doubt he talks about me much. Suh-specially with babes."

"Look, that's enough of that 'babe' shit, all right?" said Terry, sternly. She'd decided it was time to call this meeting to order. This was a lot like baby-sitting; You had to let the youngster know who's boss. "I've never spoken to your father in my life, much less *dated* him. That's assuming Maitland Crane *is* your father, which I'm not exactly convinced of, by the way. So tell me what you're doing on the *Cormorant*. He let you take it for a sail before he started on his trip?"

She took a decent look around while she was saying that. She knew they'd been sailing for hours at a pretty good clip, so they had to be a ways from Cape Enid. But they were still only a few hundred yards from shore, which was on their right-hand side; apparently this kid was heading down the coast for some reason. How far down they'd gotten, she had no idea; all the sailing that she'd done had been right around Cape Enid.

She also took a real look at the boy. She wondered if he *could* be Crane's son. Facially he didn't resemble him that much, except for both of them having long straight hair. This one had brown eyes, a nose that was more pug than roman, and a complexion that was a whole lot darker than Crane's— broken only by a few widely spaced silky little black hairs in the sideburns area and above his rather full-lipped mouth. The one way he was most like his father—if Maitland was his father—was that he had a bit of the same . . . aloofness, would that be? Of course, his stutter detracted from that and made him less attractive, on the way to pitiful.

"L-let me? N-not exactly," the boy was saying now. "I s-stole his guh-goldarn boat. I wuh-wanta shake him up, b-but good!"

Terry stared at him. "You're telling me you stole the *Cormorant?*" she said. "Just as he was getting ready to take off on an adventure?"

38

If true, that was pretty funny. But it'd probably also mean a Coast Guard cutter would be coming up at any moment, and that she'd next talk to Mone from jail. Talk about a bummer! Being brought home by Maitland Crane was one thing, but being towed back by the Coast Guard in the company of some junior juvenile delinquent was another. She'd have to go to boarding school to get away from all the hee-haws everyone would launch in her direction.

"Nice, but shouldn't you be trying to hide it and yourself?" she asked. "Before the Coast Guard catches up to you?"

His reaction to those questions—an incredibly stupid-looking blank stare—made her think that neither of those possibilities had ever occurred to him. Perhaps because he was so young; perhaps because he was a full-fledged idiot.

But—she thought, suddenly—assuming either or both of those shortcomings, maybe she could talk him into going somewhere, eventually, where *she* wanted to go, assuming they could somehow give the law the slip.

"Look," she said, loading up her voice with phony geniality, "let me tell you who I really am. I'm Terry; I'm a stowaway." She stuck her hand out, willing him to shake; he did, though not enthusiastically—he limp-fingered her. "I go to Cape Enid

High, but I decided it was time for me to split from that whole scene." Was that the way a kid his age would talk? "I needed to 'spread my wings,' as they say. I was hoping that your dad—who I don't know from Adam, as I said—might be my taxi driver to . . . wherever. Anywhere but here—and hopefully an island in the sun, somewhere between back home and Panama."

She hoped that sounded good to him. He'd taken it all in, though not looking at her steadily, because he kept throwing glances at the big mainsail, and their wake, and the shoreline. But once she thought she might have caught a glimmer of *respect*, and maybe *interest*, in his eyes.

"One thing I'm curious about, though," she went on. "If Maitland Crane's your father, how come I've never seen you around Cape Enid? I know you've never gone to school there."

The boy's first answer was a shrug. But then he took a breath, as if he'd finally made up his mind about something, and he started to talk. And once he started, he went on and on.

He said his father'd named him Mick J. Crane, after Mick Jagger of the Rolling Stones, which was his father's favorite band, but he'd been living with his mother (who preferred to call him Mikey, Mike, or Michael) almost all his life—his parents having been divorced when he was two. He'd been sent away to boarding schools starting in the fourth grade, he said (before he even had wings, Terry thought) and to summer camps as well—including sailing camp the last three years (which explained, she thought, his present expertise). All this was paid for by his father, who also sent him expensive and desirable gifts (a miniature, electric-powered Lamborghini; a genuine, handmade Indian tepee; one of Paul Gauguin's Tahitian woman paintings) at every Christmas and on his birthday. Whenever he visited his father at Cape Enid, though, he mostly watched television and talked to the servants, while Maitland Crane did other things. Mick said he was convinced his father loved him very much, but had more or less repressed those feelings by buying him presents, keeping him at "an emotional distance," and taking off on his adventures.

He explained that he could understand and "deal with" his father's problem because, unlike his father, he had been to many therapists, and therefore understood much more about "puh-people," including himself, than most kids his age.

*"Par exemple,"* he said, suddenly, "I discover zat in one of my past lives I am ze Marquis de Framboise. I was ze same age as, and a *confidant* of, she who's known to you as Joan of Arc."

Terry's mouth flopped open. She pulled an earlobe, shook her head. She didn't know any French,

41

but of course, she'd heard of Joan of Arc, the Maid of Orleans, and she certainly knew a French accent when she heard one. But the most amazing thing was that what she'd just heard coming out of Mick J. Crane were not the strident, childish sounds made by an American teenager with a medium-bad stutter. Instead, she had heard the smooth, almost seductive voice of a . . . oh, perhaps college-age Frenchman with no speech impediment whatever.

She rubbed her eyes. Yes, he even *looked* different, a lot more poised and "with it," with just the faint beginnings of a little smile playing around the corners of his unbelievably sensuous mouth. She remembered that she'd seen him naked—was that incredible or what? That the first young man she'd ever seen that way was a onetime member of the French nobility?

"Hold on," she said. Before she got too carried away, there was something that she had to get straight. "Are you saying that you were this marquis guy, or that you are him now?" To her, that made a big difference. "Were" was interesting, far-out; "are" would mean this kid was nuts, one of those "multiple personality" wackos.

"Oh, were," said the marquis's voice, with a chuckle. "His time was in ze early fifteenth century. But I can recollect him, if you will. Remember how it was when I was him."

"I see," said Terry. That was most unusual, but possible, she guessed. Previously she'd been pretty skeptical about reincarnation. Mone was of the "when you're dead, you're dead" school. But now that she thought about it, she did know other boys who often acted and sounded more like people from a different place and time—like some jungle, shortly after the discovery of fire.

"But getting back to now," she went on, "what exactly are you up to? As Mick—or Michael or whatever—Crane. Now that you've got your father's boat and everything."

"Wuh-well," he said, and proceeded to tell her, now talking totally American—like himself—again. His plan, he said, was this: to steal his father's favorite toy, the *Cormorant*, sail it down the coast, and anchor it in this secluded cove (which they were very close to now), which he'd discovered while in sailing camp. Once there, he'd simply listen to the radio. What he would hear on it, of course, would be the news of the disappearance from Cape Enid of Maitland Crane's son and Maitland Crane's boat. And as time passed, and there was no trace found of either of those things, he'd start hearing more and more about his father's anguish, of his deep concern about his missing boy.

Then, once he'd decided that his father had suffered enough, he'd row to shore and give the old man a call from the nearest telephone. He said he felt that this would be the beginning of a new relationship between his father and himself, one that would be close and warm—and, yes, respectful.

"Suh-sometimes coming close to losing suh-something shows a puh-person that he really wants that thing," Mick said.

Terry had her doubts about this story ending the way he said. Her guess was his father would be mightily pissed off and want to kill young Mick. But what concerned her most was that this plan of his was not in harmony with hers at all. If things happened to work out the way he hoped—and face it, after all the therapy he'd done, maybe he did know a lot about psychology—then she was out of luck. He'd turn this tub around and head back to Cape Enid.

She looked at him appraisingly. He'd put his silly hat back on and was staring up at the sail with his mouth gaping open like an idiot. He could have been somebody's stupid younger brother playing Captain Dress-up. The only good part of his plan was that she wouldn't have to hang around his wonky junior highnesss anymore if it worked out.

But to give him credit: She, right now, felt close to *losing* her big chance to spread her wings, and that *did* show her (yes!) how much she really *wanted* to!

With nothing else to do, she sat down on the floorboards of the cockpit and began to sulk.

# chapter 5

It wasn't long before they reached the boy's "secluded cove." Once there, Terry had to choose between either becoming his first mate, Miss Helpful, getting involved in the business of lowering sails and anchoring, or taking her sulk below, thereby informing him that if they weren't heading for the islands, this boat and anybody else aboard it could just kiss her bonny booty.

Because she'd sailed enough to have some skills she could show off, and because she didn't want to foreclose any options yet, and *particularly* because she didn't feel like hanging out in that stuffy little "cabin" of hers, she stayed topside and helped.

Watching him manuever the boat into the perfect place to anchor, and deal with all the sails and sheets and other lines, Terry decided that Crane had gotten his money's worth out of his son's sailing camp. The kid looked as if he'd spent his life on shipboard. The awkwardness she'd seen when he was trying to get his pants on was replaced by an almost monkeylike agility as he danced from here to there, up onto the foredeck and back again. Terry wondered, fleetingly, if she was looking at the downside of human evolution: that men were graceful only with their clothes *on* nowadays.

In no time at all they were anchored in fairly deep water but near one shore—actually under the brow of a steep bluff that almost sheltered them from, say, the prying eyes aboard a Coast Guard search plane. And they were also tucked in behind a spit of land, on their other side, that hid them from the open sea.

Terry didn't need her watch to tell her it was dinnertime: After more than twenty-four hours without a real meal, she was really famished, *starving*. But food seemed not to be on Mikey's mind at all. No, once he'd seen that everything that *could* be shipshape was, he flicked on the ship's big radio and fiddled with its dials.

She'd never seen him look as happy as he did right then. He looked the way *she* probably would have looked, she thought, if—at that moment—she were smelling burgers broiling in the little galley down below.

When he had the station that he wanted, they sat and listened to the local news; the station was in Dreary, the "big town" nearest to Cape Enid, where the shopping center was. That night the local news concerned the following:

A prankster or pranksters still unknown had put what was believed to be as many as eight broken brown beer bottles into the clear-glass container at the Dreary Recycling Center. The town constable was following up a number of leads.

Plans for the Fourth of July All-You-Can-Eat Supper at the Cape Enid United Church were in full swing. The menu for the occasion was *Suprêmes de Volaille Véronique* (chicken breasts with grapes), *Riz a l'Indienne* (curried rice), *Salade Lafayette* (fancy lettuce), and profiteroles (small cream puffs) with a North Coast white Burgundy to wash it all down. There was to be one seating only, at 8:00 P.M., and tickets were on sale at Sheldon's Store at $19.98 per person.

Local gardener George D. King had apparently grown a tomato in his small attached greenhouse that bore, he said, an uncanny resemblance to his late wife, Edna.

The bull moose that had wandered into the Caboose family's backyard the day before, and become

entangled in their clothesline, was still at large. Anyone seeing a moose with a sheer black chiffon
nightgown detailed with a rich satin scroll design
hanging from its antlers is asked to please give
Dotty Caboose a call at 555-5490. She reports that
the gown had been left at her residence by their son
Ernest's former wife, the one who'd moved back to
New Jersey, and she'd planned to cut it up for dust
rags.

And that was it; the nightgown was the only
missing object on the local news; no sons or boats
were mentioned. Michael sat there looking stunned,
staring at the radio and shaking his head. But after a
few long moments, he blinked his eyes and raised a
finger. He had had a new idea.

He said he bet his father just reported what had
happened to the Coast Guard, and asked them to
keep it off the news. He said of course his dad
wouldn't want local reporters coming over to the
house and pestering him for statements, or having
to field calls from all three networks' evening news
shows and the *New York Times*.

"I cuh-can pick up the cuh-Coast Guard on
short wave," he said.

And after more dial-twisting, he succeeded in
doing so. But about the only thing the military
seemed to have on its mind that early evening was
reports of nude bathing taking place off a beach

near Point Hopeful. It sounded as if a number of different Coast Guard craft were converging on the scene.

By then, Terry felt as if some weightless scavengers were gnawing at the lining of her stomach, so she threw caution and good manners to the wind and said, "I imagine there's some food on board. How about I whip us up a little supper?"

He made a gesture that she took to mean "do whatever you want, you hopelessly self-and-unimportant-matters-centered interloper," so she disappeared below and heated canned spaghetti sauce while the pasta to go with it boiled one burner over. As soon as she reached the galley, she'd chewed one end off a loaf of French bread she found in a locker; the rest of it was warming in the oven.

When everything was ready, she prepared two heaping platefuls, carried them up to the cockpit, and handed one to him. He looked at the food as if it were roadkill, and then proceeded to scarf it all down—like, one two three, no thanks to her. He didn't speak at all, in fact—even to tell her that he'd forgotten all about eating lunch, which Terry bet he had. She ate a second serving of spaghetti and another hunk of bread, but down below, before she started cleaning up.

Back in the cockpit, she found him listening to the radio again, frequently twisting the dial—almost savagely—to another station, as if by threat of physical force he might intimidate it into finding one that broadcast only news of the Crane family and its possessions. She was reminded of the temper tantrums her brother, Richard, used to throw when he was younger, and how incredibly absurd and unattractive they had made him look. Sometimes she'd used to egg Rich on by chanting "Baby-baby-baby." Now, instead of doing that, she looked away from Mick and smiled a little grown-up smile.

At one point he passed the broadcast of the Red Sox baseball game just as the announcer was getting fans caught up on the "out-of-town scoreboard." "In an afternoon game," she heard, "it was San Diego twelve and San Francisco nothing." So she could imagine Kirt Manwaring being pretty bummed by that. But she bet he was handling it a lot differently than little Mikey Crane was handling *his* disappointment. Kirt was the sort who'd tell his teammates, "We'll get 'em next time!" and "You gotta believe!" and "When the going gets tough, the tough get going." In this situation, he'd be telling her, "I wouldn't want to mess up your plans, Terry, so even though I have to play a doubleheader in St. Louis tomorrow, I'm going to drop you off onshore here with enough money for a first-class plane ticket down to Nassau in the Bahamas—an ideal place for you to spread your wings and get a great job working for Ralph Lauren." That was the difference between a Kirt Manwaring, she thought, and a spoiled-brat-baby Crane.

After a while, she found that the combination of salt air, excitement, two big helpings of slightly overcooked spaghetti (not to mention half a loaf of French bread), and nothing whatever to do was making her extremely sleepy.

So she just stood up and went below, where she got her duffel out of the bow, brushed her teeth in the little sink in the galley, used the head, and rolled onto one of the couches in the second cabin. *To hell with him,* she thought. It never crossed her mind to dive back in the duffel for her can of Mace.

The next morning she was awake before seven, and in a slighlty better mood. She could hear that the radio was on again, topside—which probably meant that he hadn't heard what he wanted to hear—and she wondered if he was even capable of preparing food, for instance getting breakfast. She made herself a quick pb & j, and a cup of tea.

When she joined him in the cockpit, he was staring at the sky, and he kept on doing that after her arrival. So she looked up herself, and saw unbroken blue; if there were Coast Guard aircraft flying, they went elsewhere.

"Would you like one of these?" she asked him,

51

pleasantly enough, waving her sandwich for attention. "It's peanut butter and jelly. And I'm having tea."

He shrugged. "Nuh-no tea," he said, and so when she finished with hers, she made him a sandwich and poured him the more traditional (and age-appropriate) glass of milk.

After the morning local news summary—the moose had not been spotted overnight—he turned off the radio and went below. When he returned, he had a binoculars case over his shoulder, and he started unfastening the *Cormorant*'s little dinghy from its place on the foredeck.

"I'm guh-going to see what's out there," he said, jerking his head in the direction of the ocean. It was pretty clear to her he didn't want her company (and vice versa, she assured herself).

When he had the dinghy launched and was starting to row away, however, she couldn't resist calling out to him.

"You're not afraid *I'll* steal this tub, I guess," she said, with a wicked smile in place.

Looking at his face, she could tell he'd never considered that possibility. Until then. He sat motionless, with both oars out of the water. She wondered if he might be *unusually* stupid, even for someone his age. Now he was trying to decide, she was pretty sure, whether to come back on board and stay there, try to drag her into the dinghy, or just keep on going.

"Yeah—*right*," he finally said, choosing door number three and trying to act cool.

When he'd landed on the little spit of land and disappeared from view, she went below and put her swimsuit on. It was a low-back tank, thin green-and-white stripes, with a pretty high-cut leg. At the last moment she'd packed a bikini, too, a blue one with a French top and kind of teeny down below, but that was not for now, or Mick J. Crane, binocular-boy.

She had a nice dip off the boat, taking a bar of soap with her, and she found and used the little ladder that made getting back on board a cinch. Afterward she dried off in the sun before going below and getting dressed again.

He came back a little after noon, looking blacker than ever. Terry made them a lunch of tuna fish sandwiches and Oreos and diet Dr Pepper—having found, she thought, ol' Maitland's junk-food locker. It was starting to seem probable, to her, that young Mick J. had been 180 degrees off the mark when he predicted that his father would realize how much he wanted a son when the one he had was missing—along with his thirty-four-foot yawl. More than likely, Maitland Crane, assuming that his worthless kid would wreck the boat and drown himself, had said "Good riddance!" to the two of them, and was already looking forward to *Cormorant II,* with its Plexiglass hull and state-of-the-art self-steering mechanisms. She could imagine him keeping a stiff upper lip when the Coast Guard showed him some pieces of wreckage, a few weeks hence, and saying, "I'm afraid the lad was just a chip off the old block. Except he didn't have my luck, God love him!"

If she was right, that meant the boy now had (it seemed to her) three choices. He could slink back to Cape Enid, explaining that he'd wanted to experience, however briefly, the kind of life his hero/dad enjoyed. Or he could maybe *sink* the *Cormorant* right where they were, hitchhike back to his mother's house, and answer any questions that came up with "What? The *Cormorant?* Dad's boat? It's *missing?* Me, I got a little homesick and decided to hike back to Mom's."

Or, best of all and about time, he could shut his yap and take her to the Caribbean and then sail off the edge of the world, for all she cared. She tried projecting that idea to him by mental telepathy—while watching him do what she used to do when *she* was a kid: take an Oreo apart and lick the filling.

"You know what I'm believing?" he said suddenly, putting down the cookie and speaking with the smooth French accent of the Marquis de Framboise. "I'm believing that he had a fatal heart attack, my poor *papa,* or possibly he drive too fast and perish on the highway. And furthermore, this much I know: He wouldn't want for me to have to deal with all the—how you say it?—*fallout* from his passing. What he would say to me is, 'My beloved son, don't weep for me and fall into depression. Instead, go out and celebrate my life; go on an adventure, just like one of mine! Sail this grand old girl down to the Caribbean. As for the stowaway—take her with, if she so chooses. Say this to her: Frankly, Red, I don't give a damn!'" He smiled and cocked a questioning eyebrow at the girl.

Terry's eyes had widened in delight as he was speaking. Now she sprang onto her feet, saluting smartly (stomach in, chest out), projecting "model shipmate," "eager-beaver crew."

"Anchors aweigh, *mi capitán,*" she said.

# chapter 6

It made sense, Terry thought—regretfully—that the Marquis de Framboise really *didn't* give a damn whether she was on board the *Cormorant* or not. After all he'd been through, growing up in the fifteenth century in drafty castles with no indoor plumbing, and possibly including seeing Joan of Arc, a confidante of his, burned at the stake, what a Cape Enid teenager did or didn't do wouldn't be likely to either make or break his day.

Watching someone you'd been a confidant of get burned at the stake would be a bummer of epic proportions, she imagined. *She'd* felt a little nauseous just listening to Mr. Relish, her eleventh-grade physics teacher, verbally dissect her classmate Max

Manusha when he'd confused the first and second laws of motion—and she had never talked with Max that much and only kissed him New Year's Eve, when everyone was kissing everybody else.

In this second appearance of his, the marquis had once again made quite an impression on Terry. There was definitely something Manwaringesque about him—about his poise, his confidence, the way he rose to an occasion. It's fair to say that if he'd stuck around, Terry would have considered trying to make him forget Joan of Arc, although she didn't have a clear idea of how to go about that.

"Did you and Joan ever discuss whether it'd be all right for both of you to be confidants of *other* kids, as well?" was something she thought she might say, for openers. "Because I'd like to tell you something kind of personal, if that'd be okay."

To which he maybe would reply, "Please do. She always said that I should also hear what's in the hearts of other girls."

"In that case," Terry then could tell him, "you should know that, unlike her, I'm not a saint."

She thought there was a good chance that her saying that would make him happy.

"I am, in truth, most pleased to have that confidence," she imagined him replying. "A saint is much to be admired—being helpful, yes, and even inspirational. But this does *not* mean such a person makes a perfect girlfriend."

"The thing is, though," Terry figured she'd be wise to add, "I'm really not much of a sinner, either." There was no telling what a fifteenth-century marquis might expect from a girl who didn't have any noble blood in her veins and wasn't a candidate for sainthood. In the old days, maybe it was open season on such girls. And she didn't ever want to be accused of getting a boyfriend under false pretenses (also known in modern times as "teasing").

Ideally, he would chuckle at that.

"Is okay," he'd say. "No problem. Back home we have a saying: We drink no wine before its time. But still, I do have one small question for you, Terry, *ma cherie*."

"What?" she'd say. "Ask anything. Feel free."

"Do you hear voices? When there's no one there?"

"No," she'd say. "Of course not."

"*Bon!*" he'd say to that. "*Trés bon!* To tell the truth, the voices that my Joan did hear? They always—how do you say it—*freak me out* a little."

The fact of the matter was, however, that the marquis hadn't stuck around, apparently, so they weren't able to have that conversation as the coastline faded in the distance and finally disappeared.

But despite his absence, Terry Talley, self-appointed first mate of the good ship *Cormorant,* found herself as happy as a hawk on a thermal: She just spread her wings and let herself float merrily along. It seemed that she was getting what she wanted—*exactly* what she wanted—and how often does that happen (she had to ask herself) to someone who is not quite seventeen and female, in a single-parent home?

Indeed, for about the first forty-eight hours of their voyage, she was so blissed out that she never even raised her voice to whine about some way the world displeased her. What's more, she didn't realize how unprecedented that was. She was still a few years from knowing that "I've never been so happy in my life," like "I'm in a jail cell for soliciting," is seldom more than a twenty-four-hour proposition.

On the third day she did begin to notice Mick J. Crane—long since back to being the "original flavor" Mick, of course—*was* becoming a bit of an annoyance. But even that, she blamed more on proximity than anything.

"What you have to understand," she imagined writing Connie once she was settled on her island, "is that the lad was somewhere near me *all the time.* You know how close a softball pitcher is when you're at bat. The length of our entire boat was not as far as that! We were always almost in each other's *pockets.* Not that he tried . . . *you* know—anything."

On that same third day, coincidentally or not, he began to "test" her sailing skills—to see if she could steer the *Cormorant,* and keep it on the course he'd set, and trim the sails so as to maximize the boat's ability to do its best in different wind conditions. He said that if she could be trusted at the helm, then he could get some real sleep in his bunk below, during the daylight hours. This would be in addition to the catnaps he admitted taking in the cockpit while alone at night.

Terry didn't mind one aspect of this testing process. She wanted to be fully confident herself that she was capable of doing all the things a single-handed sailor had to do. So learning different facts and some techniques from him was not that big a problem. The hard-to-take part was Mick's style of teaching. He did what could have been a *Saturday Night Live* takeoff on all the rotten teachers in the world—except it was so obvious he wasn't kidding.

He'd make her say stuff back to him *exactly* as he said it, and go on and on with boring stories from his time at sailing camp—the kinds of anecdotes a person *really* would have had to be there to appreciate at all. And then there were the silly poses that he struck.

"Is there suh-something funny that I'm missing here?" he asked her as she was biting the insides of her cheeks to keep from laughing out loud at the way he stood there with one finger raised, his stupid yachting cap on backward, and pulling solemnly at one corner of his upper lip as if there were, in fact, a mustache there.

"I cuh-can assure you, running into duh-duh-driftwood isn't any laughing matter," he continued.

"Right—but how about a *whale*?" she'd asked, needing to interrupt the list of completely obvious "don'ts" he'd started on, needing not to hear his preachy, condescending tone of voice for a minute or two, needing to annoy *him*, maybe, for a change. "I bet running over a whale isn't funny either—the size of some of those big mothuhs. Would whales be another 'hazard to navigation' in these waters?"

He shook his head impatiently.

"Well, that's a relief," she went on. "You know what I'd *really* hate? To be swallowed by a whale. I was thinking about that last night. Say we're caught in a calm, and I was swimming off the boat, and all of a sudden a whale came along and just gulped me down. Yuk! I'd really *hate* that." She was talking fast and trying to run some words together, Connie-style.

"Not that that's even *possible*," she continued. "D'you think? I don't know why they put that in the Bible—you know, the story where Jonah or what-everhisnamewas is eaten by some huge *leviathan*—

I love that word, don't you?—and ends up living in its *gut*? Personally, I don't see how a person could *breathe* inside a whale's tummy. Of course, they *do* have blowholes—like, remember that time on *Seinfeld* when someone hit a golf ball into one? But even if you could breathe, think how gross—*disgusting*—it'd be, just sitting in this . . . like a cave, except with *flesh walls*, in the dark, with a bunch of half-digested fish or plankton—whatevertheheck *they* are—sloshing all around you . . . !"

"If you don't *mind* . . . ," he'd interrupted, finally. "Duh-do you think we could get back onto the *subject*, now?"

Eventually they both agreed that she was fully qualified to sail the boat for a few hours, in the daytime, in good weather. And that put them on a slightly different daily schedule.

Although neither of them had ever brought the subject up, Terry'd assumed she also had the title of ship's cook. So she'd gotten food for him ever since she first came up out of her hiding place in the bow, and in their new schedule she kept on doing that. (She wasn't any French chef, but she could open cans and packages, either boil or fry whatever stuff came out of them, and by adding ketchup and some other seasonings, make almost anything taste quite a bit like pizza.) She used Mick's father's small alarm clock to wake herself at six and get their breakfast. After it, he'd go below and she'd be at the helm till it was time to wake him up, at one, when she'd make sandwiches for lunch. Then he might go back to bed again—or not; at 6:00 P.M. she'd whip up dinner, and by nine she was ready for bed. That meant the only times they spent together were some afternoon and evening hours.

It only took a couple of days for her to become convinced she could handle *that* amount of closeness—no sweat—for however long it took. Being around him still annoyed her, but like most small aches and pains, as she got used to it, it seemed to get more bearable.

One time, lying in her bunk, below, she wondered what Mick J. would do once they reached wherever he was going to let her off. She didn't think he had a plan, or even a clue. The marquis was the one who'd said that Maitland Crane was dead; did Mick J. believe it, in his heart of hearts?

She didn't ask him that—or any other questions. She decided that the less she knew about his life, the better. It was the same as why she never read the little stories or descriptions under the pictures of the homeless puppies that the Humane Society put in the *Cape Enid Shopping Guide*: She didn't want to end up feeling sorry for the kid and trying to solve his problems. The marquis had gotten him to go on this "adventure," right? Mick wasn't her responsibility. All she'd done was try to tell him, tele-pathically, to do what he was doing—but it had never worked when she'd sent messages to Connie (like: "Buy me a chocolate-and-vanilla Twistee cone, why don't you?").

Of course, the marquis could have had it right. Maybe Maitland Crane *was* dead. In that case, Mick J. Crane was probably a millionaire. She kind of hoped he was. That'd mean he had a real nice future to look forward to, at least in terms of having stuff. And it'd doubtless help him to attract a certain kind of girl. Not *her* kind, necessarily. She closed her eyes and imagined Mick behind the wheel of a little vin-tage MGB two-seater with the top down—him without the yachting cap and with a better haircut. Maybe five years older and a Williams College jun-ior, say. Would she get in and take a ride with him?

If he spoke with a French accent, say?

# chapter 7

When you're totally depressed and miserable, it's hard, sometimes, to feel certain that after a while you'll snap out of it and feel real good about yourself again. Terry was far from mastering that little trick.

But also when your clothes look good on you, you're making lucky guesses on most of the multiple-choice questions, and your sister's torn her ACL and simply *cannot* use the car you share, you seldom tell yourself: "Deep doo-doo straight ahead." Terry never had yet.

And it's the same with the weather, particularly fair weather. At sea, you can really get the feeling of being locked into a fair-weather system. And this is even more true if a person hasn't been at sea that much. Terry Talley was just such a person. It simply never occurred to her it wasn't going to be "like this" for her whole trip "to the islands." "This," she felt, was what the islands were like—why people saved all year to have vacations on them.

Her first hint of ca-ca from the weather gods took the form of rain squalls in their area. You could watch them dance across the surface of the ocean, sometimes hitting/drenching you, and sometimes not. In times, however, they turned into steady rain, and the sea began to look more troubled. Soon the *Cormorant* was riding darker, deeper swells. Mick told her the barometer was falling.

"That means?" she asked.

A change in weather, he informed her curtly. "For the wuh-wuh-worse."

She asked him how much worse and got the feeling from his shrugs he didn't know. That afternoon he didn't go below, and kept checking the barometer, tapping it with his fingers as if it were broken, or he didn't quite believe what it was telling him. But still he let her keep on steering. She'd put on Maitland Crane's extra set of "foul weather gear," a slicker and sou'wester, and thought she looked real cute in them.

Before she went below to make their dinner, he took down the sail on their second, smaller mast, the mizzenmast, and also the jib, which was, along with the staysail, one of the two small ones in front of the mainmast. He then "reefed" the two remaining sails, the mainsail and the staysail; that made them smaller. He told her that he didn't want to be "wearing too much canvas" if the wind continued to get stronger. She thought he might be showing off or trying to scare her.

After they'd eaten, though, he got out and then put on (over his T-shirt and long shorts, which were already wet, of course) a "safety harness," which was basically a bunch of straps and ropes that, when fastened to a body and a boat, would keep the person from being washed overboard, in the event a big wave broke over the cockpit. He chose to *not* put on the foul weather gear himself, knowing (she assumed) she had the cuteness contest all wrapped up. Or it *could* be he preferred the much-increased mobility that wearing fewer clothes provided.

Just as she was heading for her bunk, he told her that he wanted her to stay below under any and all circumstances, until he told her to come up again, concluding with "Thuh-that's an *order*, understand?"

His saying that not only irked her mightily but also, along with his putting on the harness, scared her quite a bit—so much so that when she finished brushing her teeth and using the head (no mean feat, sort of like riding a rodeo bull sidesaddle with your trousers at half mast), she dredged up some of the Twenty-third Psalm out of her Sunday school memory bank. "Please leadeth me beside *still* waters, really soon," Terry prayed, wishing she'd established more of a relationship with Whoever was capable of doing that. Terry, like her mother, was a person who (1.) believed there certainly *was* a God (Who didn't have a long white beard and Who could just as easily be female), (2.) *loved* the whole *idea* of heaven, and (3.) always celebrated the birth of Christ by getting even more outdoor lights, procuring fattening and expensive edibles in ridiculous quantities, and finding just the right surprises for each other's stockings (while calling other people's celebrations "too commercial"). She was also a person who, post-Sunday school, attended services at the Cape Enid United church only when the spirit moved her (mother, usually), which averaged a half dozen times a year. Both of them had pleasant singing voices and got into the hymns, especially. A mangled line from one of them, "So hear our prayer blah-blah to thee, for those in peril on the sea" popped into her mind and got repeated, along with that bit from the Twenty-third Psalm, quite a few times in the course of the night.

It turned out she didn't much enjoy either lying

down on her bunk or standing looking out a port-hole, holding on for dear life. Lying down was somewhat better in terms of comfort, but she couldn't keep herself from getting up—oh, every fifteen minutes at the most—to look in frightened fascination at what was going on outside.

She couldn't see that much; there wasn't any moon or starlight, just a little glimmer from their masthead light. But thanks to it, she could make out the shapes of the biggest waves she'd ever seen, by far, with white foam being blown from off the crests of some of them by the ferocious wind.

At one point she heard a lot of scrabbling sounds almost directly over her head, then grunts and curses and a bang; it was as if a bunch of heavy monkeys were up there, busy doing something. Something difficult, that also pissed them off. Of course, she *knew* it was Mick doing stuff with ropes or sails or maybe the dinghy, there being no heavy monkeys on board, and she took comfort in the fact that if she kept hearing him moving around up there, it meant that he was probably all right, and that she—oh, thank you, thank you, God—was not alone.

From time to time she fleetingly considered going topside herself to see if she could help—and, hardly unimportantly to show the kid how little weight she gave an "order" from a dweeb like him—but in the end her need to make that point was easily overcome by her intense desire not to be swept overboard. She didn't have a safety harness, after all—and even if there'd been another one, she wasn't sure she could have put it on; it looked incredibly uncomfortable.

But it wasn't very long after she had those thoughts that she heard the hatch fly open, and of course, she feared the worst. She ran the few steps to the other cabin.

"I have strike the mainsail," the marquis informed her, "an' from the mooring lines I improvise a species of sea anchor, which I think may slow our progress *un petit peu.*"

He was standing at the bottom of the stairs and dripping water on the indoor-outdoor carpeting. His hat was gone and the shirt and shorts he had on underneath the harness were like a second skin, plastered to his body; he looked *great*. His dark eyes twinkled merrily.

"Can I help? In any way at all?" Terry heard herself inquire, the words cascading from her lips before she'd even thought of them, it seemed.

"*Non, cherie,*" he said. "Is required only that one person steer and try to keep the wind behind; I do that job myself. When and if it starts to calm, a nice hot cup of *chocolat* would be delightful, though."

And with that he bounded up the little stair and back into the cockpit.

The marquis's return to the *Cormorant* both calmed and excited Terry, she discovered. She assumed he had at his disposal all the seafaring knowledge Mick had acquired at that sailing camp—but, in his case, layered onto the experience in getting out of tight spots anyone who'd lived and traveled in the fifteenth century would be almost bound to have had. That was the calming part.

She imagined that the fifteenth century had been one of the most dangerous periods in the world's history, a time when even the shortest of land journeys—say, the length of one from Cape Enid to Dreary—would have exposed a traveler to plague, wild boars with tusks, roadside hangings, thieving innkeepers, village idiots, peasant uprisings, and even wars over religion or between two petty fiefdoms. And bad weather like this was much too everyday and small-d democratic—the same for everyone—to be a thing that a marquis would let himself be bothered by.

The exciting thing about his reappearance was . . . well, simply *him*.

But even as Tee Talley thought those thoughts, the *Cormorant* began to pitch and roll more wildly. A huge wave came down on the boat, and there was the sound of wood splintering, followed by a crash. Terry held her breath and ran to look out the porthole. The masthead light was out, or maybe gone;

perhaps the mast had broken and washed over-board. Might Mick and the marquis, she wondered, have gone with it?

And then she heard the bilge pump being worked. He was in the cockpit still, and coping. Terry thanked God most sincerely and repeatedly. Perhaps, she thought, the two of them had started a relationship. It'd be a kick, she thought, for her to wheel on down the road of life and have God at her side. Or maybe (she amended) that should be the other way around: God driving, Talley riding shotgun.

The storm continued to rage on that night. The *Cormorant* was a wild, bucking bronco, soaring up, then diving, crashing down, only to (once more) leap straight up again, whinnying and groaning as it went. The wind shrieked and whipped great sheets of foam and rain against the tiny vessel. From time to time another monster wave crashed down on it, threatening to break it right in half, or push it way deep under, sink the little thing. Two or three times Terry heard a heavy object scrape across the cabin roof.

She supposed they were racking up a lot of miles, going so fast for so long—but in what direction was another story. It was almost certain they were way off course, pushed by a wind that didn't give a hoot about the destination that they had in mind. Because they'd been so far from land when the storm started, she didn't think it likely that they'd run aground anywhere—and hopefully they wouldn't hit a major piece of driftwood (or a whale). A greater danger might be posed, she thought, by something like another boat—a cruise ship, say, or even the wreck of some craft their own size. If their mast was down or if their sails had ripped away, the marquis wouldn't be able to steer around . . . well, anything, even if he saw it way ahead of time, which, of course, he wouldn't.

*Yikes*—she thought, at one point—might they be right now, this minute, in the dread "Bermuda Triangle"? That was (she knew) an area where many ships and even planes had disappeared without a trace. Her earth science teacher had mentioned it in passing a couple of years before, and everyone in the class had thought it'd be cool to crack the mystery of those disappearances. But no one had wanted to do that by first becoming the most recent one—which was exactly what the *Cormorant* could be (she thought) before this night was over.

Even as ideas like that swirled through her brain, Terry kept on going back and forth between the porthole and her bunk. Because it seemed to her the sea had gotten just a little bit less rough, she actually got into bed one time, to see if tucked-in sheets and blankets possibly might work a little like a safety belt and hold her body in one place. They did. She closed her eyes for just a second . . .

When she woke up, absolutely everything had changed—a lot. For one thing, it was light outside; for another, they were moving very differently: rocking now, instead of plunging up and down.

*Oh, my gosh,* she thought, *the marquis's cocoa!* In a flash she was in the little galley, starting water boiling and looking in the food lockers for marshmallows. It wasn't long before, with steaming mug in hand, she was going up the little steps and out into the cockpit once again.

The first thing that she noticed was the tiller, lashed in place by two strong lines. Mick had explained that was a thing a single-handed sailor did quite often, when he had to leave the helm to deal with something way up front, or even up the mast. A lashed tiller would keep the boat from going round in circles.

The second thing she noticed was, she didn't notice anyone up front, or up the mast, either. Indeed, there wasn't any mast, or any boom, or any dinghy. And in the cockpit there, she saw the remnants of a ripped-up safety harness.

The terrible reality sank in, in spite of her resistance to it. She was alone on board the *Cormorant.*

Mick J. and the marquis were missing. They had saved their little ship, and her, but in the process they had lost their lives—*his* life, whatever.

Terry sat down on the floorboards, fat tears running down her cheeks, and sipped the marquis's *chocolat*.

# chapter 8

As Terry sat there, crying in her cocoa, she tried to imagine what someone like Kirt Manwaring would do if he were to find himself in comparably dire straits. Say, for instance, he was traded to the Houston Astros, which'd mean he'd have to play his future home games *indoors,* in the crummy old Astrodome, till they built the new stadium. What would he be apt to tell himself?

Well (she told *her*self), he'd probably say something like, "So Kirt old man, cheer up; there's nothing to be gained by moping, really. You've still got your health and your rugged good looks, and there are still a lotta fans out there you can count on. The doggone trade was a *management* decision; it might look like a disaster right now, but face it, buddy, you've survived it, and it isn't up to you to second-guess the boss. Sure, you're gonna miss your old teammates, but guys like Barry Bonds and Matt Williams wouldn't want you going into some big slump because of that. They'd say for you to just hang in there and—who knows?—something really good might come of this. Perhaps they'll trade you to the Rockies!"

Thinking the way Kirt might have did a lot for Terry Talley's state of mind. She shouldn't second-guess The Big Boss either, she decided; a lot of kids she knew said everything happened for a *reason*, whenever something happened they could see no earthly reason for. And she absolutely *did* owe it to Connie and the rest of her fans—er, *friends*—as well as her family, to "just hang in there," and do whatever she could to make something positive out of this seemingly negative situation. If she didn't at least *try*, then Mick J. and the marquis would have died in vain, whatever that meant, and she was not about to let it happen.

So, fortified by the cocoa and inspired by the spin she'd put on everything, she thought she'd see if she could lay her hands on Mick's binoculars and have a look around. Perhaps the storm had carried her into "the shipping lanes," and the poor old *Cormorant* was now the equivalent of a broken-down

Ford Fairlane parked on the shoulder with its hood up, waiting for some passing trucker to use his CB radio and summon help for it.

As she got to her feet, she glanced in the direction that the crippled craft was floating—and almost jumped for joy. In what she'd call the "middle distance"—in other words, too far to paddle but easily seen by the naked eye—there was *land* of some sort. It seemed to be, she thought, an island, but not just a cartoon island with a single palm tree and a fat man in an undershirt on it. This one stretched for quite a distance, shaped sort of like a turtle's back, and rose high above the sea. And near one end of it she saw . . . yes, surely, it was something *moving*. Was it—could it be—a boat?

She lunged at the locker underneath the helmsman's bench; the binoculars were there. In no time she had them out of their case and focused. It was definitely a boat, a powerboat, like one of the big fast ones in Cape Enid harbor, the ones that club members used for fishing, cruising, and (they hoped) impressing women other than their wives. Terry was definitely jumping then, for joy and from excitement. Soon she would no longer be "in peril on the sea!" She was going to be rescued. It seemed the people on the boat had seen the *Cormorant* and were heading straight for her!

It would still be a little while before they got

there, though. And Terry realized there were two ways she could prep for their arrival. Would it be best to look bedraggled—pitiful—a wreck just like the *Cormorant?* Or should she try to make the best impression possible? As she was dressed right then, she occupied a kind of middle ground, in pants and a T-shirt that looked as if they'd been slept in, but which surely didn't shout "Unfortunate survivor!" or "Pathetic!" on the one hand, or "Drop dead gorgeous" on the other.

There was time for her to go below and change, either up or down. *What would Mone advise?* she asked herself. That was an easy one. She hurried down the stairs and into the forward cabin, stripping as she went.

Her choice was an engaging little sundress in a floral print, light and swirly, made of an amazingly wrinkled-resistant synthetic fabric. It showed off her bare arms and nice long legs, but wasn't short enough to be provocative, she didn't think. She had good color from those many sunny days they'd had, and the rain that had drenched her short red hair before she'd found the sou'wester had left it looking soft and shiny. She gave it a good brushing, and after a fast application of nearly natural lipstick and a tiny touch of eyeliner, she felt absolutely ready to be rescued.

• • •

The cruiser, when it reached her, was a reassuring sight. Its paint job, white with gold trim, looked brand-new; its woodwork positively glowed, and its brass fixtures sparkled in the sun. *The owner of a boat like this might draw a blank at "Kirt Manwaring" or "Oasis" or "Smashing Pumpkins," but would greet a name like "Merrill Lynch" with nods and knowing smiles,* Tee thought.

She wasn't exactly sure how a person being rescued ought to look, other than grateful, so again with Mone in mind, she settled for "poised." She stood and put her back against the mizzenmast, gripping it with her left hand below her waist, while waving with her right hand, shoulder-high and side to side. On the evening news she'd once seen Mrs. Clinton wave like that.

Whoever was steering the cruiser knew what he was doing, smoothly bringing his boat alongside the *Cormorant*. As soon as he'd done so, a pair of pint-sized people popped up from behind the cruiser's rail. Terry thought that they were Asians, at first glance. They quickly tossed four fat fenders over the side of their boat; these, hanging there, kept the *Cormorant*'s hull from scraping up against their nice white paint. Then the two hopped onto Terry's deck, both holding nylon lines which they expertly belayed around two cleats up near the *Cormorant*'s bow. Apparently they knew what steps to take when giving some poor wreck a tow job.

It was while they were doing this "making fast" business that Terry realized the two were not only not Asians, but not even grown-ups. They were children—kids—one a boy and one a girl, a good deal younger than Mick J. (maybe ten, eleven, twelve years old), and very much alike. They were barefoot, wearing cutoff shorts and tank tops, his dark blue and hers a lovely shade of lavender. Both had shiny, straight black hair; hers was parted on the side and pulled back in a ponytail, while his was a traditional Prince Valiant. Around both of their left wrists were by far the biggest, heaviest, woven-gold ID bracelets Terry'd ever seen. *Much* too much of a good thing for kids that age, she thought. Not that it was any of her beeswax.

It seemed she wasn't the only person admiring their expertise, though.

"Bravo! Well done, you beastly brats!" boomed out from the cruiser's covered control center. It was a man's voice, not a *young* man's voice, a voice, Tee thought, that rang with confidence, authority, and mixed together, affection and contempt. Altogether not unlike the voice of Mr. Pettifogg, principal of old Cape Enid High.

"You rotten little swamp scum," he concluded.

Looking delighted, the pair plunked themselves down on the roof of the *Cormorant*'s cabin with their dirty feet dangling into the cockpit. They were a comely pair, who really did resemble one another, having huge dark eyes and eyebrows, shapely little noses, perfect straight white teeth, smooth even tans, and—unmistakably—bad attitudes. Those dark eyes had one question in them: "Yeah—why *should* I?" Terry'd seen their kind before at the Cape Enid Club, smoking cigarettes behind the tennis backboard.

"Now . . . " The captain of the cruiser took a big deep breath and let it out, not quietly. Terry thought it was a getting-down-to-business sort of sound.

"Halloo there, fair young maiden—greetings, cutie-pie," he started. "Please accept my heartfelt deep condolences—I'd like to say *our* deep condolences, except these savage young 'uns have no manners and perhaps no feelings—greed excepted. It's all their mother's fault, she's never . . . but that's no concern of yours, and anyway—what am I thinking of? Profound, *profound* apologies! For all I know, you haven't understood a word I've said. Or *have* you? Let me see. . . . " He took another breath and cranked the volume up still higher. "DO YOU UN-DERSTAND THE ENGLISH? PARLEY-VOO ANGLAY, NESSPA?"

Terry nodded. The area his voice was coming from was glass-enclosed, but the glass was tinted, like a limosine's. It was difficult deciding how she felt about this invisible man. On the one hand, he seemed friendly (if long-winded), but she also thought that he might have a mean, sarcastic side. Like Mr. Pettifogg, again.

"*Excellante!* Good! We share some common ground," he then continued. "Where was I? Let's see. . . . 'Deep condolences,' was that it? Yes! But now your frightening ordeal is over; you've scaled the Matterhorn and now are starting down the other side. You're safe—and unless my eyes deceive me— supersound. Even to the point of pulchritude—not that that would be an issue, either way. So let's get down to business, eh? Suppose you call your father or your uncle or your other shipmates topside, bringing with them your ship's papers. Once they put them in my hands, I'll fire up the wireless and send out joyful tidings to a waiting world. Think how frantic they've all been back home!"

"Hm," said Terry, "I'm afraid I don't have any shipmates. My father and my uncles never were on board. There was another . . . person, but he was . . . well, swept overboard, last night. He's surely dead by now"—a tear ran down her cheek, provoked by that word "dead"—"I guess."

"Oh, what a *pity*," said the other. "Pity, pity, *pity!* And, you know, I'd feared as much. Every time we have a real monsoon—this one's name was Murray, by the way—we're apt to find a . . . stranger, washed up on our beach come morning. Other than alive, I'm sad to say. Today it was a slender, blond, attractive lad—long hair with sideburns. Would that be your . . . other person? Quite the young Greek god? Maybe twenty, twenty-one, or -two? A little tiger tattooed on his . . . *derriere?*" The sound of that word made his kiddy crew look quickly at each other and begin to giggle.

"No," said Terry, deciding to ignore them. "Kirt was twenty-eight or -nine, I think. He had short brown hair and a muscular physique. No tattoos, but a surgical scar on his right, or throwing, hand." She didn't know what prompted her to give this totally misleading description of Mick, even going so far as to call him "Kirt"; she just did.

"I *see,*" he said, and stepped—one might say "waddled"—out of his enclosure. "Well, if you're the sole survivor, maybe we should move along to introductions. *I* am Captain William Horatio Francis Cormac Bonny Bartholomew Avery Gold— 'Short Bill Gold'—for short."

And "short," he was indeed, no more than five foot three or four, by Terry's reckoning. If he'd been her brother Richard's age, they would have called him "husky," but her label for his shape was "fat." His face was florid and clean-shaven, except for a pointed white Vandyke beard; he had plump cheeks and a broad little nose, and his eyes were those of a friendly potbellied pig, small but also merry. He was quite elegantly dressed from top to bottom, beginning with a yachting cap exactly like Mick's, but powder blue instead of white and with a lot of gold braid on the visor. His leisure suit was also powder blue, and its trousers were bell-bottoms; from below them peeked a pair of black Air Jordans. Around his neck was a dark blue ascot with white polka dots, and a sizable black bird was perched on his right shoulder. Terry was very glad she'd dressed the way she had.

"How do you do?" she said, politely. "My name is Terry Talley."

"So, Terry," said the captain. "That's a lovely name. Now, if you'd just get me your ship's papers . . ."

"I don't know where they are," she said, quite truthfully. "I *guess* they're somewhere in the cabin. Kirt took care of all that kind of stuff. If you could tell me what to look for, I'll gladly—"

"No need to bother," he informed her. "That's why God makes kiddies, isn't it? To run our errands for us? *Papers,* you young scallawags. Go fetch!"

With that the two slid off the cabin roof into the cockpit, then down the hatch; they were as quick and smooth as otters.

Terry remembered Mone advising her to always make a point of knowing everybody's names, whenever she found herself in an awkward, unfamiliar situation. "People *like* it when you use their names," Mone said. "It flatters them."

"They're awfully cute, those two," she said, gesturing toward the hatch the twins had just gone down. "What would *their* names be?"

"Cherubim and Seraphin," the captain said. "Those were my ideas, of course; little did I know how they'd turn out. Cherry's the girl and Serry's the other one. Last name's Holly. Their mother mostly opts for 'Buddy' for the boy—that's typical of how her mind works, I'm afraid. I had to talk her out of her original plan, which was to christen him 'Bowser.' As in 'Deck the halls with Bowser Holly'— get it?"

Terry nodded, smiling weakly. She wondered where the children's mother was, and if she was related to the captain.

"And the crow?" she asked, nodding at the bird on his shoulder. "What do you call him? Or is it a her?"

"He's not a crow," Bill Gold corrected her. "He's a myna bird. Different species altogether, member of the starling family. Mentally and stylistically superior to crows. Aren't you?" he said, looking over at the bird. "Tell this pretty little lady what to call you."

"Call me Ishmael," said the bird, quite clearly. And he followed that amazing, even literary, statement with the loudest, most piercing two-tone wolf whistle Terry'd ever heard.

She clapped her hands with pleasure, feeling silly, but still flattered by the bird's opinion. "Gladly, Ishmael," she said to him. "And I'm very glad to meet you."

"Are you a myna bird?" Ishmael asked her, poking his long beak in her direction.

"No," she told him. "I'm a girl, like Cherry, except older. My name even rhymes with hers. It's Terry."

"Hi," said the bird, drawing out the word so as to make it . . . well, *suggestive*, Terry thought. And then following it with another tremendous double whistle.

"He's taken quite a shine to you," said Captain Gold. "As a rule, he's not that fond of females. Can't stand Cherry, for example. Which proves that he's a bird of sense and sensibility, I'd say."

As if responding to this latest mention of her name, Cherry burst out of the *Cormorant*'s cabin, followed closely by her brother. She had papers in her hand; he held nothing but a grudge, as it turned out.

"No fair!" he screamed. "She wouldn't let me up on the cap'n's bunk. And they were in the locker right behind his pillow."

"Tough. You thought that they were with the

charts, you little half-wit. And you had dibs on where to look," she told him, rubbing it in. "You stink at finding stuff. You couldn't find your whatsis in your underwear!"

"*Silencio!*" the captain shouted. "Name and owner, read 'em to me, gutter-mouth. Be quick about it."

"The yawl's name is the *Cormorant*," said Cherry, reciting in a goody-goody tone of voice. "And she's owned by Mr. Maitland Crane."

"*Maitland Crane?*" The captain almost sang the words. "Did you say 'Maitland Crane'?"

"Uh-huh," the girl replied.

"*Oooh,*" he said. "*Delightful!*"

"*Hi,*" said Ishmael, again.

# chapter 9

Having the *Cormorant*'s papers in his hand did not cause Short Bill Gold to "crank up the wireless" as he'd said it would, Terry noticed. Apparently the waiting world was going to have to wait a little longer for the glad tidings of the yawl's (and her) deliverance. No, the captain, after rolling the owner's name around in his mouth another time or two, simply popped the papers into a cabinet near his steering wheel and suggested that she climb aboard.

As she did so, she added to her name collection by glancing at one of the cruiser's life preservers. Painted on it in black and gold letters was the boat's name, which was the *Kidd Me Not,* and its home port of Isla Muela Negra—words the *presidenta* of the Cape Enid High Spanish Club correctly translated as "Black Molar Island." (*Gross,* she thought.)

Terry hadn't yet had time to figure out all the possible effects the "rescue" might have on that master plan of hers—which was to start a new and independent life down on some island with a pleasant name that she (and people like J. Peterman, Donna Karan, and whoever owned The Gap) had heard of. Perhaps she'd made a big mistake by telling Captain Gold *her* real name. If it ever got into the ears of tell-alls like Tom Brokaw of NBC, or, worse yet, the various announcers on NPR's *Morning Edition,* Mone'd be at Logan Airport within minutes and somewhere in her vicinity in hours. So she was just as glad that Captain Gold seemed more concerned with getting the *Cormorant* in position to be towed than trying to reach the mainland telegraphically. He was leaning over the cruiser's stern at that moment with his fat little rump in the air, maybe making sure his towing lines were clear of the *Kidd Me Not*'s propellers.

She'd assumed the twins were somehow helping with the salvage operation when they appeared out of the cruiser's cabin carrying about an eight foot piece of wide and heavy lumber—what in construction work is called a two-by-ten. This they then proceeded to fasten to bolts set in the cruiser's foredeck so it stuck out like . . . hey, a diving board!

This wasn't out of character—for them to have their own agenda—Terry thought. When they disappeared below again, she guessed they'd gone to change into their bathing suits.

So it was a big surprise to her when they returned still dressed the same, but holding very large old-fashioned pistols, along with lengths of nylon line.

"Hey, Uncle Bill—you want that we should tie her hands behind her or in front?" the boy twin yelled in the direction of the captain.

He looked to Terry like a "Buddy" at that shocking moment. "Buddy" was an alias, the sort of name that hid a criminal identity. "Buddys" ended up in penitentiaries—the ones who weren't rock and roll immortals.

"Dibbies on doing the blindfold," said his sister.

"What?" Gold turned around and saw the heavily armed pair, and then the board projecting off the vessel's bow. "Oh, no, no, no—you little imbeciles! Have you lost *all* the marbles in your toy chests? Go put those things back where you found them, and leave the girl alone. Nobody's going to tie her up"— he leered—"for any purpose whatsoever."

"You mean she isn't going to walk the plank?" said Cherry.

"Before we left the island, you *said* that there were signs of life on board—that you'd seen that through your spyglass," the boy chimed in. "You *promised* we could make 'em walk, whoever was on board. You said they'd all be 'fish food.'"

"That's *right*," his sister confirmed. "If you hadn't *promised*, I never would have come. I'm sick of taking prizes when it's just some dumb old boat with no one on it. We didn't have to help today; Roger could have come."

The captain sighed a weary sigh. "What you two little chowderheads still have to learn is to expect the unexpected in this business. Every prize is different. You never know, when you leave port, exactly what you'll have to do to maximize your profits from the . . . deal. Sometimes circumstances call for bloodshed, and there's loss of life, and even *lives*. I don't remember hearing anybody whine when we were forced to open fire on the gentlemen in that fast speedboat with the ruptured gas line. The ones with all the thousand-dollar bills they didn't want to share with us? We didn't know what we might have to do until we got to them, and chatted—learning they were . . . pharmaceutical suppliers, and ungenerous."

"Oh, yeah—the Colombian drug biggies. That was fun," said little Buddy Holly with great relish. "*Pow-pow-pow!* Boy, were they surprised or what? They never thought a fat old guy and two fifth graders would do a thing like that—put a bunch of real big holes in them." He shook his head and chortled at the recollection. "*Pow-pow-pow! Adios, muchachos.*"

"Surprise can be a leveler of playing fields, my boy," the captain said. "Today's surprise, however, is a ring-tailed doozy."

Terry had to go along with that. If she could believe her ears, which had definitely heard the twins use expressions like "taking prizes" and "walk the plank," the captain of the *Kidd Me Not* was, if not Captain Kidd, someone in the same profession. A man who, if she hadn't been on a boat that was property of Maitland Crane, would have let two murderous middle graders turn her into "fish food." Even as she thought those thoughts, he was explaining to the little psychopaths who Maitland Crane was, and what this Terry Talley person might be worth to them.

"To convince him that we really do have her, we'll send him a photo of her with some identifiable piece of the *Cormorant,* probably the stern transom where her name is. That'll be after we've winched her out of the water and cut her up for parts, of course." The captain smiled and nodded.

"I can see the girl being worth a million in unmarked bills," he went on. "And on top of that, these vintage sailing boats are hugely valuable, even one in this condition. You don't see decking like that nowadays—or portholes, or cabinetry, or fittings. In six months' time, bits and pieces of her will probably be skimming o'er the Persian Gulf, incorporated into quite a few old oil sheiks' pleasure dhows. No, the *Cormorant* would be a real prize even if it wasn't bearing babes—*a* babe—as well. I wonder what this Terry is to Crane. Could be his daughter *or* a firm, young mistress, I suppose. In any case, a pretty bauble. He'll be *very* glad to get her back, I warrant."

It was then that Terry finally found her voice.

"You're *pirates!*" she exclaimed. "You run a chop shop! You're kidnappers, black marketeers, extortionists, and murderers! And for your information, I'm not *anybody's* mistress!"

"Mistress, mattress—the only thing I care about your being is a *treasure,*" Short Bill Gold informed her. "That's what *I* see you as. Maybe not as valuable as the one that's buried *there*, somewhere"—he nodded in the direction of the island—"but you know what they say about a bird in the hand. . . . "

"Are you a myna bird?" asked Ishmael again, reacting to that mention of his kind, perhaps.

"Oh, shut up, Ishmael," said Cherry Holly, apparently still in a bad mood after having been deprived of her afternoon's entertainment. Terry wanted to tell her she'd felt that exact same way some years before when Mone told her she couldn't stay up to watch *Hill Street Blues*, which absolutely everyone she knew *could* watch.

"Yeah, shut your hole, you stupid bird," young Buddy added.

"Pieces of shit, pieces of shit," cried Ishmael, turning his head toward each of the twins in turn—and repeating words the captain had taught him.

"That's pieces of *eight*, you moron," Buddy howled. "Can't you learn *anything*? You'll never make a pirate's parrot."

By then the captain had the cruiser heading for the island at a good clip, pulling the *Cormorant* along behind it.

"There's a treasure buried on your island?" Terry asked. Having gotten over the initial shock of learning that her rescuers were pirates and that she was going to be held for ransom, she was anxious to find out everything she could about the situation she was in, however irrelevant that information might appear to be to . . . her escape, for instance. (This was sort of the same, she thought, as when Connie'd loaned her her copy of *The Joy of Sex*. "You may not plan to use the facts in here for quite a while," her friend had said. "But still, they're awfully interesting.")

"*Supposedly* there's a treasure," said Cherry, still not in the best of moods, but maybe interested herself in having an older girl around, someone she could talk to. "It's meant to be a box of pirate loot from the old days. Silver pieces of eight and gold doubloons, and emeralds and rubies and sapphires. A lotta junk like that. We had a map once."

"Wow," said Tee, a little excited in spite of her predicament. "A *treasure* map? That'd show you where a treasure *chest* was buried? Did X mark the spot and all that?" She was babbling, but she thought: *So what?* "But you said 'had' a map. What happened, did you lose it? Or have it stolen by some *other* pirates?"

"Worse than that," said Captain Gold. "We think it just blew off a table out on the veranda. And into Bubba's pen. It's possible he ate it, though as a rule he sticks to meat, both fresh and . . . other-wise."

"Bubba? Who's Bubba?" Terry asked, think-ing—maybe—watchdog.

"Bubba's a Komodo dragon," said Bill Gold. "The world's largest living lizard. He's my sister's . . . sort of *pet*—although nobody pets him. They're native to some island over there in Indonesia and they're get-ting very rare—and valuable. She won him from a Chinese trader in a mah-jong game. I wanted to cut the sucker open and look for the map, but she'd have none of it. She's a pretty strong-willed person. Roger calls her 'the Dragon Lady.' And I'm not about to tell you that the name don't fit."

"I've never heard of a Komodo dragon," Terry said. "How big are they?"

"Bubba's about ten feet," said Cherry. "But Mom says he's still growing."

"World's largest living lizard," Captain Gold repeated.

"Wow," Terry said, again. "He sounds . . . disgusting."

She was learning a lot of interesting stuff, though. For instance: Captain Gold was Cherry and Buddy's uncle, and his sister was the Dragon Lady and the children's mom. Also, for the second time she'd heard there was another pirate, Roger.

The boy, Buddy, had been sitting up on the *Kidd Me Not*'s foredeck during this exchange, and now he was pointing ahead and yelling excitedly to the captain.

"*S. S. Flotsam* off the port bow," he hollered. "Can we sink it with the cannon, Uncle Bill? Please-please-*please*? You owe us something, be a sport, come *on!*"

"All right, I guess," said Short Bill Gold, throttling down. "If it'll shut you up. Go get the cannon, if you want."

The "cannon," when the kids had brought it topside, didn't much resemble the big guns on a battleship or destroyer. Instead, it looked like a cross between a bazooka and something you might see at a football game, and it turned out there was also a place where you could fasten it on the foredeck.

What Buddy called the "*S. S. Flotsam*" wasn't a steamship, but some ordinary flotsam—driftwood—bobbing in the waves a couple of hundred yards ahead.

When the gun was in place, the children did a lot of excited capering about, while arguing at the top of their voices about who was going to do what, and when. Out of all that came some aiming and, eventually, some firing. The captain allowed them a total of six shots—or three apiece—and two of those appeared to find their intended target. The cannon seemed to fire cannonballs rather than explosive shells.

"Sighted junk, sank same!" cried Buddy, though in fact some bits of driftwood drifted still.

"The flagship *Kidd Me Not* records still another kill," said Cherry, grimly. It seemed this bit of shooting had revived the twins' good humor.

"So I don't want to hear a single bit of bitching to your mom," said Captain William Gold.

# chapter 10

The cannon shots were fired fairly close to the island, so they may have warned its other human inhabitants of the *Kidd Me Not*'s imminent arrival. Or maybe they'd been watching through a spyglass the whole time. Whatever the explanation, they were waiting on the long wooden pier in the harbor when the pirate ship and its prize slid up beside it. Terry didn't need the captain's introductions to tell the two of them apart.

"Terry Something, shipwreck survivor and—imagine this!—related somehow to *the* Maitland Crane, allow me to present my sister, Hildegarde Holly, the junior member of our tribe," said Short Bill Gold.

"How do you do?" said Terry, thinking: *very, very junior*. Hildegarde Holly was somewhere between her own age and Mone's, early thirties at the most, a whole lot younger than the captain. And where her brother's body type took after Santa Claus, hers was more a fashion model's, or Winona Ryder dressed for training animals in shiny black boots, tight tan riding britches, and a tailored white silk shirt. In one hand she held a whippy, leather-covered swagger stick.

In terms of features, she resembled her two kids—somewhat. That is to say, her nose and mouth and chin were regularly shaped and similar to theirs, and her eyes, like theirs, were rather wide apart. Her complexion, too, was dark and smooth, unblemished, and her hair was long and black and straight, with bangs. But overall her face seemed much more *chiseled*—much, much *meaner*. It was as if living twenty years longer than the twins had . . . well, *disgusted* her. Terry thought she looked like she could chew up glass and spit out icicles—or, conversely, swallow jalapeños and breathe fire. Roger's *nom de ridicule* for her, the Dragon Lady, absolutely suited her.

But the captain had continued talking. "And next to her, my first mate, Jolly Roger."

Jolly Roger looked like a pirate right out of central casting. *And it's about time*, Terry thought. He was angular and dark, with a scruffy beard; a gold hoop earring dangled from one ear, and his head was covered by a dirty blue bandanna. His only other articles of clothing were a pair of black trousers (pantaloons?) with their legs chopped off midcalf, and some soft black boots that went up just about that high, and had a cuff on top. He was middle-aged (forty or so, to Terry) and maybe a little worn, but he didn't look weak. His long-nosed face seemed set in a permanent scowl. Stuck in his wide black belt was an unsheathed machete. *Or would that be a cutlass?* Terry wondered.

"Where you gonna put 'er?" he asked Captain Gold, jerking his thumb in Terry's direction.

"How about the Honeymoon Cottage?" suggested his boss.

"All the same to me," grumped Jolly Roger.

The Honeymoon Cottage turned out to be a ramshackle one-room wooden structure, built of weathered plywood with a palm-frond roof. It was, however, just off a pure white beach, down a steep wooded path from the "Plantation House" and the compound that surrounded it.

Terry got to it the long way, carrying her duffel bag from the *Cormorant* and escorted by Roger and the twins—while the captain and his sister stayed behind, admiring their latest prize. In the course of her leisurely stroll, Tee was able to get a good idea of the island's flora, fauna, and topography, and to understand how Muela Negra got its name.

Seem from above, she realized, it did indeed look like an extracted human molar, lying on its side, a dark shape half buried in the blue-green sea. The two slightly curving spits of land that enclosed the harbor were its roots, and the rest of it, rounded, higher, slightly flattened at the top, would be the molar's neck and crown.

In addition to the pier, the harbor had moorings for a number of boats: another fast cruiser, a cargo vessel a good deal larger than the *Kidd Me Not*, a pair of smaller speedboats, and a very fancy yacht that Terry took to be another recent prize. Onshore there was an immense gasoline storage tank, a drydock, some small sheds, and a huge boathouse the size of an airplane hangar. Terry supposed that this was where the *Cormorant* would be divided into many parts and, that way, "disappear."

From the harbor, they walked up a wide gravel road to the Plantation House, which was a sprawling one-story building with a long veranda all along the front of it, and many doors and windows opening onto that veranda. The Plantation House, Terry learned, contained the compound's communal kitchen, a spacious living-dining room, Short Bill Gold's apartment, and a room-sized stainless steel walk-in vault and freezer combination which held not only loot and personal valuables but also meat and vegetables and ice cream, as well as quite a few cases of fine Jamaican rum.

Just past this structure was Bubba the Komodo dragon's pen. It was at least the size of a couple of football fields, had a stream running through it, and was covered with dense vegetation, trees and shrubs, some of them imported from Bubba's native Indonesia, Roger said. Every day, "treats" (both living and dead) were put inside a gate or tossed over the ten-foot chain-link fence that surrounded the pen, so as to satisfy Bubba's carnivorous appetites. An occasional wind shift would carry an aroma, described by Cherry as "totally vomitous" to the Plantation House side of the pen. This was due, she said, to Bubba's taste for meat he had allowed to "ripen" in the sun.

The Dragon Lady and the twins occupied a lesser, but still sizeable, two-story bungalow on the other side of the pen. It had an old-looking tavern sign beside its front door that read THE BUCKET O' BLOOD above a painting of a pail that had red liquid overflowing down its sides.

"Mom found that at a tag sale in Key West," said Buddy. "She said the painting's copied from a Sherwin-Williams sign."

A building known as the "Guest House" ("Where my uncle's business associates stay," said

Cherry), some workshops and storage buildings, a big garage, and a few animal pens and chicken houses completed the compound. Several large generators that provided electricity for the compound kept up a steady hum.

Roger's little house was on the island's highest point—even up above the plateau where the island's airport was—a grassy landing strip long enough to accommodate a medium-sized cargo plane. Roger said one needed "aircraft" in this business nowadays. It turned out he was a former Royal Air Force pilot, and it was he who flew the pirates' plane. Terry noticed by the time they reached the house site he had gotten downright chatty, and he hadn't scowled in quite a while. He rhapsodized about the view he had before they reached his house—the "Crow's Nest," as he called it—and Terry was impressed with it herself. Apparently the only drawback to the site he'd chosen was its vulnerability to the monsoon winds. He said that a couple of times each season, his house would simply "blow away." "I hang my hammock in the cellar now," he told her with a chuckle.

Walking around the island on the different roads and paths, Terry came to realize the place was a veritable game preserve. There were frequent rustlings in the underbrush, and from time to time she got a glimpse of animals that ranged from short and squat and slow to antelopey, as well as birds of many feathers, some of them extremely plump. Isla Muela's vegetation suggested that the heavy rain the *Cormorant* had encountered wasn't that uncommon. This wasn't any desert island by a long shot. Everything was lush and healthy-looking, and there was no shortage of colorful flowers and flowering vines. "Frangipani," Terry said inside her head, and "Peccaries."

One unusual thing she noticed was that there were quite a number of dug, but seemingly unused, *graves* in the forest, with piles of dirt beside them. She could tell from the dirt piles that some of them were quite recent; others must have been a few months old. At first she figured that every time there was a storm, the pirates feared the worst— like having a big bunch of drowned "boat people" wash up on the island's beaches, people who'd fled from Cuba, or maybe Haiti, in crude craft made out of inner tubes and old screen doors. But eventually Cherry told her she was seeing "treasure hunters' holes." Apparently all five of the permanent human inhabitants of the island had gold (and silver, ruby, emerald, and sapphire) fever, and it seemed the rich loam of the island wasn't hard to dig in, even for kids. Everyone was constantly getting "hunches," Roger added, or they were told things about the treasure's whereabouts by their

Ouija boards or divining rods or dreams. For a little while, Buddy said, the captain believed—nobody knew why—that the myna bird would lead him to the right spot by "pooping on it" (Buddy giggled), but he'd had to abandon the idea when Ishmael contracted "die-a-rear."

When she was finally dropped off by the others at the Honeymoon Cottage, Terry took stock of her situation. Her living quarters were a little house that contained a writing table, a straight-backed wooden chair, a beanbag chair, and a saggy double bed with a single cotton blanket folded at the foot of it. There was also a cupboard with a faded flowered curtain across the front of it that held some plastic plates and cups and bowls and knives and forks and spoons—the sort of stuff you might take on a picnic. There were also some bottles and jars that once held ketchup, mustard, mayonnaise, and probably Chianti, and a single bar of soap in a COMPLIMENTS OF THE TAJ MAHAL wrapper. In the table's drawer were three wax crayons—a red, a blue, and a green—and a yellow stub of a pencil, and a copy of the novel *Moby Dick*. Back in the trees, just off the beach, there was an outhouse; the ocean's waves were all the running water she had access to down there.

There was only one positive thing that she could think to do. She took the pencil stub out of the writing table's drawer and tore out the last blank page from the back of *Moby Dick*. On it she printed the following:

> *Dear Connie,*
>     *I'm being held captive on Isla Muela Negra by Short Bill Gold and his pirate crew. No kidding. The island is shaped like a pulled-out back tooth, lying on its side. If you ever want to see me again, you'd better do something fast. They are a bloodthirsty crew.*
>
> 

*Your endangered friend,*
*Terry Talley*
> 

Then she put the note into the empty Chianti (or whatever) bottle and pushed its cork way in. Wading a little way into the gentle surf, she kissed the bottle and laid it carefully on the outgoing tide.

With that done, she returned to her cottage, took off her clothes, unwrapped the bar of soap, and waded back into the blue-green water, her big bathtub.

After that, she dressed for dinner.

# chapter 11

It was sort of like when she was still on the *Cormorant* and she'd seen the *Kidd Me Not* for the first time, coming toward her, coming to *rescue* her, as she'd thought at the time. Then, she'd also had to decide what sort of a first impression she wanted to make: pathetic-slash-bedraggled or (what Mone would call) well put together.

So now she had to make another clothes and style decision, though a different kind of one. "A mess" was not an option this time. She was, in one sense of the word, safe—and had been for several hours. She'd had time to unpack and take a bath. She was living in a beach house on a lovely island. Hers was not a fate one beat one's breast and rent one's garments over. Not for the time being, anyway.

No, what she had to chose between were the options that faced all motion picture people—all producers and directors, anyway—at the time they made decisions dealing with a movie's content. Did they want the picture rated G, PG, PG-13, or R? (As a rule, NC-17 was not considered by filmmakers, Terry knew, for distribution reasons, and she didn't weigh it as an option for herself. "Full frontal nudity," in public, was definitely not her thing at this point in her life, even on an island in the sun.)

Back in Cape Enid, Terry'd gone through some similar debates with herself before going out on dates. How bad a case of "turnonitis" (as she called it) did she want to give her escort for the evening? The answer almost always was "a *very* mild one." That meant that she'd slip on a cami or a T-shirt underneath whatever shirt or dress she'd chosen—and forget an outfit like a bra top with some short shorts altogether.

In this case, on Isla Muela Negra, the debate was made different by the fact that she was dealing with some unknown quantities; two older men and (in a different way) the classic "older" woman. What would attract a man of Bill Gold's age—and was there something basically disgusting about "attracting" such a man at all? And the same applied to Roger, although a different set of things was "wrong" with him. The trouble was: Part of her brain was telling her that if she managed to survive (escape?), it'd be because somebody'd *helped* her. What would it take to get such help? She really didn't know, exactly. She almost didn't want to know.

And to complicate matters, something told her it'd be a real poor idea to get on the wrong side of the Dragon Lady. Hildegarde Holly hadn't struck Terry as the sort of woman who'd enjoy—permit— another player in the queen bee competition.

In the end she kind of chickened out, going with a little slip dress, navy with white polka dots, with buttons down the front. A rather "little girly" dress, she thought. It had a nice fit and flare shape, but it wasn't particularly low cut, and if its thin straps showed off her arms and shoulders nicely, its just-above-the-knee length made it pretty modest, down below. The only semidaring thing she did was go without a bra, which she had always done with that particular dress at home, without collecting any "looks" from Mone. Overall, she thought, she rated a PG—PG-13, perhaps, if she leaned over.

She'd been told that dinner on the island was at seven, so she showed up at the Plantation House at exactly five of, in time to "help," if called upon, but not early enough to have to deal with any major cooking project. Feeding Mick J. Crane was one thing; these people were a different matter, taste-bud-wise. You could tell from looking at them.

When she arrived, she found the twins setting the big refectory table in the dining area (using heavy silver, cloth napkins, and stemmed glass-ware—along with much bad language, talking to each other); the three adults had gathered in the kitchen. There seemed to be two explanations for their presence there, the first being the preparation of the meal (by Captain Gold) and the criticism of his work (by Roger and the Dragon Lady). The sec-ond thing that drew them to the kitchen, Terry thought, was the open bottle of rum on the counter by the stove, and the stubby glasses (with a wedge of lime in each) firmly clutched in everybody's hands. Ishmael, perched on the captain's shoulder, was looking down his beak at the assemblage—disap-provingly, it seemed to Terry.

Both Roger and the Dragon Lady had changed for dinner, Terry couldn't help but notice, while the captain had stayed in his powder blue uniform. The change that Roger'd made was both so marked and unexpected, she almost didn't recognize the man.

It was as if he'd really been in costume, earlier, dressed by central casting for the "pirate" part that he'd been playing. Now he was clean-shaven, except for a pencil-thin mustache. His hair, previously hid-den by that dirty bandanna, was short and neatly parted on one side; it shone, from either recent washing or, perhaps, a dab of styling mousse. He'd also put a shirt on, a khaki one, with those straps on the tops of the shoulders that military men wear bars or stars or eagles on. Instead of black pantaloons, he sported a well-tailored pair of white linen Bermuda shorts; below them he wore shiny penny loafers (with no socks). He raised his glass to Terry when he saw her entering the kitchen.

"What ho!" he cried. "Our princess cometh!" Terry wondered if he thought that she was Jewish.

Roger's greeting caused the Dragon Lady to swivel around so quickly that a little liquid flew out of her glass and splashed on the floor. Her outfit wasn't like anything that Tee had seen before, except in a Victoria's Secret catalogue. It was a long, slinky black dress, cut low in front and back, with a fitted bodice and spaghetti straps, and a sweeping side-slit skirt that gave the world a look at more or less three quarters of a beautiful bare leg.

"Oh, yes," the Dragon Lady said, in lieu of greeting. "Her."

"I like your frock, m'dear," the captain said to Tee. "Seems like the two of us are *also* twins." He gurgled a laugh and pointed at the ascot knotted at his throat. Terry'd forgotten it was blue with small white polka dots, something like her dress.

"Is there something I can do?" she asked. "To help?"

"Not now," the Dragon Lady answered. "Later. Here's the way it's going to work. Cherry and Buddy set the table. Billy or I cook and serve. You've been appointed scullery maid, which means you get to do the washing up. Roger"—she laid her palm against his upper arm, as if she were about to stroke him—"being a bachelor, has no domestic skills, so he observes, consumes, and, hopefully, expresses gratitude."

Although she'd obviously been given the scuzziest, most menial, and long-lasting job, Terry didn't waste her breath demanding justice—as she would have done at home or school. She was resolved to make no enemies; her goal was to become the one everybody had nice things to say about. So that, someday, some*one* would help to save her butt, somehow.

"Fine," she told the Dragon Lady and the others now. "I'm certainly experienced. I do the washing up at Daddy's house on Thursday nights, the maids' night off. And I'm so glad to just be off that boat of his and on dry land again."

Although she hadn't planned to break it to them all that soon, Terry had decided on the walk up from the Honeymoon Cottage that she would tell them she was Maitland's daughter. That seemed like the best alternative. For one thing, it'd put to rest that "mistress" crap. And it required the least amount of explanation concerning her presence on the boat—not to mention making her supremely valuable.

She saw the three of them exchange quick glances almost as soon as the *D* word was out of her mouth. Message received, quite clearly. But it wasn't until they'd picked up the serving platters and bowls (medallions of pork in a thick, tomatoey sauce, and buttered noodles, and eggplant parmagiana, and a big green salad), and filed into the dining room, and everybody'd taken his or her seat and started chowing down, that Short Bill Gold revisited the subject of her bloodlines.

He was sitting at what he probably believed was the head of the table, with Terry on his right and Buddy at *her* right. The Dragon Lady was at the other end, with Jolly Roger on her right and Cherry just past him, which put her on the captain's left. When not forking food into her mouth, Cherry kept her eyes on Terry (maybe wondering how long before she'd own that polka-dotted dress, Tee thought).

"So you are Maitland Crane's presumably most darling daughter," mused the captain. "But hey, your last name's different—Valli or Tassey, or whatever you said. Why-come is that, young Terry?"

"Are you a myna bird?" asked Ishmael.

Terry decided to deal with the captain's question first.

"Well, my parents were divorced when I was small, and *Talley* was my mother's maiden name," she said. "Mom switched both our names before I knew what was going on. But I've always visited my dad during school vacations, so we've gotten really close. And no, Ishmael, I'm not a myna bird, unfortunately."

There was a silence, during which the adults nodded, chewing on that information (along with bites of pork and noodles, vegetables and salad). Ishmael, apparently well pleased with Terry's answer to his question, leaned toward her, making little throaty sounds.

Terry saw that everybody had good appetites. The food, in fact, was excellent, and apparently the same could be said for the rum. The bottle had made it to the table, thanks to Roger. "Another tot, old crumpets?" he said at that point, and without waiting for an answer, poured generous rations into all three glasses.

"I *kept* my husband's name after his . . . unfortunate demise," the Dragon Lady said. "I love gold bars and rings, but I never liked it much in teeth, or as a name. 'Holly' has a better ring to it than 'Gold.' My husband's mother had a chauffeur once, a man by the name of Richard, and he wrote a song about her—did you know this, Billy? 'Good Golly, Miz Holly,' it was called. But Mother Holly made him change the title when he turned professional and got a big recording contract. That's what she told me, anyway."

Terry looked at her respectfully as she explained all that. Based on her experience observing this one friend of Mone's who always said she'd "love a little sherry" any time she dropped in at the Talleys', she believed the Dragon Lady was half bombed.

"Right, yes, I did know that, Hildy," Short Bill Gold said mildly. And then he turned back to Terry. "I see—your mother's maiden name is Talley. And so your dad lent you and . . . *Art*, is it? . . . his boat? Now, who is—or *was*, I'm sorry to say—this Art, exactly?"

Terry dropped her eyes and then blinked a couple of times before she answered. And that wasn't a complete act. She'd never known someone her age, or younger, who had died, before. But she knew she had to keep her wits together.

"Oh—*Kirt*," she said. "He was my father's captain. I think he was a former baseball player, maybe in the major leagues. He looked after all my father's boats. And sailed with him in the big races sometimes, like the one to Bermuda, I think it is." This was the kind of stuff she'd heard at the Cape Enid Club.

"So you and this chap Kirt," said Roger, "you were bound for . . . *where*, old dear?"

"Nowhere in particular, I guess," said Terry sadly. "Daddy wanted me to get to know . . . the islands. Let's see . . . Jamaica and Barbados and Saint Somethings—Kitts? Those were three I think he said. He would have taken me himself, but something came up with some business he was doing, and he got Kirt to take me."

"This Captain Kirk," the Dragon Lady said, leaning over and talking to Roger, "was going to beam her down, I bet. Perhaps he taught her how to 'come about,' already." She winked and giggled, giving Roger, Terry saw, a long look down her dècolletage.

"Captain Kirk?" said Buddy. "You mean the guy on the real old *Star Treks? He's* the one who ended up in Davy Jones' locker?"

"Not exactly," said his mother. "Why don't you and Cherry go and stick a movie in the VCR? This is grown-up time."

"I'm just about a grown-up," Cherry said. "I bet I get my period this year. I want to stay and listen."

"You'll be a grown-up when I say you are, and not one day before," her mother snapped. "Vamoose. And you can get a Dove bar from the freezer if you take off now."

Apparently the promise of an ice cream treat was sufficient balm to soothe young Cherry's blasted adult aspirations. Both she and her brother spun out of their seats and sped out of the room.

"Now, getting back to 'Daddy'—where would

he be now, d'you think?" asked Captain Gold of Terry. "At home?" She shrugged, then nodded. "Okay. Then we'll be needing that address. We'd like to get in touch ASAP." He uncapped the gold fountain pen he'd fished out of an inside pocket, along with a small, leather-bound address book.

"To set his—doubtlessly—troubled mind to rest, of course," the Dragon Lady said.

"And get him bloody well started stackin' up some coin," said Roger.

Terry gave them "Box 100" in Cape Enid, knowing that anything that had Maitland Crane's name on it would end up in the proper slot. She was thinking it would matter quite a bit, though, whether he was alive or not. If he *was* alive, the pirates' ransom note and accompanying photo might very well pique his curiosity; he was an adventurer, after all. And as such, he might decide to look into this whole situation, just on his own; presumably the pirates would have warned him not to call the U. S. Navy or the FBI, "or else." If he showed the photo around town, somebody'd probably recognize her and tell him who his "daughter" really was. If he was dead, however, some old lawyer'd open all his mail and doubtless toss the ransom note away, thinking it was just another crude attempt to scam a millionaire's estate. The lawyer'd *know* Crane didn't have a daughter.

Yikes, thought Tee; the marquis'd better *not* be right.

The meal concluded shortly after that. The adult pirates didn't eat dessert, apparently. The Dragon Lady said she was going home "to slip into something more comfortable," aiming that at Roger, Terry thought, though it was Ishmael who whistled. The two men headed for the big upholstered chairs in the living area, where, as the captain said, they could "settle that fine meal" with a glass or two of port and a cigar.

This they did while Terry attended to the dishes. There were a lot of them, plus pots and pans and silver and glasses. Mone had had a dishwasher all of Terry's life, so doing all those greasy things by hand was something new—and not appealing—to her. But she soldiered through the job, pretending she was a fifteenth-century serving wench, working at a marquis's castle—one who knew his lordship had his eye on her (and that there wasn't a marquise upstairs). She didn't want to think of poor drowned Mick and *that* marquis, but imagining herself to be a clean and comely peasant girl, the fairest of the servants at the manor, was a fantasy that helped to pass the time.

When she was finally done and ready to leave the Plantation House, Roger sprang to his feet in the living room and announced that he'd "toddle along" with her, lighting their way with a kerosene lantern. But then the captain told him "No-no-no," and just about insisted *he* would be the one to see her to her "fair abode," using his big five-cell flashlight to be sure they didn't wander off the path. The two men argued back and forth a while, both clearly wanting to be Terry's one and only escort. In the end, they compromised. Neither of them went with her, but both gave her their lights to carry down the hill. She was extremely glad—to have the lights, and neither of the guides. The lantern, she could use for light inside the cottage—perhaps she'd get around to reading *Moby Dick*. And the flashlight would be great for going to the outhouse after dark, and making sure, when there, she didn't sit on . . . a tarantula, for instance.

She used it for exactly that, that night, and then took it with her to the water's edge when she went down to brush her teeth. It was a little weird, brushing with salt water, and as she walked back toward the cottage across the hard wet sand exposed by the retreating tide, she was thinking about how totally different her life had become since leaving Cape Enid.

Because of this reverie, she almost missed it. Not *it*, itself—she couldn't help but see it when the flashlight beam passed over it, right near the high-water mark—but its significance. After all, it was a thing you always saw on beaches, and never thought about at all.

But this night, two steps after she had seen it, she stopped short, and turned, went back, and knelt beside it for a closer look. "It" was a footprint of a bare left foot, one a great deal bigger than her own!

# chapter 12

Much, much later, Terry wondered if she had "stood like one thunderstruck"—as if she "had seen an apparition"—the way Robinson Crusoe said *he* had, in similar circumstances. The footprint was much too sizeable to have been made by one of the captain's fat little tootsies, and she was pretty sure her own size eight and a halfs were also bigger than Buddy's feet, or Cherry's or the Dragon Lady's. And surely Roger hadn't been down on the beach since she'd bathed and dressed for dinner, had he? Although he hadn't had socks on under his penny loafers when she arrived at the Plantation House kitchen, he'd looked like a man who'd been devoting himself to cocktails for a while, rather than someone who'd just raced up from the beach, through the underbrush.

But if the footprint wasn't Roger's, whose could it be? Captain Gold had said dead bodies often washed up on the island's shore, after a monsoon. Could there have been, this time, a live survivor of the storm—in addition to herself?

Of course, it did occur to her the footprint might be Mick's, but when that thought dropped in her mind, she didn't let it stay for milk and cookies. It'd be a Big Mistake, she felt, to start imagining that she'd have outside help any time soon. Maybe, much, much later on, Maitland Crane might try to do something. But for now, she almost certainly was on her own. If there was, in fact, another living shipwreck victim on the island, he'd probably turn out to be a person of no earthly use to her at all, a vacuum cleaner salesman or, perhaps, a talk-show host.

So, shortly after thinking those thoughts and returning with her toothbrush to the Honeymoon Cottage, Terry flopped down on her bed and blew out the lantern, resolved to get a good night's sleep.

Among Tee Talley's many unneurotic qualities was this one: She never wasted time or energy bemoaning things she'd done that couldn't be undone. And so, before she fell asleep that night, her thoughts were not about the past, and her decision to stow away on the *Cormorant;* they focused on her present situation and the future.

The present seemed chock-full of positives, and she quickly made a mental list of them.

She was alive and in good health, and on a gorgeous tropical island. Delicious meals, it seemed, would be regularly available to her, at no charge. Her little cottage, which she didn't have to share with her mother and her brother—or anyone else, for that matter—was on a private beach, and the water off that beach was just the perfect temperature, far warmer than the ocean off Cape Enid. The air around her wasn't at all humid, and during the day a pleasant breeze made the heat completely bearable. The clothes she'd brought with her seemed ideal for the situation in which she found herself, and she'd yet to be bitten by an insect. It even seemed likely that, in a few days' time, she'd have, in the girl Cherry, a little friend who'd want to hang out some, and also might turn out to be a good source of information about what the adults on the island were saying about her. All in all, her present situation wasn't one she could complain about.

As far as the future was concerned . . . it was, of course, a question mark. Or really, one big question mark made up of many, many smaller ones. Such as: If the two mature male pirates "liked" her, as they seemed to, how would each of them "express" (the

Dragon Lady's word) that liking? But if you put such questions, the ones about specifics, to one side (as Terry was inclined to do when answers to them weren't readily available), the future was, in general, something she looked forward to.

As in the past, she didn't stop to analyze *why* she believed that things would work out for her; she just did. Of course, she knew she didn't happen to be a high school dropout, or a teenaged mother on welfare who smoked a pack of Winston Lights a day and did a line whenever she was offered one. Her last name didn't end in *o* or *ez,* and her race was like the color of this page. And if she was asked about such things, she would have readily admitted that she'd had regular exercise, breathed clean air, and eaten nutritious food all her life, and that she'd only had one cavity so far and frequent compliments about her looks. Yet she couldn't give herself credit for any of those things, or even for being, as a rule, a hopeful person, one who didn't dwell on gloom and doom. She'd read that scientists believed a person's tendency to be an optimist—*or* a pessimist—depended mostly on her genes; that she didn't have a choice, in other words, and was merely following a program.

But she also was a bit of a . . . traditionalist. She'd placed that key ring with the little can of Mace attached to it on the floor beside her bed before she lay down on it. After all, that was sort of where she'd kept the thing, back home.

Although it woke her up, the tapping on her door was so soft she had to sit up in bed and listen hard in order to be sure she wasn't hearing things. But once convinced, she got right up and tiptoed toward the door.

It—that door—was just a piece of plywood, and the "lock" on it was one of those hook-and-eyelet deals; it wouldn't take much strength, she knew, to bust right in. So she figured, what the heck, she might as well. . . .

Not that it wasn't a little scary, answering your front door in the middle of the night wearing just a T-shirt and your underpants. But at least with the help of the captain's flashlight, she'd learn who was standing on her doorstep before he—small chance it was a female!—got to see how she was dressed.

"Yes?" She said that softly with her lips near the little crack where the side of the door almost met the jamb. The fingers of her free hand were on the little hook; she'd forgotten—or neglected—to pick up the can of Mace.

"So tell me, please," was whispered back to her, "what happen to my nice hot cup of *chocolat?*"

"*Marquis!*" The word flew out of her on one big gust of breath as she pulled the hook up and the door open. At the same time she flipped the flashlight backward toward the bed. This meant that she had both hands free to wrap around his body in the hug of hugs and to end up flattened on his warm, bare back.

He smelled of . . . well, the seashore; he smelled *great!* Hugging him seemed necessary and proper; she was overjoyed to learn he was alive, that he'd survived, somehow. And clearly, he was glad to find her, too.

"Ter-*ree! Cherie!*" he said, his mouth beside her ear. His body shook, maybe with happy laughter, perhaps from crying in relief. She couldn't tell, and she was not about to ask.

Some seconds passed. Slowly she began to think more ordinary thoughts. When had he gone over-board? How come he hadn't drowned? How long had he been on this island?

And then one further question. His back was totally and absolutely bare: WHAT ABOUT THE REST OF HIM? Sure, she'd seen him naked once, already, but that had been by accident and . . . well, before she *knew* him. Knowing someone made things different.

She realized it was time to terminate the hug. So she relaxed her right arm first and let it fall, just casually, in such a way that as it dropped, her hand brushed up against his side, below the waist.

Whew! She'd touched material; it felt like terry cloth, a towel.

And so it was. When she stepped back and (finally) looked at him—by the light of a fraction of a moon and a million of the brightest stars she'd ever seen—she saw he had a towel, her towel, in fact, securely wrapped around his waist. She'd hung that towel on a line outside her house after her bath. She assumed until he saw it he'd been . . . going native.

Once she'd satisifed her curiosity about . . . well, *that,* she let her gaze go up and down and take in all the rest of him. He seemed to be quite fine: He bore no major cuts or bruises she could see in that dim light. She decided that she really liked the sort of body that he had: smooth and on the slender side. The pumping-iron, hairy, muscle-type never had attracted her. She supposed a marquis would have gotten into shape by doing lots of riding and getting heart-lung exercise in sword-fight classes.

"I can't believe you're safe," she told him, stepping back so he could come inside. There were tears in *her* eyes now. She didn't care if he could see them—in fact, she hoped he would. She lit the lantern with a match, but turned the flame down low.

"I buh-barely can myself," said Mick J. Crane.

She turned away and dabbed at her eyes with the hem of her T-shirt. She was very glad that Mick was safe, too; it was just that she'd forgotten about him in the excitement of the previous moments. He went and took a seat on the straight-backed chair by the table, and she realized he didn't look half bad himself. Maybe a shipwreck made a guy look older.

For the next fifteen minutes or so she mostly listened to their story, and it was "their" story, told by both of them. This was something new. One would say some things, and then the other would; it was like listening to two friends (who just happened to inhabit one body) describe a shared experience. Terry thought Mick stuttered less, and his style seemed different than before—more relaxed and understated, much less pompous.

But no matter who was speaking, Terry found herself caught up in a tale in which skill and bravery, luck, determination, and resiliency all played a part.

It was Mick who'd been washed overboard—at least in the telling. That happened just after he'd removed his safety harness to struggle into a life jacket, having noticed that the marquis should have put that jacket on long, long ago. It also seemed to him that possibly the seas had started settling a bit, as dawn began to break. Like the good sailor that he was, he'd lashed the tiller before he slipped out of the harness.

But another monster wave arrived just as he'd

finished fastening the jacket. It picked him up and absolutely *threw* him overboard—and he very nearly drowned, not once but half a dozen times, when other big waves buried him and turned him upside down. Luckily, Mick had learned to swim as a baby; water didn't scare him, so he kept his cool; and when the swells diminished and full morning came, and he saw some major chunks of driftwood in the area, he swam right over to them.

"I ride on one of these," the marquis said, "like it was from the stable of my father. Swimming is a thing I'm less familiar with."

"I honestly buh-lieve I fell asleep a little while, holding on to this big piece of some boat's life raft," Mick J. added.

In any case, at some point the survivor had been awake enough, and the day bright enough, for him to look beyond his immediate surroundings and see two things that very much excited him. First, he'd noticed there was *land*—it seemed to him to be an island—not that far away, and he was drifting toward it. And second he'd noticed that a large powerboat he hadn't seen or heard before had gotten a line attached to the *Cormorant* (which the boy[s] hadn't seen either, since being washed out of it) and was towing it in the same direction.

The marquis's first thought was to start flapping his arms and maybe hollering, so as to get the powerboat's attention, but before he could do so, a cannon shot was fired from that craft which very nearly hit him!

"What am I to think?" he said to Terry. "Other than they want this Frenchman dead for reasons quite unknown to him? I assume their target is the yellow of this jacket Mick put on."

So it was Mick who quickly took the jacket off and slid his dark blue T-shirt over it—he'd lost his shorts soon after he'd gone overboard, he'd said, effectively depantsed by some great wave. A few more shots were fired and a couple of direct hits were scored on the driftwood near the piece he'd ducked behind, but then the boat sped off toward shore, still towing the *Cormorant*. Mick then used the wrapped-up life jacket like a kickboard and headed in the same direction (if nowhere near as fast). He guessed the people in the powerboat believed they'd gotten him, "the bastards."

When he finally made it to the island and staggered onto dry land, he spent a while just recuperating from his ordeal, lying in the shelter of the nearest tree line. But when he had the strength to move again, he made, in less than an hour's time, two most welcome—not to say incredible—discoveries.

The second of these was what he found inside the little cottage by the beach: Terry's duffel bag with, unmistakably, her clothes—including her Red Sox baseball cap—that she'd unpacked from it!

Knowing she was still alive, and *there*, was, Mick said, "about the buh-best news I've ever gotten in my life.

"Even *supérieur*," the marquis added, "to that which we discover just a little time before."

Terry clapped her hands and started laughing when she heard what *that* was. Apparently the first thing the boy thought to do when he felt strong enough to do anything was to get up and bury that yellow life jacket so there wouldn't be any way the cannon shooters might come upon it and conclude they hadn't killed him after all.

Lacking any tools, he'd started digging with both hands, doggy fashion, in a sandy stretch among some palms. And no more than a foot and a half down, he'd hit what he believed to be, at first, a good-sized stone.

"I break a nail on her, *voilà*," the marquis said, holding out a hand for her inspection. She took ahold of it and even turned the flashlight on for a better look. And yes, his middle finger's nail was broken, although not too badly. This was the first time she'd paid such close attention to a hand of his. It was a lovely one, she thought, with long tapering fingers growing from a sturdy, muscled palm—an artist's hand, but an artist who could also wield an axe (logging or battle), or twist the top from off a jar of honey or spaghetti sauce.

"But once I brushed the sand off," Mick went on, "I saw it was a wooden box with metal strapping on it."

Yes, it was the treasure chest! The boy had found it totally by accident, after all those pirates and their progeny had spent . . . oh, God knew how long searching for the thing, digging all those holes and holes!

"Its contents are remind me of this one *boîte* my father have, back in the strong room of our castle," said the marquis. "When I was little boy, my mother let me play with all those shiny, precious things, on rainy days."

What he'd done, he said, was leave the chest right where it was, after pulling the sand back into the hole and then carefully smoothing it over. Then he'd buried the life jacket in another sandy spot, among a different group of palm trees.

"And now it's your turn," Mick informed Tee Talley. "How did *you* survive the storm? Who *are* those people in the powerboat? And how the huh-huh-hell do we get out of here?"

# chapter 13

Terry was a little embarrassed, telling her story; it was so much less of an epic—less exciting, complicated, and heroic—than his. It wasn't just that she hadn't come close to drowning half a dozen times; she'd never left the *Cormorant* until it docked; she hadn't even gotten any of her clothes wet! But she gave him a blow-by-blow account of everything that had happened anyway, and she certainly couldn't find fault with his reactions. Even in dim lantern light she could see him looking horrified when she got to the part about her almost being "fed to the fishes" by the youngest pirates. And he was obviously gratified by the news that it was only his father's ownership of the *Cormorant* that had saved her from a watery grave. She wasn't sure exactly how he felt, though—amused? conflicted?—when he heard of her decision to pass herself off as Maitland Crane's daughter (in other words, his sister).

"Just think," Mick said, "I thought you were his guh-guh-girlfriend, that first day."

"That seems a long, *long* time ago now," said Terry, quickly, not liking to remember what a silver-plated jerk she'd thought he was, the first few days they were together, and thankful, once again, to Monsoon Murray for blowing that idiotic yachting cap of his into the foam-flecked sea. His losing it had made her fully understand—for the first time—a thing old-timers in Cape Enid liked to say: "It's an ill wind that blows no good."

Mick, and sometimes the marquis, also wanted to hear everything she could tell them about Short Bill Gold, the pirate captain; Roger, his mate; the Dragon Lady, his sister; his niece and nephew, Cherry and Buddy; and the Komodo dragon, Bubba.

Terry figured that the marquis had probably heard lots of tales about pirates and highwaymen back in the fifteenth century, and had maybe even seen a few of each get hung in various marketplaces (while a mob of peasants, shopkeepers, and pickpockets shouted, "Dance, you varlets, dance!"—except in French), but hearing of big Bubba made his eyes bug out.

"Is like a de-no-saur, *n'est-ce pas?*" he said. "*Ce Monseiur Boobba.* I think I like to see this creature very much."

"Right. Though probably not close up," said Terry, dryly. "They say he's got huge teeth and claws and a terrific sense of smell. Besides being a really fast runner for his size. He's the world's largest living lizard, you know."

The marquis made a face and nodded, clearly much impressed.

Terry then went on to explain in some detail—she was afraid that this part was a little boring—the physical layout of the pirates' compound, where all the buildings and Bubba's pen were, in relation to each other. And after that she described her duties as the scullery maid up there, and the mess she'd had to clean up after dinner. During that last bit Mick first sat up straight, then twitched a little in his chair.

"My gosh," she said, clued in by that, "I didn't think. You must be *starving!*" How could she have prattled on about lizards and outbuildings when what he wanted most to know about was food, and how he might meet up with some? "When did you last eat?" Stupid question. So she answered it herself. "Back on the boat, of course. And water! Did you find a spring or anything since you got here?"

"I'm pretty hungry," Mick admitted. "And

thirsty, too." He was looking around the cottage as if he maybe thought he'd see a bag of chips and maybe a couple of cups of Gatorade, just lying around.

But as he did, he told her he had found some edible fruit and munched on that, and its juices had slaked his thirst a little.

Terry promised she would bring fresh water down to the cottage right after breakfast; saying she could even do that openly, that the pirates would understand her need for some down there. She said she'd put it, along with any leftovers she could slip into her pockets, in the thicket that was right behind the outhouse.

"That'll be a real good place for me to leave things for you," she said. "It's only natural for me to be heading in that direction lots of times. But you know what I wish I had, for food smuggling? A pair of really baggy sweatpants. Then I could snag a piece of food and in two seconds drop it down the front of them—some toast, or waffles, bacon even. Whatever."

"*Bien entendu*," the marquis said, nodding and grinning. "Some scrambled eggs, a piece of custard pie—whatever."

She said that after the pirates' dinner would probably be when she could get the most food for him, because by the time she finished washing up, all of them would probably have gone to bed, and she could walk out with a heaping plateful.

"Then I could put a lantern on the windowsill when I got back," she said. "Just like they do in storybooks."

As soon as she said that, she remembered that in storybooks when the girl put the light in the window it was usually to let her boyfriend know he could come and get *her,* instead of the blue plate special. And that made her realize that the question of where Mick was going to spend the night, then and in the future, had yet to be addressed—or even thought about, at least by her.

But before she could start to tiptoe toward that subject, he brought up another one—escape— showing he had other matters on his mind and besides such basic human wants as food and . . . well, *you* know.

"Now, so I understand," the marquis said, "the plan of *les pirates* would be to hold you for some— how you say it?—*ransom,* yes? Thinking *Monsieur* Crane would gladly pay to save his daughter."

"Um, yes, I suppose so," Terry said. He'd touched on a subject that required delicate handling: whether Maitland Crane was still able to do *anything,* never mind "gladly."

"I think they're planning to send him a photo of me with a recognizable hunk of the *Cormorant,*" she said. "A picture that'd be, like, proof the boat was wrecked and I was captured. Or so they think, anyway." She paused.

"Of course, I realize," she added, "that there's one big trouble with their plan."

Mick made a snorting sound. "Oh, you mean if Maitland Crane was dead," he said. "The way I said he probably was, before we left the States."

She nodded, trying to look a little sorrowful—or at least respectful.

"Well, that was bullshit," he informed her. "I was just talking. I didn't want to face the fact he duh-didn't care enough about me to call up the cuh-cuh-Coast Guard."

There was another silence. Terry wasn't sure what she should say. It would have been nice to have Mone there then. Mone was great at filling silences, sucking all the poison out of them by saying something unexpected, often on an entirely different subject than the one that caused the silence in the first place. "I read an awfully funny piece in the paper about what sort of undershorts were favored by the last few presidents, beginning with Jack Kennedy," she might have said. "See if you can guess who liked white cotton briefs, the kind that little boys wear."

But in her absence the marquis filled in. He didn't change the subject, just took it in a new direction.

"A photograph, such as the one you just describe, along with a ransom note referring to his daughter—these are things that Maitland Crane cannot ignore," he said. "I doubt that he believes this *very* pretty girl has stole his boat alone; more likely he will think his son run off with her. And possibly that makes him proud. Good boy, he thinks, becoming more like me—*un aventurier, n'est-ce pas?* And also he will probably discover that the very pretty girl is from Cape Enid, too. How would it look if he ignored the note—made no attempt to get her safely home? By saying she's his daughter, she is almost asking him for help, *vraiment.*"

Terry couldn't argue with any of that, especially the "*very* pretty girl" part. But still . . .

"The trouble is," she said, "he'd have to find out where we are and who these pirates are, and that won't be easy. I can't see the captain sending him a ransom note with 'Short Bill Gold, Isla Muela Negra, the Bermuda Triangle' on the envelope. He's not that kind of out-of-it."

"You know what I'd like best," said Mick J. suddenly, "is for us to just escape—without my father's help or anybody's. That'd show him. S'pose we got our hands on the key that starts Gold's powerboat. I can drive that sucker. And with a full tank of gas we could get beyond the range of any of their other boats . . ." His voice got more and more excited. "We'd work the radio and send out SOS's. Somebody'd hear us, before we even got somewhere, I bet."

Terry thought that sounded like a fine idea—until she noticed Mick J. Crane hadn't stopped looking straight at her since he'd said, "S'pose we get our hands on . . . " And that now he had his eyebrows sort of up, like, "Well . . . ?" It looked to her as if he was thinking *she* would be the one to steal, or otherwise obtain, that key from Short Bill Gold. Somehow. By any means at her disposal, at her *feminine* disposal. Sure.

She didn't smile and wag her tail—at all. In fact, she frowned. But before she had to say something, the marquis spoke up again.

"What you could maybe do," he said to her, "is ascertain if there is someone in their group who we can . . . let us say, *persuade* to help us. After all, we have information of great value: where the treasure is. Might not, for instance, Roger"—he pronounced the name *Ro-jay*—"want to do a favor for *la belle Ter-ree*—if doing so would cause him to become a millionaire?"

Terry felt her face relax. She'd jumped to a conclusion and been wrong, apparently. The boy was not suggesting she should . . . have an affair (which sounded so much better than "do it") with the captain. He'd had bribery in mind all along. Just as she had now, but on another subject.

"That's definitely worth looking into," she said, "once I get to know them all a little better. But meanwhile—this is something I could do tomorrow, I think—how about I see if I can get some clothes for you?"

What she thought that she could do was tell young Cherry that what girls Tee's age back home were wearing was men's clothing, the baggier the better—and that she'd love to get her hands on some of Roger's things that, when she was ransomed and back in the States, would be like a souvenir of her time as a pirate captive. But, she'd say, she didn't want to approach Roger directly; she was sure he'd probably make fun of her, the way a lot of grown-ups do when faced with kids' ideas and fashions. So what she was wondering, she'd say, was if maybe Cherry—for, say fifty dollars (U.S.)—would "borrow" like a shirt and a pair of pants from him, for her.

"Unless I miss my guess, she'd *love* to do a thing like that," said Tee. "The little bandit."

Mick seemed a little embarrassed by being reminded of his present state of undress. He pressed his knees together and tugged at the towel, trying to get it to cover more of the side of his thigh.

"It'd be nice to have some clothes," he said. "N-no matter what you think"—and he smiled a little smile—"I'm really not a nuh-nuh-nudist."

"Okay," she said. "So it looks as if I'll have a busy day tomorrow. But at the moment . . ."

She yawned. She couldn't help it. So now she simply had to face the question of where he was going to sleep. And she really didn't see how she could let him go into the night, wearing only a towel, to face whatever wild and hungry predators might be on the prowl out there.

She took a deep breath, and then the bull by the horns, so to speak.

"Look," she said to him, "I've got a double bed in here, and you have nowhere else to sleep. Have you ever heard of 'bundling'?" He shook his head, looked quizzical. "That's what they used to do in colonial times, when no one had guest rooms in their houses and people had to share beds with passing relatives and even strangers, I guess, sometimes. Everybody wore a lot of clothes and didn't touch—that's what our history teacher, Mrs. Simmons, said. We can bundle now. I'll get dressed, and you can roll up in that blanket there— and we'll go straight to sleep, all right?"

"Oh, sure. Of course." She thought he sounded serious, like . . . a consenting adult, so she got up and without further ado got out her blue jeans and sweatshirt and pulled them on. By the time she'd finished doing that, he'd gotten the blanket wrapped around him so he looked like a caterpillar in a shabby gray cocoon and was lying on the far side of the bed, facing away from her. So she blew out the lantern and lay down on the extreme near side, facing away from *him*.

But even at that distance she could hear him whisper, "I'm really, *really* glad you're still alive."

"Me, too," she answered, meaning something quite different from that, that had to do with him—but still, she didn't add to those two words. She smiled to herself, though. She'd always thought she'd say a bunch of other things the first time she was with a naked boy in bed.

# chapter 14

When Terry rolled over in bed, deep in the darkness of that tropical night, her right arm whipped around and caused her open hand to land on Mick J.'s blanket-covered back. She came awake at once, knowing in that very instant what she'd done, to whom. "Sorry, sorry," she said softly, so he'd know it was an accident and not some kind of wake-up call or . . . invitation. If and when she ever had one to deliver, it wouldn't come from her unconscious, Terry vowed.

She could have saved her breath. Mick didn't stir. Both he and the marquis lay loglike, fast asleep. For their minds and shared body, this was payback time for all that it'd been through the last few days.

She probably could have picked him up off the bed, thrown him onto the beanbag chair facedown, patted him over for concealed weapons, and read him the Miranda warning at the top of her lungs—and he still wouldn't have woken up.

By eight o'clock in the morning there hadn't been much change in his situation, but she'd been down to the ocean and up to the outhouse, to wash her face in the former and pee and change her clothes in the latter. Back in the cottage, as she began to brush her hair, she also started singing, choosing the Simon and Garfunkel song, "Scarborough Fair," a great favorite of her mother's. She hoped that she could wake him sweetly, gently. She would be like his clock radio, set to a golden oldies station.

It worked. He rolled over, then sat up and looked at her.

"Wow, great voice," he said. It seemed he'd gone from fast asleep to wide-awake in seconds. He stretched, arms up, straight overhead; the blanket fell off his shoulders and down around his waist. "And boy, did I sleep well!"

She saw he had some lines on one side of his face, where his cheek had pressed against the mattress, and his dark hair was a little mussed. But his eyes were bright and smiley. In the morning light she could also see he had a bit of a sunburn, nothing serious, and she remembered how smooth and warm and nice his skin had felt the night before, when they had hugged hello.

"Good," she said, suddenly a little shy—and in a hurry. "I have to go now. They may have started breakfast, and I shouldn't be too late. I've got to just act normal." She was babbling, she realized, talking to herself as much as to him.

"Let's see," she said, trying to slow down. "We talked about food and water, and where I'll leave them, right? So maybe you'd better get up soon and find a good hiding place. Those kids may roam around a lot during the day."

It was amazing, she thought, how much she was already counting on him being there that night, how important he'd become to her, just by showing up. She'd been okay alone when she believed that he was . . . lost, maybe because she'd never really dwelt on that. But now, after having gone through such a feeling of relief, such a rush of happiness . . . everything was different. It was so weird. She bobbed her head at him with a little half smile on her face, and hurried out of the cottage.

She was halfway up to the Plantation House when she remembered she'd forgotten to tell him he should keep the towel and take her Red Sox cap if he wanted—and be really careful not to get too much sun. She was going to be all right, but she worried about him. She would have to make it very clear to him, she thought, that she would never again go along with any plan that had him taking all the risks while she stayed safely in the cabin, so to speak. Why she felt that way was unimportant; she just did. "I don't even know myself," she told herself, out loud.

The entire pirate "family" was seated at the dining room table when she arrived, each in his or her own zone.

Roger, who hadn't shaved or combed his hair, looked surly and out of sorts again; he had on what looked to be a mechanic's coverall, navy blue with dark grease stains here and there, and ROG in red thread just above the left breast pocket. His breakfast seemed to consist of tomato juice, coffee, and a liverwurst and Bermuda onion sandwich on pumpernickel.

The children, wearing the stunned look of the recently awakened, were alternately spooning cereal into their mouths and staring at its point of origin, a box of DoubleChockyFruiteeNuttyOs. They were dressed in their previous day's outfits, as was their mother, in her boots and riding britches. Her breakfast was coffee and hot milk, which she poured into a large cup from her differently shaped silver pitchers. As she sipped, she read an article in *Cosmopolitan*. Terry, passing right behind her, saw its title:

"YOU DON'T EVER HAVE TO DO WITHOUT ..." (and then in smaller letters just below) "the Satisfaction You Deserve."

So, of the group, only Short Bill Gold and Ishmael took happy note of Terry's arrival, the bird with his standard whistle, and the captain with a smarmy smile. Ishmael was still in basic black, but Gold, apparently just out of the shower, had on a fluffy "shorty" bathrobe made of clean white terry cloth, all cotton. It was the first time Terry'd seen him without his yachting cap on. His round pink head was very nearly bald on top, with just a few wet strands of shiny white hair thrown over it, from left to right.

"Say, look who's here," he chirped, "our welcome guest and *most* negotiable security, the divine Miss T. herself. Join us, my dear. I can recommend the drippingly sweet papaya, already sliced"—he gestured toward the sideboard—"and in the kitchen you can toast yourself some whole-grain bread and boil a little hen fruit, same as I did." He had an egg cup in front of him, into which he'd broken bits of toast and spooned a couple of runny ones. "It's all hands for themselves at breakfast-making time, so seldom is heard a dissatisfied word—or any word at all, for that matter."

"I see," said Terry. "Okey-doke. A lot of people don't like to talk first thing in the morning. And I *will* have eggs and toast, if that's all right. I like my eggs hard-boiled," she prattled on, "which Daddy always says is funny, 'cause that's just the opposite of how I am!"

The Dragon Lady shot a glance at her when she said that, and Terry hoped she hadn't overdone the "Daddy" thing. What she'd actually been thinking was that toast and hard-boiled eggs would be easy foods to take down to Mick, and left to its own devices, her mouth had just kept going.

And so did she—into the privacy of the kitchen, where she boiled four eggs and toasted four pieces of bread, but only carried one of each back to her place at the dining room table.

She'd barely started eating when the Dragon Lady got up to go. But before she left the room, she had some words for Terry.

"This is the day you get to star," she said sneeringly, "in your very own picture show—all color stills, in this case. Ten A.M. at the boathouse, you looking cute and natural as Cover Girl can make you, please. Oh—and bring a swimsuit, a bikini if you have one. We'll want to show dear Daddy what he wants the most to know, won't we?" She switched to baby talk. "That his widdle girl don't have a single boo-boo on her pwetty body—even though his sailboat got all wecked." And with a smirky grin on her face, she made her exit.

"Good thought," her brother said to her departing back. And then to Terry: "That'll be great fun. You can pretend you're a *Sports Illustrated* swimsuit model. I bet they'd love to do their shoot down here one year. We've got everything they look for: perfect weather, beaches, scenery, and palm trees up the bippy. There's just one trouble, though." He shook his head, seemingly in genuine regret. "Being in *S. I.* would put us on the map. Greetings, Mr. Rand; howdy-do, McNally. And that's not just a no-no, it's a no-no-no." The captain wiggled his arms and shoulders, like a ballroom dancer moving to a Latin beat.

"You mean, nobody knows this island's here?" said Terry. "That can't be; that's impossible."

"Oh, of course some people know it *exists*," the captain said. "But hardly anyone has ever paid attention to it, other than some old-days pirates and ourselves. It's just too out of the way, not to mention being in the spooky old B. T.—that's the Boomooda Twiangle, to you."

"But how about the people who you've held for ransom, and their families pay the ransom and you let them go?" persisted Tee. "Wouldn't they be apt to tell the FBI or someone where they were and where you are?"

"Oh, *them*," the captain said, and stopped—suddenly at a loss for words, it seemed. He looked down at his scummy egg cup and drummed his fingers on the tabletop. "Well, the thing is . . . what we do is spin 'em around a few times before they go," he finally said. "That makes 'em good and dizzy and—shazam!—they absolutely lose all track of where they've been."

Terry wondered what kind of a Gullible Gerty he thought she was. Or was it that he didn't care? He was obviously lying through his teeth. What the pirates doubtless did was collect the ransom and then feed their hapless, helpless captives to the fishes—which was exactly what they planned to do with her. But she didn't want to have him think she knew all that, so she put on a wide-eyed look and said, "Oh, right! Like in Pin the Tail on the Donkey," and then got up and started collecting dirty dishes.

And as she did so, she brought up the matter of fresh water for the cottage, and the captain, probably delighted (she thought) with the change of subject, bustled around and found a nice orange-and-white plastic two-gallon thermos jug for her, the kind with a little spigot on the front of it. So when she headed down the hill after her washing up was done, she had it in one hand and her sweatshirt in the other, folded around three eggs with (sorry, Mick) unbuttered toast. In her mind, of course, was one more reason for the two of them to figure out a Great Escape Plan.

# chapter 15

At five of ten outside the boathouse, it looked as if the photos to be shot would be of crowd scenes. Everyone was there, not all of them by invitation, it turned out.

But as Terry approached, the Dragon Lady, with a big Polaroid on a colorful woven strap around her neck, and a black equipment bag dangling from one shoulder, started barking orders through a little megaphone.

"Okay," she announced, with one hand on the boathouse door. "Bill, Cherry, Buddy—scram, vamoose. Yes, you too, Ishmael. There's nothing here for you. I don't need your help, advice, suggestions, *presence*—not in any way, shape, form, type, or description. So get lost!" She took the megaphone away from her mouth and continued in a very different tone of voice. "Roger, you can stay and watch, and maybe we could cool off with a swim or have a champagne cocktail, after."

"Er, yes," he said. "Either one would be delightful." But then he smacked himself a good one on the forehead. "Except I just remembered—dammit!—I forgot to do me preflight checkoff on the plane. And I guess we'll want to be getting your photos to a mainland post box right away, chop-chop, eh what?"

And without waiting for an answer, he turned and hurried away. The D. L. watched him go, looking, Terry thought, like a spider who has just been told her web would need some serious reweaving.

Cherry, meanwhile, had considered her dismissal and decided that it wasn't fair.

"Why can't I stay?" she hollered at her mother. "I want to see the photo shoot. I think I want to be a model someday."

"You? A model?" said her brother. "Like, for what? A barf-bag commercial? I could see that. Or a do-it-yourself enema kit?" With a nasty laugh, he took off, running.

"I wouldn't mind it if you stayed," Terry said to Cherry, just as her mother told her, "Absolutely not. Forget it," and the girl herself picked up a broken piece of oar that had been leaning on the boathouse wall and started after Buddy, shouting, "I'll give *you* an enema, you little booger!"

Inside the boathouse, Terry discovered that the pirates had already done a lot of the chopping that would turn the *Cormorant* into valuable used parts. There were stacks of decking, of portholes, and of lockers, as well as little heaps of brass fittings. The stern transom, with the boat's name and home port on it in black and gold lettering, had been placed on a scaffold they'd made, which served as a kind of display rack for it. Big windows, set sideways and a good seven or eight feet off the cement floor, lined both sides of the hangar-like boathouse, so it was nice and light inside, perfect for photography.

"All right," the Dragon Lady said in a businesslike tone of voice, "let's get the paperwork out of the way first." And she went over to what looked like a high desk, or a speaker's lectern that had a ledger lying open on it, with an inkwell and pen alongside.

"I keep a record of all of our ... activities," she said. "That's because I'm going to write the story of my life someday, and unless I miss my guess, it'll be a runaway bestseller. As long as people have a taste for a rich confection of violence, intrigue, scandal, and depravity, thickly coated with a yummy layer of S-E-X, it can't miss. Of course, I'll have to use a pseudonym, which is too bad in a way. But how does Portia S. DeWinter strike you? Classical, yet nicely understated, yes? Lady Gwyneth Moseby might work too; you know how Americans suck up to titles."

Terry doubted that the Dragon Lady wanted her opinion, so she simply smiled and nodded at all this. But moments later she was asked for (quite directly), and supplied, some true hard facts: that her full name was Teresa Fremont Talley, and she was sixteen and three quarters years old, five feet eight inches tall, and a hundred and twenty pounds, with red hair and hazel eyes.

"Any distinguishing tattoos, scars, or birthmarks?" asked the Dragon Lady next, and Tee admitted she'd had an appendectomy the previous winter—which had left a tiny scar on her lower right ab.

"Okay, fine. I guess we're ready, then," the D. L. said. "You can toss your clothes on that pile of decking and change into your swimsuit over there. You do have a bikini, don't you?" Terry held it up: two pieces, not a lot of cloth in either one. "Oh, that *does* look good. If we have to, we can roll the bottom down a smidge so we can get a good shot of that scar. We'll see. Unless *he* does, our dearest daddy won't be sure this Terry is the real McCoy, now will he?"

Terry didn't see any point in telling her her *father* never would have seen that scar. She figured that'd just lead to more rude remarks about her sex life by the Dragon Lady, who was obviously convinced that Maitland Crane's relationship with her was other than paternal. Tee would have liked to know exactly why it was she'd come to that conclusion. Was it something about *her*? How could an almost seventeen-year-old virgin give off "loose woman" vibes? Were Roger and the captain getting the same message? How about Mick and the marquis? And how come being perceived as some kind of a practicing jezebel didn't make her drop-dead furious?

While thinking all of that, she did as she'd been told and undressed and got into her swimsuit. Teeny as its bottom was, she knew it still covered up her appendectomy scar, just barely, so without being told, she rolled it down a tad, thinking: *Well, all right, so there.*

The Dragon Lady checked, and nodded her approval. She seemed to have thought out exactly what she wanted in the way of poses. For her first shot, she had Terry stand beside the transom with one arm raised, pointing at the *C* in *Cormorant*.

In that pose, Tee's head was tilted slightly up, and that meant an unexpected happening in one of the big windows couldn't help but catch her eye. It was the pudgy fingers of somebody's hand curling over the windowsill—and then the equally pudgy fingers of somebody's other hand doing the same thing, perhaps a foot and a half away from the first one. The nails on all those fingers seemed to be well manicured.

Then, as Terry watched, there slowly, slowly appeared an all-too-familiar yachting cap, baby blue with gold braid on its visor, and a pink face under it, now even pinker than usual, its eyes bugged out by effort. And off to the side of it, a black bird's head, from the open beak of which there came . . . a shrill, enthusiastic, two-note whistle!

"Shit!" the Dragon Lady cried. "The goddamn blackbird and our own little peeping William!"

She dropped the camera and ran for the door, reaching in the pocket of her riding pants, from which she pulled a stubby little derringer, the perfect lady's gun (it seemed to Terry). She threw the door open and disappeared outside; three shots rang out, like: *Blat-blat-blat!* And a moment later she was back inside.

"I hope I scared the living wee-wee out of him," she said. "I swear, though—he *is* hopeless. Silly me, I thought a *Playboy* gift subscription might, like, satisfy his needs, but no such luck." She shook her head. "I just wish that what he's got was real contagious." And she sighed.

Three poses later, they were done and Terry got to put her clothes back on. Outside the boathouse, she saw Cherry sitting on the pier—waiting for her mother, Tee supposed. But she walked over to her anyway, still hoping to strike up some kind of friendship with the little girl.

"Hi," she said. "Waiting for your mom? She ought to be right out; we just got finished."

"No, I'm just sitting here," said Cherry. "I wish I could have watched—thanks for trying to get her to let me. Did Mom shoot Uncle Bill or Ishmael? I saw them hauling ass around the corner, but I didn't bother to check on them." She shrugged. "So how do you like being held for ransom? Does it make you feel important? I'll give you some really good advice, if you don't ask me to explain it."

Terry nodded and then raised one eyebrow.

"Get off your diet if you're on one," Cherry said. "Pig out, in fact, on all the stuff you feel you shouldn't eat 'cause it's too fattening. Like Dove bars, which we've got a ton of—yum. You won't ever regret doing what I just said—and that's a promise."

Because of the captain's earlier goof, Terry "got" what she was being told, which was that she wasn't going to live long enough to get fat. (*Gee,* she thought, *this kid must really like me.*) But she didn't tell Cherry she was on to . . . everything. Instead, she played it cool and shrugged, as if to say "Oh, yeah?" and, out loud, put this question to her little (sort of) friend.

"How'd you like to make a hundred bucks, U. S.?"

# chapter 16

It wasn't that Terry didn't remember she'd told Mick that she planned to offer Cherry the perfectly respectable sum of fifty bucks to "borrow" the clothes from Roger. She did, she did. But when the time came, she decided it might be wise to double the . . . incentive. Her reasoning was that the girl had been brought up in an atmosphere in which money didn't simply talk—it monopolized most conversations. To a kid like that, half a *C*-note might sound pretty chintzy.

But the look on Cherry's face, after Tee'd explained what she wanted for her money, and why, told her that she probably could've gotten the job done for nothing. Clearly the Dragon Lady's daughter, like Terry's Daddy Maitland, had a taste for adventure. On top of that, she'd reached the age—what is it? twelve? six? two?—when dissing adults was part of her job description—by word or deed, whatever. Also, it turned out that she was sufficiently xenophobic and gender-conscious to enjoy victimizing an English *man* for the sake of a fellow American female. And finally, with a past history that included acts of both planned and unpremeditated murder, a little petty larceny was not about to trouble her well-callused conscience.

"I can do the job right now," said Cherry, eyes asparkle. "It'll be a piece of cake. Rodge-Podge said he had to go check out the plane; I heard him tell Mom that. So the coast oughta be clear. You can come with me if you like. You can hide in the bushes and be lookout. Even if he caught me, it'd be no sweat. I'd just tell him my mom wanted something that smelled of him, but she was too shy to ask or something." Laughter gurgled out of her.

Terry had trouble imagining the Dragon Lady being too shy to do anything, but she held her tongue. She sort of admired Cherry's nerveless confidence; she could see her as one of a future pair of legendary bank robbers, and the movie somebody would make about them: *Cherry and Clyde: The Sequel.*

On their uphill walk from the boathouse, it was

as if, for months or years, Cherry'd stockpiled things to say until she had a girlfriend.

"Later on," she started, "I thought I'd do some treasure hunting. There's lots of places where nobody's dug. I'd like to ask you to help, but I can't. Mom says if Buddy or I find it, we should tell her quick like a bunny—but not a word to anybody else, meaning Uncle Bill and Roger mostly, I guess. She's pretty sure they wouldn't share with us if one of them found it. Pirates aren't into sharing, Mom says. If they have their men bury a treasure, they then have to kill 'em all. That's so they don't have to share, later. When we get enough money, the three of us are moving to the States. Mom'd like to live in Malibu—that's in California and right on the Pacific Ocean. Have you ever been to California?" Terry shook her head. "I bet it's neat, except for the earthquakes and stuff. Mom says it'd be like living here, only better on account of all the movie stars we'd have for neighbors. She gets really sick of being around Uncle Bill all the time. I think I know what she means: He's got a real bad case of diarrhea of the mouth." She looked up at Tee again to see how she had taken that . . . expression, and Terry rushed a little smile into position.

"One big problem we'd have, moving," Cherry went on, "would be finding a place where it'd be all right to have Bubba. Mom would never put him in a zoo or anything like that, and she said a lot of places don't allow pets. Bubba needs to have his space, too—just like Mom does, she says. And here we can give him all the food he likes, such as wild pigs and deer and stuff. That's what he grew up on, back in Komodo, wherever that is. An' you know what else he likes, his favorite treat? Those dead bodies that wash up on the beaches after a storm. I guess they're nice and salty. Bubba'd rather eat during the day, same as a person. Sometimes he goes hunting in his pen. Some big fat birds, like chickens, fly in there sometimes. You can hear it when he catches something. Mom says he gets in a real bad mood when he's hungry—same as Uncle Bill."

"I'd think everyone'd be in a *good* mood, here," said Terry, "living in a place as nice as this. Though I suppose if you capture people off one of your 'prizes,' and they aren't worth holding for ransom, they'd be pretty depressed. Has anybody ever tired to escape from here, that you know of?"

"Well," said Cherry, "there *was* this fat old lady who, like, disappeared one time. We think she swam for it. But there's really no place you can swim to from here, so she probably ended up in Davy Jones's locker anyway."

"One way or the other, she was food for the fishes," Tee suggested, trying to enter into the spirit of things.

"Yeah. Or the crabs." Cherry giggled and made pincers out of both her hands, clawing at the air around her, imagining it to be (her companion supposed) the old fat lady's flesh.

They were approaching the island's landing strip as she said that, and Terry could see the pirates' plane sitting on the end of the runway. It was a big twin-engined job with space inside, Cherry'd said, for cargo and for a dozen or so people on bench seats running up and down both sides.

"I don't see Roger anywhere," said Tee, peering around a tree.

"He might be in the plane," said Cherry. "Or I guess he could have finished checking and gone up to his place. You remember it from yesterday, right? His little Crow's Nest? Maybe we should check it out. You want to?"

"Sure, I guess. Seeing as we've come this far," said Terry. "Maybe he won't be there. Maybe he went . . . I don't know—swimming?"

But when they got close to the Crow's Nest, Cherry scouted ahead and after a bit returned to say, "No luck. He went back home." It seems she'd seen him through an open window, writing a letter or something.

"You want to try and wait him out?" she said to Terry, next. "He's got to go sometime."

But before Tee got to answer, they heard what

sounded like a person coming up the path.

Half a minute later, the two girls were sprawled on their bellies, hidden in the underbrush, and watching as the Dragon Lady passed on by. She'd changed from boots and riding britches into a simple, very light, white shift and sandals, with a diaphanous cerise silk scarf loosely tied around her neck. She also had a big red flower in her hair. Looking at her, Terry got the feeling that she wasn't wearing any underwear.

In one hand the Dragon Lady held a small blue box, in the other a big bulging envelope.

"She's bringing him the ransom note and those photos of you, I bet, and a little box of mints or something," Cherry whispered, and Terry nodded even though she thought the box resembled one that Connie'd "borrowed" from her older brother's room to show her once, and it had held a dozen condoms.

"I think I'll go back down," said Terry when she'd passed. "They'll probably be . . . talking for a while. Maybe he won't leave till after lunch."

"I guess I'll stay a little longer," Cherry said. "But if I have to, I can come back up this afternoon. Either way, I'll bring the stuff to your place right before dinner, if that's okay."

"Great. I'll have your money ready," Terry promised, and the two of them exchanged high fives, both grinning. "See you down at lunch, I guess."

They arrived at the Plantation House for the midday meal at almost the same time. When she saw Terry, Cherry gave her head a little shake and shrugged her shoulders; apparently her wait had been in vain. For the first few minutes of the meal, it was just them and the captain—and the sumptuous make-your-own sandwich spread that he'd laid out. But then Buddy arrived, dirty and sweaty and very much out of sorts, after still another unsuccessful treasure hunt, it turned out.

"I don't think there *is* any pissy old treasure," he told his uncle as he sat down. "What'd you have to go and lose the map for? Can't you think a little harder and remember where the X that marked the spot was?"

The captain pursed his lips in irritation. He'd almost finished constructing an enormous sandwich for himself: curried egg salad under crisp strips of bacon, under glistening tomato slices, all on thick Italian bread. But now he put the salt and pepper shakers he'd been using down and gave his nephew's questions his complete attention.

"Of course I can't," he told the boy. "If I could've, I would've found that damn box long ago. And I can't remember 'cause I never really looked to see exactly where it was—the X, I mean." He shook his head and sighed, then turned toward Terry and continued.

"There wasn't any need to," he explained, apparently anxious to justify himself to a new, impartial witness, "as I'm sure *you'll* understand. I . . . obtained the map one midnight from a blind man in his home—his *hovel*, really—on the island of Tortola. Because this chap was blind, he had no lights inside; indeed, when I approached the place, I feared he wasn't home. But still, I knocked and, hearing no reply, I tried the door. It wasn't locked, and so I entered.

"'Halloo,' I sez. 'You there?' And this voice come from the dark and sez, 'Yessir. Right straight in front of you, Cap'n. Just keep followin' your nose.'"

"And that's exactly what I did. My nose gave me directions, and I followed 'em. Old Chew—that was his name, Hugh Chew: old, blind, onetime Able Seaman Chew—he really stunk, worse and worse as you got closer. When I was right up next to him, he tells me, 'Here's the map, Yer Honor. And so where's me money?'

"Well, sir"—Short Bill Gold smiled at the recollection—"moments later he had handed me the map and in return had got . . . what he had coming to him. I took one peek at it under a streetlight when I was out the door—just making sure it was a map, and not a place mat from some pizza parlor, say—then hightailed it back down to my ship. And that map stayed folded in my pocket till I climbed the steps to the veranda, right out there." He gestured in the direction of the Plantation House porch.

"I think you know the rest of the story," he said to Tee. "I laid the map down on the table and went into the house to get my sister and a bottle of champagne I had on ice—Dom Perignon, it was—so we could have a proper celebration. While I was gone inside, a little breeze sprang up and . . . whoosh, it blew my golden treasure map away, forever, I suppose."

"Mom says she can't believe you were that stupid," Buddy said. "I'm just a kid, but I'd have taken a lot more than one peek at the map if I'd been you. I would have looked at it, and looked at it, the whole way home."

"That's because you're an untutored little prepubescent pecker-head," his uncle told him, "lacking any sense of style or ceremony—the proper way to do things. This wasn't like a message in a fortune cookie that you just unfold and read and toss into the trash. No, what I laid reverently on that veranda table was a page from buccaneering history, my boy: a classic treasure map, drawn by a dull and stubby pencil, no doubt, on a rumpled paper napkin." He sighed again. "Someday you'll know that waiting for the proper moment to enjoy . . . well, almost any-thing—a piece of art, a piece of cake, a piece of . . . sassafras—can make that moment all the sweeter!"

With which he slapped a bread lid on his sand-wich, cut the huge thing in two big halves, picked one up, and took a healthy bite of it.

"Ah!" he said, after he had chewed and swal-lowed. "Yes! How sweet it is!"

Before Short Bill Gold had started on the sec-ond half of his sandwich, they were joined by the Dragon Lady. The moment Terry saw her, she was pretty sure that things had not . . . worked out for her at Roger's. In addition to the dissatisfied frown she wore, the tip-off was that big red flower in her hair: It hadn't moved, or wilted (from more heat than it was used to, even).

"Well, our flyboy's in the wild blue yonder," she announced. "He gave me some big line of crap about having to take off right away so's he could make the five o'clock pickup at the mailbox at the airport. *I* said he could take our packet straight to the post office, but no—*he* said there were eagle-eyed postal inspectors hanging around the place, and they might see him and remember who it was who mailed"—her voice went up another couple of levels on the sarcasm scale—"that *real* suspicious-looking packet. A British-pilot-looking guy, they'd say." And she snorted.

"'Into the air, junior birdman. Into the air, upside down . . .'" the captain sang, with a malicious grin on his face. But then, putting on a comic English accent, he added, "But it's jolly good he didn't tarry, *eckshually*. The wireless informs us there's a big blow on the way: Hurricane Jackson, by name. With luck, the bloody thing will stay at sea and then go shooting up toward Nova Scotia. But at best there'll be some wind and rain, both here and there, by eventide."

The Dragon Lady snorted again. But after that she settled down and made herself an exceedingly appetizing-looking chef's salad, using all the lettuce Bill had washed for sandwiches—before Terry'd snagged some for herself.

So she made a BLT without the L and ate it slowly, very slowly, along with some handfuls of potato chips and two tall glasses of iced tea; she was, as she had planned to be, the last to finish.

After washing up, she threw together a really big ham and cheese sandwich for Mick and wrapped it in a couple of paper napkins before slipping it under her skirt. When she started down the path to her cottage, she was sipping from a third tall glass of iced tea, into which she'd stirred four spoons of sugar. Mick, she figured, might be pretty bored, and possibly would like to have a little sugar buzz. She found that she was wishing it were time for her to put her lantern in the window.

It occurred to her on the way down that no-body—herself included—had thought to comment on the Captain's Peeping Tom routine and his sister's spirited reaction to it. She guessed that meant these were, like, ho-hum what-do-you-expect-type happenings on this peculiar island paradise.

# chapter 17

Terry spent part of the afternoon sweeping the cottage floor with a homemade broom she'd fashioned out of palm fronds, and generally tidying up her little house so it'd be looking nice when Mick and the marquis returned that night. Then she put her bikini back on and went down to the ocean for a swim and a bath. The wind had picked up, and the surf with it, so she had a little trouble keeping her balance when she crouched down in the water and tried to soap her body with her swimsuit partway off. Before she'd known Mick was on the island, she'd washed the way she'd showered at home, more or less, without any clothes on and in water not even up to her knees. But now, for all she knew, he was lying in the underbrush, looking out in her direction. It made sense for him to choose a hiding place that had an ocean view.

She'd thought about whether she'd mind Mick seeing her naked, and decided that she would. It wasn't that she was ashamed of her body; she'd long since decided it was okay or better. As a matter of fact, she'd even imagined being a model for an art class and being paid to pose nude, if she really needed the money. She wouldn't go *looking* for the job, but she could imagine doing it, particularly if the class consisted of just women. But she didn't feel ready to have a boy she knew see her that way. The fact that she'd accidentally stumbled on an unclothed Mick didn't mean she "owed" him a similar view of her, absolutely not. She realized that she believed a boy should wait until he'd *earned* the right to see a girl naked—somehow. She wasn't exactly sure how he'd go about that, though. In the olden days a knight could go on a quest for something like the Holy Grail, or he could slay a dragon, or carry some keepsake his girlfriend had given him into battle. Any of those things would prove he was sincere. But nowadays? Just talking nice to a girl certainly wouldn't be enough. That wasn't any proof at all. Hanging around the Cape Enid Club, she'd overheard some guys—college age and older—who'd made smooth talking into an art form, and she had major doubts concerning their sincerity.

Walking back from her bath, she realized she didn't have a towel anymore, so she shook herself like a dog before she went back inside the cottage. Then, after walking around air-drying for a few minutes, she patted the remaining wet spots with the sundress she'd put on for her rescue from the *Cormorant*. It did an okay job, and being made entirely of synthetics, it dried again, completely wrinkle-free, in no time flat. She was pleased to feel she was adjusting well to Isla Muela Negra life.

By the time Cherry showed up, a windswept drizzle had begun, but the little girl had snagged a couple of umbrellas (one for Tee), and so the bundle that she carried wasn't even damp.

She hadn't overdone the "borrowing," having only liberated two pieces of Roger's wardrobe, but she was very pleased with one of them, a pair of madras pants. Terry'd seen their twin at the Club; they were the kind that looked a great deal like a patchwork quilt, and she thought that they were really hideous, but to Cherry they were "totally cool." She begged Tee to model the baggy things at once, and cracked up when she did so. Terry told her they were sure to be a huge hit at home, that all her friends would be completely sick with envy; Cherry looked away without a word when she said that. The other thing she'd swiped was ho-hum by comparison: a dark blue pocket T-shirt.

Tee had the money ready, as she'd said she would, and Cherry smacked her lips at the sight of it.

"I'm saving this for Malibu," she said. "I want a surfboard, really bad. Uncle Bill has all these cool old Beach Boy albums he lets us listen to. That's the life for me, I'm pretty sure—hanging out at the beach with a bunch of friends, and seeing who could ride the biggest killer wave."

"Right," said Terry, noncommittally. She could imagine Cherry doing that in Malibu. Surfing killer waves, she thought, called for some of the same qualities that robbing banks did, like daring and stupidity.

Tee got her little friend to start up the hill before she did by telling her she had to write in her diary for a while. She'd never owned a diary, but she needed a chance to go pick up Mick's water jug without being questioned about its odd whereabouts. When dinnertime approached, it was raining pretty hard, and she didn't even want to think about poor Mick.

The meal was a lot less festive than the one night before. Roger wasn't back, and the Dragon

Lady was still in a sour mood—plus it was her night to cook. The menu that she'd chosen might have been one of those "misery loves company" deals, Tee thought, being liver and onions with rather gummy brown rice and definitely "crispy" broccoli.

Terry, though, was used to food like that. Her mother was the sort of person who loved to go on different health kicks, so Tee'd been faced with many "organ meats" (like liver), "natural whole grains" (like brown rice), and "steamed green vegetables" (like broccoli), and had actually come to like all three. Buddy and Cherry, however, took one look at what came out of the kitchen and accused their mother of trying to make them so weak from throwing up that they wouldn't be able to get out of bed in the morning, and would just lie there while they slowly starved to death. They made themselves pb & j, on white.

Short Bill Gold had thought to bring the rum bottle to the table, so he washed his dinner down with frequent swallows of his drink *du jour,* which was rum and Coke. The Dragon Lady kept him company, and her mood improved during the course of the meal. So even before dessert she'd accepted her brother's challenge to a game of Scrabble, after—only providing that the game be played on her "home court" and that all obscenities would count as double word scores. Dessert was something no one lingered over: gingerbread men, pretty badly burned on the bottom, who were wearing what appeared to be aviator's caps and coveralls.

After dinner, once everyone had left for the D.L.'s house and her washing up was done, Terry made three big sandwiches for Mick out of lunch leftovers. These she carried down to the Honeymoon Cottage along with her flashlight, a bag of potato chips, and the filled water jug. The weather had gotten even worse, in terms of wind and rain, and she wondered if the captain had been misinformed and Hurricane Jackson was actually heading straight for the island, with winds up to 125 mph. All she needed (she thought) was to have her little house's roof and walls blown off, all in one piece, causing her to tie herself to a palm tree while a thirty-foot tidal wave bore down on her.

So when she got to the cottage, she put the lantern in the window right away. If she was going to end up tied to some old palm tree, she wanted Mick and the marquis to be right there with her.

He must have been nearby, because he came almost at once. But once again he knocked, instead of rushing right on in the way a lot of people would've done if they were half as miserable as he appeared to be.

He was soaked—"drowned rat" kind of soaked—with his hair plastered to his head (again!) and water dripping off his skin and off the sodden towel around his waist. At least, thought Tee, they weren't in Cape Enid; anywhere but in the tropics, he'd be also suffering from hypothermia. But here, he even managed cheerfulness.

"Well, I didn't get a sunburn," he told Terry. "And guess what? I'm not the least bit thirsty!"

"You've got to get dried off!" she said. "Poor you! Could you find *any* shelter? Look, you can use this dress for a towel—and here are some clothes for you. She only got two things—aren't these pants awful? I hope they fit all right. Take your time; I'll just be over here"—she walked over to the cupboard—"looking at these dishes."

Terry thought it was pretty cool, the way she'd handled that—letting him know she wasn't going to stare while he dried off and dressed. He tried to say he shouldn't get her dress all wet, but she told him to shut up, that she'd used it as a towel herself already. After that, for the next few minutes, she just listened to the sounds that everybody makes when they're drying themselves and putting clothes on: the rubbing and the stepping and the sighing. It could have been her mother there behind her, she thought, or Maitland Crane, or Connie. The sounds, for sure, were unisex.

"Ta-*da!*" he finally said. She turned around and there he was, in clothes again. He was clutching those ugly pants at the waist (he'd need a clothesline belt), but otherwise he looked just fine. A little silly maybe, but fine. It was *very* good to see him.

While he ate, she told him everything she'd seen and done and heard that day. She figured two heads were better than one, and for them to come up with a plan that'd get them off the island, he needed to know everything that she knew. So he quickly learned about the captain peeping at the photo shoot, how Roger had avoided the Dragon Lady's advances, Cherry's hopes to move to California, Bubba's eating habits, and the story of the treasure map.

Mick chewed on all this information along with potato chips, bread, cheese, smoked turkey, and a number of other cold cuts. From time to time—and this was different than on shipboard—he'd interrupt Tee's narrative to say how good the food was and how "wonderful" she was to take such perfect care of him.

"I can't imagine what I would have done," he said at one point, "without your being here."

Terry couldn't imagine how she'd be feeling if he weren't there either, but she didn't want to go into that just then. She got a little confused when she tried to analyze her feelings about him. Was needing someone the same as liking someone a lot? She could see that if you knew you really *liked* someone, you could get to feel you needed to have him around, in order to be at your happiest. But did it work the other way, necessarily? You could *need* a bodyguard, and hire a good one, but still not like the person at all. She wondered if maybe Mick was just her bodyguard against loneliness and depression, and other similiarly awful feelings.

When she'd finished with the story of her day, they both just sat there for a moment, Mick with his head down, gnawing at his lower lip. Then he looked up at her.

"So now, perhaps, it's needed that we ask ourselves"—it was the marquis speaking—"if there is some . . . some member of the enemy that we can *use* somehow. Not in the manner that we used this little Cherry, though—more connected to our leaving here alive."

"Well," said Tee, "we have the treasure—or at least you know where it is. It'd make a pretty juicy bribe."

"*Absolument*," the marquis said. "Without a doubt. Possessing such a treasure, the *maman* of Cherry could purchase half the waterfront at Malibu. And from what you say, she'd also take great pleasure having much more riches than the others."

"And the same would be true of the captain and Roger," Terry said. "I think the Dragon Lady's right: None of them is into sharing."

The marquis nodded with a little smile. Terry

thought this kind of intrigue turned him on, a little. She imagined that in fifteenth-century France the various dukes and counts and marquises were constantly making and breaking treaties, double-crossing one another, staging sneak attacks, and—most joyfully of all—plunging their arms elbow-deep into treasure chests containing gold and jewels, the "spoils" they'd won in battles with their neighbors.

"I see one big *difficulté*," he said. "Who can we trust to keep their word—to make a deal and stick to it? All of them are pirates, masters of the double cross—you see that on their flag, the skull and crossbones. To lie, deceive, is second nature to such people. Let's say we wish to trade the treasure for the *Kidd Me Not*. I doubt they are about to let us have the ship until they have the treasure. And once they have the treasure"—he cocked his head, and smiled, and shrugged—"*au revoir* to all agreements, no?"

Terry saw his point. When you were a kid and someone took your mitten and wouldn't give it back, you'd run and get ahold of their wool hat. And then you'd trade: Each of you'd hold on to both the stolen items, and on the count of three you'd both let go of the thing you were trading. But you couldn't do that very well with a treasure chest and a powerboat.

"But the trouble is," she said, "the treasure is about the only whatchamacallit . . . *bargaining chip* we have."

There was another momentary silence, during which the marquis looked down at the floor again.

"Not exactly," he said, finally. "There is one other thing." Terry thought he said that grudgingly, almost as if he didn't want to.

"Like what?" she asked.

"Oh, like that fondness which the captain has for looking at *jeunes filles*—in swimsuits or *au naturel*," the marquis said. "Which we have learn from what you say he did this morning at the boathouse."

Terry hadn't been prepared for that. Oh, sure, the thought had crossed her mind earlier that in this kind of situation her "feminine viles" *could* come in handy. But that thought had never gotten serious or detailed—beyond her wondering which dress to wear to dinner. She certainly had never considered *doing* anything. Now here was the marquis suggesting . . . what? Some sort of sex-for-powerboat exchange? Unthinkable! How could he? She sat there stunned, not knowing what to say.

But the marquis'd raised his eyes by then and noticed her discomfort.

"Don't misunderstand, I beg of you," he started. "All I'm thinking is perhaps there is a strategy. . . . It just now starts to come together in my head.

Suppose you ask the captain to go swimming with you, here. Let's say he changes clothes—puts on his suit—inside your cottage. You have to wait outside, of course. Then, when he's in the water, I sneak in and search his pockets, relieve him of the key for *Kidd Me Not* from off the ring of keys a man like this is almost sure to carry. He trusts no one, don't forget." He made a gesture with both hands and raised his eyebrows.

"So all I'd have to do," said Terry, wanting to be sure she had this right, "is let him see me in my bathing suit and take a swim with him?" To say she was relieved would be a major understatement.

"*Exactement*," the marquis said. "*Peut-être* the thing that you could say to him is that there's something at the cottage which you'd like it if he fixed. The door latch or whatever—we can break it just a little. And that if he brought his suit, in addition to his tools, maybe you would join him in a brief swim, after."

"I think that I could do that," Terry said. And then she had a brainstorm. She could use aromatherapy on Short Bill Gold. "And I could heat up some essential oil in here, beforehand. Oil of lavender, for instance, which is very calming. That'd help to keep the captain from getting . . . all excited."

"*Bon*," the marquis said. "And I will be nearby, in any case. Not visible, but near. And with a big stick by my side. I can always give him *bim-bam-boom,* if need be. I'd never let him hurt you."

They agreed that if the weather cleared, next day, Tee would try to get the captain down there in the late morning, a little before lunchtime. And with all of that decided, they were both soon ready to retire for the night. It had been a long, exciting (or soaking) day.

Mick, in his new clothes, began to wrap himself in Tee's gray blanket once again, but she told him that he didn't have to bother. For no reason in particular, she'd decided she could trust him.

They said good night and told each other to sleep well; soon they both had started doing that. When, at some point in the night, Tee rolled over and her shoulder came to rest against his back, she woke, smiled sleepily, and left it there.

⚓

# chapter 18

If there are laws that govern the behavior of weather systems like Hurricane Jackson, they are—alas—still mostly unknown to trained meteorologists and amateur forecasters alike. Aided by computers (or flare-ups of their grandma's "rheumatiz"), these may make "best guesses," but Atlantic storms often seem to have minds of their own. In the case of Hurricane Jackson, the mind behind the storm decided it should keep its distance from Isla Muela Negra and track northward in a tearing hurry.

So when Mick and Terry greeted the new day, they found it just delightful—a little windy still, but sparkling in the early morning sunshine. That made it very nice for swimming.

Tee was glad of that. She'd always been the type who, once she'd decided on a course of action, couldn't wait to get started. Postponements only made a person nervous or, in this case, more nervous. She believed the marquis had come up with a workable plan to separate the key from the captain, but it wasn't the marquis who'd have to get undressed and join the little pirate in the water, sort of be his rubber ducky.

"Right before whenever they eat lunch probably would be best." Mick cleared his throat nervously after making that reminder. "That way, there won't be any time for him to try some hanky-panky, after."

Terry was a little surprised to hear him use a word like "hanky-panky," but she didn't say anything. She couldn't give an exact definition of the word, but she figured it was something the marquis would be apt to know more about than Mick. It sounded like the kind of thing that probably went on all the time in France, in both the 1400s and right now—and had a lot to do with haystacks and excursions into ladies' underwear.

She arrived at the breakfast table before the Dragon Lady and her kids had gotten there, and Roger's place was also empty. It seemed likely that he'd spent the night at wherever he'd flown off to, and was having what Tee's mother called "a change of scenery."

Terry was delighted by those absences and the chance they gave her to invite the captain to her house and for a swim without there being a critical audience on hand. In light of what had happened at the photo shoot the day before, such an invitation would sound pretty nutsy to . . . well, anyone with any sense at all. Though not, she was quite sure, to Short Bill Gold; fat old men with lots of money seem to be convinced that young and pretty girls all find them irresistible.

"Hi-ho, hi-ho, hi-ho," he said when Tee walked in the dining room, sounding even jollier than usual. "Ain't this a fine Muela Negra morning, now? According to the mainland weather service, the ugly mess of wind and wet and wave, Mr. Hurricane Jackson, has stayed a ways away from us and now is speeding ever northward. By the time he reaches Nova Scotia—or wherever—he'll barely have the strength to blow out candles on a birthday cake, I'll bet."

"That's wonderful," said Terry, giving him a carefree, happy grin to sort of set the tone for what she hoped would follow. "Daddy's not afraid of hurricanes, but he surely does respect them. I believe he rode one out in *Cormorant* in ninety-four, somewhere in the South Pacific."

"You don't say!" the captain said. "Amazing! He's a daddy in a million—which is what I'm sure he'll gladly pay to have his darling daughter home again: one million dollars cash, ten thousand used and unmarked hundred-dollar bills. I know I'd fork it over just like *that*"—he snapped his pudgy fingers—"if *I* were in his Gucci loafers."

Terry nodded cheerfully and grinned at him again. She hoped she looked impressed and grateful, although in fact she was a little . . . disappointed. A million didn't seem like much to ask for her, the supposed daughter of a Maitland Crane. Mone had told her waterfront estates in the Cape Enid area started at two milllion five. And she'd read that a Japanese businessman kidnapped down in Mexico (where everything was cheaper than up here) had brought *six* million in ransom. This was for a man four times her age and, going by his picture in the paper, not great-looking.

But she put any hurt feelings to one side and segued into the matter of her broken door latch and her hope that maybe he could fix it for her. She didn't say "a big strong manikins like you," but let her tone imply that.

And then she hit him with the carrot, adding maybe he would like to join her for a cooling and refreshing dip, once he'd made her little home, her castle, all secure again.

The captain bounced with pleasure in his chair, rising to that beautifully presented bait.

"Count me in!" he promised. "I'd love to. First I'll strap my tool belt on—Mr. Fix-it is my middle name—and once my work is done, we can have our little paddle in the Big Pond, using the buddy system, I assume. And that should put us in the mood to"—he licked his lips with eyes half closed—"have ourselves a fine, hot—

"—*lunch*," he finished as the Dragon Lady strolled into the dining room wearing a floor-length white terry cloth bathrobe, with her long straight hair still wet from a morning shower. Buddy and Cherry trudged in after her, both looking totally displeased with the whole idea of morning.

Having them arrive meant that Terry didn't have to keep on chatting with the captain, which so pleased her that she leaped to her feet and volunteered to fix the Hollys's breakfasts at the same time that she made her own.

"Thanks a lot. That's really nice of you," the Dragon Lady said—or at least that's what Terry decided she meant by the wordless shrug she gave, more or less in her direction.

So she hustled off into the kitchen where she boiled eggs for herself and Mick, got out cereal and milk for the two kids, and heated milk and coffee for their mother. She felt her day had started well. At that moment she thought the marquis's "workable plan" was looking like A Truly Great Idea.

Once everyone had finished eating, and she had done the cleaning up and hidden Mick's breakfast and drinking water behind the outhouse, Terry started wandering around the island. Aimlessly, you ask? Not quite. She had twin purposes, in fact. The first was to avoid Bill Gold; she didn't want to see him till the time she said she'd meet him at the cottage. She didn't want to deal with him five minutes longer than she had to.

Her second purpose, though, was positive: She was looking for something. She hoped to find a wheel-barrow, a garden cart, or even a little red wagon, that wasn't under lock and key. Although she didn't know how much the pirate treasure weighed, she imagined that it could be quite a lot, even more than she and Mick could lug between them. And she was not about to leave that chest behind; it was going with them when they got on board the *Kidd Me Not*.

Greed was not her motivation; she was pretty sure of that. There wasn't a whole lot of stuff she wanted that she wouldn't get from Mone at some point, or from her father—both of them were kind and generous. Plus, she'd never ruled out the possibility of making quite a lot of money herself, working at some job that was a lot of fun and at which she also was outstanding.

No, she wanted the treasure for two other reasons. The main one had to do with, basically, her *homecoming*. It had never been her plan to stay away from home forever. She loved her mother dearly, and her brother and her absent father too—not to mention her friends, like Connie. But she'd realized from the moment she decided to stow away on the *Cormorant* that when the time came for her to return from her great adventure, there might be a little . . . awkwardness.

The thing was, she'd made an agreement with Mone about three years before in which she'd said—promised—that she'd at least talk over (with Mone) any major changes in her lifestyle, before putting them into practice. At that time she'd figured the agreement had to do with sex and not much else, but now she had to admit that running away from home did constitute a pretty major lifestyle change. So, with that being the case, it might be nice to have another focal point for conversation (once she arrived back home) in addition to "How could you?" and "You promised!" A pirate treasure, she felt sure, would be a thing that anyone would enjoy talking about and that everyone would be completely glad to see.

The second reason for her wanting to bring the

treasure home was much less selfish; it had to do with Mick. She figured that some treasure might make Maitland Crane a lot less pissed at him for stealing *Cormorant* and losing it.

So when she spied a sturdy two-wheeled garden cart up near the gate of Bubba's pen, she gave a little grunt of satisfaction. Seeing nobody around, she quickly hid it in the underbrush a little way off the path that led down to her cottage. It would be there when they needed it, probably that very night, if all went well.

# chapter 19

When it was time to go meet the captain, Terry found she felt the way she used to feel before a Cape Enid High School baseball game. Then—as now—she felt some nervousness, but she also knew that she was ready. In each case there were things she had to do before the game could start. Back home, she had to have the bases and the baseballs and the bats all in their proper places; she also had to have the checks for the umpires in her pocket, and the score book and two sharpened pencils laid out on the scorer's table. Here she had to have—and she had taken care of this before she left her house that morning—her one-piece swimsuit on the line. And there was one other thing that she'd forgotten to set up: aromatherapy! She'd wanted to have the cottage *reeking* of lavender when he arrived; the calmer Bill Gold was, the better she'd like him, she was sure.

But he was waiting by the cottage when she got there, with his leather tool belt strapped around his ample waist, over his painter's overalls; a pair of batik swimming trunks dangled from one hand. *Damn!* she thought. The little so-and-so had showed up early. It seemed the captain was extremely ready.

So he got right at the job, which was to reset the little hook and eye that served to "lock" the cottage door from the inside. Mick had pulled them both out of the partly rotted door and frame before he left, that morning. Whistling between his teeth, the captain made a big show of taking measurements and asking Terry to decide how high up she wanted her latch to be this time, and marking two big *X*s with a carpenter's pencil before he screwed the pieces in. A good ten minutes passed before the job was done.

"So now . . . ?" said Short Bill Gold. He rubbed his hands together (like somebody ready to have *fun*, thought Terry, now more nervously).

"Let's call this our cabana," she began. They were standing right outside the cottage. "Why don't you change first? And then I'll follow, after."

"Okey-doke," the captain said, and disappeared

inside the little house, closing (but not latching) the door behind him.

In fact, Tee's plan was rather different than she'd said. She was going to change right where she was, while he was changing. That'd take care of any peeping he had planned. By the time he reappeared, she'd be all ready for their swim. Like most women, Terry could change clothes at lightning speed when time was of the essence.

So as soon as the door to the cottage closed, she sprang into action. Off went the sundress and the little T she'd had on under it; down went her under-pants as well. But she was only starting to reach for the green and white striped tank suit when the cot-tage door flew open, a merry voice cried, "Coming, ready or not!" and out came Short Bill Gold, bare naked, arms outstretched, looking like a man who planned to win a "catch the greased pig" contest.

Terry took one look at him and fled. But that one look was all she'd needed to find out two things. First, that Short Bill Gold was (at least for now, thank God) well named. And second, that the marquis's brilliant plan was going to be a bust. For though the captain had no clothing on, he still wore . . . *jewelry*—a heavy golden chain around his neck, from which there hung a good-sized ring of keys!

Tee decided to run up the beach, instead of

heading for the water right away; she was sure he couldn't catch her, running. She was slender, he was fat; she was young, he was old; she didn't smoke or drink, while he abused both lungs and liver. Her plan—once she was able to begin to put a plan together—was to get him a good distance away from the cottage and then, avoiding him somehow, run quickly back to it, grab some clothes, and head on up the hill. Once at the compound, she felt quite sure the Dragon Lady would protect her.

It didn't occur to her until she was a good way up the beach—perhaps a quarter mile—that Mick was watching this whole . . . what? *performance* from the shelter of the underbrush, holding, more than likely, his big stick—the one he'd said that he could bim-bam-boom with. *Damn!* she thought again. He hadn't earned the right to see her naked. The only reason this was happening was that his plan had been a washout. But then she thought perhaps he didn't know that; perhaps he couldn't tell from where he was that the captain had the keys around his neck. Perhaps instead of watching her (and him) run up the beach, Mick (or the marquis) was in the cottage, going through the captain's pockets.

After she'd gone another hundred yards or so, she looked over to see how her pursuer was doing. He'd fallen quite a ways behind and didn't have much foot-speed, but amazingly, he was still waddling along. Did he think he'd ever catch her? Did he think she'd think it over and decide she wanted him? Was the little caveman thinking anything other than a big fat *"Gimme!"*?

"Wait, wait," she heard him calling out to her. "I want to tell you something."

*Sure*, she thought. *Sure you do. You want to tell me something with your little wagger-pagger.* Suddenly she got very conscious of the fact that she was naked and he was watching, seeing her that way. She turned sharp left and waded into the ocean.

The surf was no longer the foaming, crashing beast that it had been the day before, so she could keep on walking until the water was up to her chin. Then she stopped and faced the shore and waited.

When he got to where she was, but not yet in the water, he cupped his hands around his mouth and shouted—between taking big gulps of air—that he was her friend, and that she shouldn't be afraid of him.

"Is that all you wanted to tell me?" she called back. She started sliding sideways in the water, back in the direction of the cottage. He was wading toward her now.

"No, there's more," Short Bill Gold replied. "My sister wants to *kill* you, once your father's paid the ransom. I'm going to save you, though; I have a plan. But I'll need your . . . well, *cooperation*. I need to know that you're my friend." By then, he'd gotten waist-deep in the water.

"That's baloney," she informed him, still slipping sideways. "She told me if you gave me any trouble, just to let her know and she'd take care of it. Just the way she almost did outside the boathouse yesterday. She said she'd give you a lead catheter if you even looked at me funny." She paused. "Whatever that means," she finished lamely, blushing.

As soon as she'd said what she had, Terry couldn't believe she'd said it. She'd never been a person who could make up lies at the drop of a hat—let alone lies that are unusual, disgusting threats.

The captain winced. "No, no," he said. "You can't believe the woman; she's been a pathological liar ever since she learned to talk. She lied so much they couldn't even potty-train her. I'm the only one who can protect you." He'd been a grade-A liar all his life himself.

At that point he was treading water, no longer able to touch bottom.

"If you'll just put yourself in my hands . . . " he added, probably thoughtlessly.

"Never, you old lech," said Tee, and cupping a hand (as she had done in many a Cape Enid water fight), she sent a jet of salty ocean $H_2O$ right into his face. Then, angling away from him, she put her head down, pushed off the sandy bottom, and swam hard toward the shore.

In no time she was on the beach and running once again, now faster even than before. When she'd covered half the distance to the cottage, she looked back and saw he'd given up; he wasn't even walking fast. But she did not slow down at all. When she got to the cottage, she was still a little wet, but she put her clothes back on without bothering to dry off, then headed up the path to the Plantation House.

Their plan had been a big, fat failure; there wasn't any point in denying that. And what's more, she now knew the captain always had his keys in his possession—that chances were he even slept with them around his neck. She'd also learned that he, beyond a doubt, had what her mother called "designs" (Mone's version of "the hots") for her. Those were that morning's minuses.

Pluses were a little harder to come up with, but Terry was the sort who always looked for them. And—yes!—she had escaped the guy; that was a big one. And the marquis hadn't had to do any *bim-bam-booming*, which meant the pirates were still unaware that he was hiding on the island. (The thought that maybe they could *kill* the captain and obtain the key that way had not yet entered Terry's mind. Credit the way she was brought up. Talleys simply weren't killers. Mone hadn't even had to tell her that; she just *knew*.)

A final plus was that her door latch was back on, and more secure than ever, actually.

She was walking up the Plantation House steps when she remembered she'd forgotten Mick's water jug. *Mmm*, she thought—*too bad*. But it was too bad for her that she'd had to run up and down the beach naked, while he was lying in the shade, watching. She figured she'd had a much worse day, so far, than he had; he could stand to be a little thirsty.

# chapter 20

Terry didn't have to think back and try to remember the last time she'd been eating lunch and had been joined by a man who'd recently seen her *sans culottes*. There absolutely hadn't been such a time. In a place like Cape Enid that would have been, if not unheard of, unforgettable at least.

So when the captain showed up in the Plantation House dining room some ten minutes after his regular feeding time, she wasn't sure what sort of attitude to take. Earlier she'd decided that, at least for the time being, she wasn't going to "tell on" him. Her decision wasn't based on there being two children in the room who wouldn't . . . "understand"; Cherry and Buddy, after all, had perpetrated even worse crimes than the one their uncle had sort of attempted. No, it was more her feeling that perhaps the incident was something she'd be wise to "save" until some future time when she could use it even more effectively.

Bill Gold didn't look at her as he slid onto his chair, as unobtrusively as possible. But he didn't escape his sister's notice.

"Make a note of the date," she advised the group already at the table, which included Roger, looking dapper in his aviator's togs. "We have here an historic moment. Never before, in all of recorded time, has William Gold been tardy for a meal. Watcha been doin', Willie? No, let me guess. Roger left an open box of Mallomars on the plane, and you, having caught the scent of them, investigated. Is that it, hmm? Is Hildy right again?"

Terry, who was watching him out of the corner of her eye, thought that though he might have colored slightly, he probably was more relieved than anything. The Dragon Lady not only hadn't pulled a gun on him, she also hadn't even hinted that she might be planning to.

"For your information," he informed her, grandly, "I'd had to go and try to locate Ishmael. He flew away while I was looking for a place where two palm trees had blown over and fallen one on top of the other, but crossing so's to make an X. I dreamed that—"

"The treasure chest was right under the *X*—wasn't that it, Uncle Bill?" Buddy interrupted, excitedly. "So where it is *now?*" He turned to his mother. "I bet the old fart found the pirates' treasure, Mom. That's why he's late for lunch. Make him share it with us, Mommy!"

"Oh, pipe down, you small excrescence," said his uncle. "I never even found the trees. But I finally did find Ishmael, thank God. He'd flown back home and was sleeping in his cage, the lazy little bugger."

Still not looking at Terry, he helped himself to the lightly curried tuna and potato salad that the Dragon Lady must have made. Tee had already eaten most of her large helping; the excitement and that run had put a fine edge on her always healthy appetite.

"Now, if I could trouble you for a roll, my dear . . . "

The rolls were just to Terry's right, so she realized she had to be the "my dear" he was addressing. She picked up the plate and swung it around in the captain's direction.

He reached for a roll, but because he was looking at her rather than the plate, his wrist made contact with its edge, jarring the plate in such a way that a roll flew off its other side and landed on the table.

"Oh, sorry, *sorry,*" said the captain, as he scooped up the errant kaiser. "My mistake. I really am most awfully sorry."

Terry made no answer. She wondered if his words had a double meaning: that he was saying he was sorry for knocking the roll off *and* sorry for what had happened earlier. But he hadn't sounded all that sorry. He'd sounded more . . . annoyed than anything. Frustrated, too. He hadn't gotten his way and he was pissed about that. His was a tone of voice she recognized, one that was not uncommon in Cape Enid conversations. Her hometown was a place where many people thought they had the right to "have it all."

When she happened to glance at the captain a little later, an awful thought occurred to her: Maybe, when he looked at her, it was like in those cartoons where a man is looking at a fully dressed woman (on the street, in a bar—anywhere, really), but in the balloon over his head it's made clear that he's imagining how she'd look without any clothes on. Because he'd actually seen her naked, that'd be easy for Short Bill Gold to do. She *hated* that idea.

And then, unbidden, what should pop into her mind but how *he'd* be looking, sitting there unclothed. She wrinkled up her nose and pushed her plate away. This was getting more and more disgusting, this fall-out from the morning's . . . foul-up.

The Dragon Lady finished moments later and got up, which gave Terry reason to get up herself and begin to clear the table. Cherry, uncharacteristically, gave her a hand and, as she carried her and Buddy's plates out of the dining room, asked her if she'd like to come and "see my room," that afternoon. Terry said, "I'd love to," loud enough for the captain to hear. That'd let him know, she thought, that he didn't have a chance of finding her alone that day—in case he still had . . . aspirations.

After she'd done the cleaning up, she took a quick trip down the hill in order to leave Mick some lunch (out of the kindness of her heart, she also brought him another big glass of iced tea), but then went right back up again and on to The Bucket O' Blood and Cherry's surprisingly pink and little-girly room.

That early afternoon, Terry got to look at all of Cherry's "special things," starting with her scrapbooks.

There were two of these. The first one, titled "California," was page after page of pictures of that state—mostly surf and sand and young people in swimsuits playing volleyball and having cookouts, but some of hillside houses looking down on the above. The second book just had "Private! Do Not Open!!" on its cover, and Cherry said she'd never shown it to anyone in her life, before. It was filled with photos of, and articles about, the film star Leonardo DiCaprio, who Cherry called "Leo." She told Tee his favorite drink was lemonade and that he liked the Beatles, Jack Nicholson, and Ernest Hemingway's *The Old Man and the Sea,* and Terry said, "Gee, so do I!" instead of what she really thought, which was *"Yeah, right!"*

After that, they looked at Cherry's other treasures, including her charm collection (for her around-the-waist choker) and the clip-on silver hoops her mother wouldn't let her wear that, when attached to different parts of her body, gave her the "pierced look" without actual piercing.

When she wasn't feeing forty-five years old and cynical, Terry was pleased and touched by the younger girl's willingness to confide and share with her—Cherry's almost *need* for approval. She could remember being Cherry's age and having her own strange obsessions and struggles to be cool, although she thought she'd been—as a result of living in cosmopolitan Cape Enid instead of on a nowhere island—a lot more involved with the "real world" than Cherry was.

But by midafternoon she'd had to change her tune on that a little, as a result of watching (and helping) Cherry do her "job."

She hadn't known what to expect when her little friend announced that it was time for her to go and "feed the pets"—and would she like to come with her? Tee said, "Sure, why not?" and when they'd poured Purina Cat Chow into two small bowls on the porch, she sort of figured that was it.

But not at all. Cherry left the porch and headed for Bubba the Komodo dragon's pen. But when she got to the tall chain-link fence surrounding it, she stopped, looked left and right, and stamped a foot while saying, "Damn that Buddy, anyway!"

"What?" said Terry. "What's the matter?"

"That brat—he stole my cart," she said. "And now I'll have to drag his food, not just to here"—she nodded at the pen's well-bolted gate—"but all the way around to the door on the other side."

"Oh," said Terry, getting it. "When you said 'feed the pets,' I didn't think of Bubba. But doesn't he eat . . . "

"Carcasses," said Cherry, "an' some guts and stuff. That's in addition to whatever he can catch inside the pen, like stupid guinea hens that fly in there, or birds of paradise, or rodents."

"*Carcasses?*" said Terry. "Where do you get carcasses?"

"Back there." Cherry pointed to one of the small sheds over beside the animal pens. "Uncle Bill and Roger hunt, and dress whatever game they kill, so all I have to do is come and get the stuff they leave for me. Maybe you can help me lug it, seeing as I haven't got the cart."

"Yeah, I guess," said Terry, as she reluctantly approached the designated shed. And sure enough, when Cherry opened its door, there inside it was not just a rotten odor the likes of which Tee Talley'd never smelled before, but also the carcass of a small wild pig, hanging from a hook. On the ground beside it was a bucket more than halfway full of what she guessed were pig's . . . insides.

"Gross!" said Terry, almost gagging at the sight and smell.

"Oh, you get used to it," said Cherry, coolly, as she lifted the pig's carcass off the hook. "So what do you want—this or the bucket?"

"*That,* I guess," said Terry, making herself take hold of the pig's hind feet, then quickly pulling it into the fresh air outside.

"Smart," said Cherry, picking up the pail. "You can't drag a bucket, and this stuff can slop on your leg if you're not careful."

Tee, dragging the pig's carcass, let the little girl lead the way, and they followed a path all the way around the pen to its opposite side. En route Cherry explained that her mother couldn't stand the sound of Bubba eating (much as she loved him), and that was why they had to lug his meals so far. When they got to the gate on the other side, Terry slid back the bolt and they took the food inside and collected the empty bucket from the day before. Cherry explained that Bubba liked to let his meat warm up in the sun for a bit before he chowed down, and that was why they didn't see him. "He's back there in the shade somewhere," she said.

"But he doesn't like it if I'm late," she added. "This one time, we were all out collecting a prize, and so it was almost dark by the time we got back and brought him his dinner. Roger had to help me, 'cause Bubba was right here by the fence and we didn't dare open the gate. Rog tossed the carcass over the fence, and you shoulda heard the racket Bubba made when he got into eating it." She giggled.

"*Yuck*," said Terry. "Sounds disgusting." She was glad when they got back to the compound without hearing anything and were able to relax with a glass of "Leo's" favorite beverage on The Bucket O' Blood's front porch.


Tee hung out with Cherry until it was getting closer to dinnertime, when she learned (from the Dragon Lady, who was cooking) that the captain had "something he had to do with Roger" on a part of the island nowhere near her cottage. So she ran down the hill, had a swim, changed her clothes, and remembering the water jug this time, climbed up the hill in time to eat.

The meal was about halfway done (ham and scalloped potatoes and sugar snap peas) when Short

Bill Gold turned toward her and said, off-handedly, "Oh, by the way, Roger and I came across that side-kick of yours from the *Cormorant* this afternoon. What did you say his name was? Kirt? Nice-looking young fella, but not much of a conversationalist." He sniggered, as if he'd just said something funny.

"That's Cap'n *Kirk*," his sister said. She'd been going at the rum pretty actively again.

"Well, whatever his name was," said the captain, "he made a fine dessert for Bubba."

# chapter 21

Later, Terry thought she might have reacted differently to what the captain said if she hadn't, that same afternoon, gotten involved with Bubba's tastes in food, and learned about his ... eating style—or at least the kinds of sounds he made while dining. Knowing what she did made the idea of feeding a human being to the great lizard all the more horrific, and the thought of having Mick become the dragon's "dessert" totally beyond imagining.

The reaction that she *did* have was bizarre, to say the least. It was as if the world shut down. She heard no noises for a while, no sounds of knives cutting through ham, or children wiggling, or rum decanted over ice, or the Dragon Lady slurring words. There was just some vacant space and herself in it, not sitting anymore or standing on a floor—not even having any body, but just being there with emptiness around her and inside her even, and the certainty that she was lost. And she stayed there in that space, in that condition, for she didn't know how long, paralyzed by what she'd heard the captain say.

The next thing she knew, she had the knuckle of her pointer finger in her mouth, and she'd bit down on it so hard that she said "Oh!" not loudly. But that brought her back to being in the dining room again, in the Plantation House again, on Isla Muela Negra and a captive of this strangely dreadful pirate band. And her conscious mind began to work again.

It could be, she told herself, that Roger and the captain had come upon a dead body, washed up on one of the island's beaches—the body of some poor sailor who'd drowned when Hurricane Jackson tore his ship apart and sank it. Hadn't the captain said that bodies often came ashore in the aftermath of a major storm? Her description of the fictional "Kirt," her father's captain, had been general enough to fit a lot of guys who spent their time on boats. And any dead person would be, in Bill Gold's words, "not much of a conversationalist."

She flat refused to dwell on the possibility that Roger and the captain had found Mick, murdered him, and fed him to the Dragon Lady's huge, disgusting pet.

In part, that was because the thought of being all alone again was totally unbearable. And it wasn't just aloneness she dreaded—it was being *without*. In just the little while since he had reappeared, Mick and the marquis had come to be . . . important to her. Earlier that day, she wouldn't have said that she "loved" Mick (if someone like Connie had asked her, for instance). "Love" was something she had more or less reserved for later on, sometime. But now she wouldn't want to say. Mick wasn't a Kirt Manwaring in terms of looks or style, but that didn't seem to matter very much.

Somehow she got through the meal without either fainting or having hysterics—possibly because she'd always said she wasn't "the type" for either one of those. After finishing the cleanup—and the scalloped-potatoes casserole dish was a bitch to get all the gunk off—she filled the water jug and made three huge ham sandwiches. Doing so, she felt, was a simple but important act of faith. Her alert and kindly God would reward her by making it not be Mick that Bubba was digesting.

But by the time she got down to the cottage she felt less certain that her making the sandwiches could have had any effect on anything. She'd done that long after God had decided whether it would be Mick or some stranger they'd toss into Bubba's pen. So maybe God had had to decide Mick's fate on the basis of *Mick's* doings and not-doings, rather than hers. God hadn't let him drown in the storm that wrecked the *Cormorant;* maybe that was a good sign, she thought. Maybe God liked him as much as it seemed she did. She put her lantern in the window and lay down on the bed to wait.

When she heard the knock on the door, her eyes got very big, and she took a breath and held it. The knock had *sounded* like one of Mick's—well, hadn't it?

Except . . . perhaps the captain also knocked that way!

She slid off the bed and padded, barefoot, to the door.

"Who is it?" she said softly, with her mouth by the newly installed, chest-high latch.

She heard a soft chuckle, then a whisper that came from just the other side of the door where her mouth was.

"Is cam-*air*-a crew from—how you say?—*Wide World of Sports?*" she heard.

Probably, she later thought, the marquis—who had no idea that maybe he'd been killed and eaten—was totally surprised to see the door fly open, and be yanked inside, where, with her arms wrapped tightly around him, Terry started sobbing up against his chest.

She was quite surprised herself. But it did make them even: She was pretty sure Mick had cried when he came to the cottage that first time and found her there. Relief could make a person cry, especially when the cause of that relief is someone you care about. Tee was so relieved she didn't even mind anymore that he had seen her naked. He'd earned that right—that one time, anyway—by not being dead. And now there were two things they were even on—she liked that.

After a bit she was able to wipe her eyes, and laugh, and explain herself—telling him about the bombshell that the captain had dropped at dinner. She found herself touching him a lot in the course of the story, as if to reassure herself it really was him. Mick said he hadn't come close to being killed, that he'd lain low all day and was probably never more than a quarter of a mile from where he was right then. And that reminded her. . . .

"So," she said, "I take it that you saw our little game of tag—our shall we say, *unusual* little game?—with both the players out of uniform?"

"Ah, *oui*—I suppose I did," he said, trying—unsuccessfully—not to smile. "Though I was such a way away I cannot see so well. Mostly I see *shapes*, you know? One, *parfait!*" Then he wrinkled up his nose. "And the other . . . *dégoûtant!*"

"Yeah, sure," said Terry, grinning. "I'll bet that's

all you saw! But you probably couldn't see he had the keys around his neck."

"*Vraiment,* I do not see that," the marquis said. "So I come in here, look in his pockets, and find nothing. Then I go back to my hiding place and observe you running back. As before, I think there is no need for bim-bam-boom. This time the little fat one doesn't even run. I tell myself is better he don't know that I exist."

Terry nodded; she agreed. And she was pleased by the gentlemanly way he'd described what he'd seen out on the beach. She could imagine the remarks and sign language she'd have had to put up with if she'd been observed in that condition by one of the boys at the Cape Enid Club. She went over and sat on the bed, letting him perch on the straight-backed chair beside it while he started on his sandwiches.

As he ate, she told him about the rest of her day, how things went at lunch, her visit to Cherry's room, and (in some detail) how and what and when big Bubba got fed.

He listened attentively to everything, taking it all in (along with his food). That was another thing she liked about him: He gave her his complete attention when she told him stuff. A lot of boys she knew seemed to think that what they had to say (in class or out) was always more important than anything a mere female could come up with. She was starting to believe that he was actually real smart.

"I have a little news m-myself," Mick said, when she was done. He reached into the breast pocket of his (formerly Roger's) T-shirt and produced a folded piece of notebook paper.

"Read this." He handed it to her. "I found it right in this same pocket; Roger must have shoved it in there and forgotten it. It has to be the rough draft of the letter he sent to m-my dad, along with your photograph. He's double-crossing the captain and the Dragon Lady—or hopes to, anyway."

Terry unfolded the paper. It looked like a first draft, handwritten and messy with some crossings-out and changes.

*My dear Mr. Crane (she read),*

*I regret to inform you that an ~~evil~~ ruffi-anly pirate crew has captured both your ship (yawl* Cormorant) *and your nubile "daughter" (Terry Talley). Though ostensibly a member of said ~~crew~~ organization, the undersigned has come to ~~feel~~ believe that piracy, kidnapping, murder, et cetera ~~is~~ are unacceptable in civilized society.*

*So, for a "~~finders~~ salvage fee" of $500,000 (U.S.) the undersigned will ~~fly~~ extricate the aforesaid Terry from the buc-caneers' ~~island~~ custody and ~~fly~~ escort her to* *a mutually agreeable location. If you agree to this ~~plan~~ arrangement, and to absolve the undersigned of any and all ~~fault~~ criminality in this matter, please arrange to have the following message appear on the Florida Marlins baseball scoreboard during one of the games this week: R.—Of course I will. Love, M."*

*~~As soon as you do~~ Shortly after the message is received, you will be given further instructions concerning the transfer of this ~~very~~ exceptionally attractive young ~~woman~~ person, hopefully in the same ~~shape~~ condition as when you last saw her.*

> *Urgently yours,*
> *Roger Person-Potright*

"Wow," said Terry when she'd finished reading. "What a double-crossing *jerk!*" She almost couldn't believe that the asking price for her—low to begin with—had been cut in half (though she did give the double-crosser credit for "exceptionally").

"I guess he's got a confederate in Miami—I bet it's a girlfriend," she continued. "That'd be the reason he keeps kissing off the Dragon Lady. She'll probably radio him here, the girlfriend, as soon as she sees the message. Assuming that there *is* a message . . ."

Mick nodded. "Until I read this," he said, "I was thinking Roger might be someone we could make a deal with: the treasure in exchange for him flying us out. B-but now . . . we'd be plain nuts to trust him."

"That's the damn trouble with all of them," Terry agreed. "They'll all screw anyone to get their way. Except I don't think the Dragon Lady would ever kill her kids, or Bubba. But other than that . . . " She shook her head, and in the ensuing silence she could barely hear Mick chewing the last of his ham sandwiches, and swallowing. *No Bubba him,* Tee thought.

*"Alors"*—it was the marquis who broke the silence— "clearly we must make a plan which takes account of who they are . . . "

"Like, ruthless, greedy, and suspicious of each other," Terry finished for him.

The marquis nodded. "Yes," he said. "And so, tonight, I vow to think on this. All night, if *nécessaire. Je suis sûr* there is some way we can escape, but first we have to think of it!"

"Good luck," said Terry, and she meant it. She believed that if anyone could come up with a workable plan, it'd be the marquis. In fifteenth-century France, before there were weapons of mass destruction—not to mention computer technology, rapid transit, fast food, and instant gratification—clever planning must have been particularly vital.

"Me, I need some sleep before I even *try* to think of something," she went on. "Today has kind of worn me out."

She'd been sitting on the bed with her legs tucked under her, but now she flopped over on her side, stretched out, and looked up at him with a sleepy smile.

He got up and blew out the lantern, then came over and lay down on his side of the bed. A moment later, and very tentatively, he reached out and touched her shoulder; the way he did that told her he was Mick and not a member of the French nobility, and that was fine with her. She gave a little wriggle, moving her body closer to his; emboldened, he slid his hand around her back and pulled her toward him. She came willingly, and seconds later they were kissing for the first time, lips to lips, and then with opened mouths and with a lot of . . . meaning (Terry thought).

Later, she decided she'd never before got herself into a kiss so completely. And that wasn't, she was sure, because there was no way her mother, or his mother, or one of the Cape Enid town constables might "catch" them. Nor was it because she was maybe going to die soon, and so would never meet anyone else worth kissing for the rest of her life. No, that kiss had had to do with liking someone at a level she hadn't known she could reach, at a wild "I'm yours" type of level.

It wasn't that she wanted to "do it" then—or do anything else besides kiss, just then. But in the future, assuming survival, assuming the availability of birth control, assuming opportunity in some delightful setting, anything might happen, she acknowledged. And she could imagine saying that to Mone ahead of time, just as she'd agreed to.

She didn't exactly kiss herself to sleep. When she finally rolled over and away from him, she did thank God for keeping him alive. And then she also said a little prayer for "Kirt," both Kirts, in fact; the one Roger and the captain found, and the other one, Kirt Manwaring, the baseball player who had been a useful model for so long. But who she really had no need of, anymore.

# chapter 22

When Terry woke up the next morning, he was sitting in the beanbag chair near the foot of the bed, looking straight at her and smiling. It was light outside, but very early still.

He got up, came over to the bed, and crawled up beside her.

"Did you sleep at all?" she asked. She smoothed his hair, as if he were a little boy she was taking care of.

He leaned toward her and kissed her quickly on the lips; it was their first kiss in the daytime, in the light. She could see that he looked happy, and she knew she was. That kiss had not seemed little-boyish.

"How long have you been awake?" she asked him this time.

"Oh, since last night, I guess," he said, and laughed. He swung his feet off the bed and got up and stretched.

"But it was worth it," he went on. "I think I almost have a plan to get us out of here. What's taking so long is that it's complicated. Like we said last night, the kind of people that they are is kinda key." He laughed again.

"So tell me what you've got," said Tee. "The suspense is killing me." She'd been sure that he'd come up with something; him, the marquis, it was all the same, really.

"Here's the thing," he said. "First of all, we b-better act real fast. If Roger gets a message back, he'll want to fly you off the island right away. I don't think he'll kill you until later on. That's because he'll know my dad'd want some more proof you're alive and he has you, before he forks over any money. I think that's why the others haven't killed you, too."

"O-kay," Tee said slowly, not all that crazy about this killing-Terry talk. "We're going to act fast. But how?"

"Step one," he said, "is just for me. I need to check something out, up near their main house, whatever it's called."

"The Plantation House," said Terry.

"Yeah," he said. "The one with the big veranda, right? Where you'll be having breakfast."

"That's the one," she said.

"So does everyone get there about the same time every morning?" he asked.

"Pretty much," she said. "They seem to actually have mealtimes, even for breakfast."

"Good," he said. "So once everyone's in there, I'll have my look around. It won't take long, but it's important—kind of the last piece of the plan depends on what I see. If I go up now, I can find a good place to hide, where I can see when everyone's inside."

"Okay," she said again. "And then what?"

"Well," he said, "I'll probably be back here before you finish breakfast, even. I'll be needing to pick up a couple of things. As far as *your* day goes, try to spend a lot of time with Cherry again, okay? It'd really be good if you can help her feed Bubba again."

Terry made a face. She wasn't hearing what she'd call "the stuff of which great plans are made."

"Sure," she said. "Feeding Bubba's *such* a fun activity. I'd like to see *you* take a whiff of the carcass shack sometime. I bet you'd lose whatever lousy lunch I'd fixed you."

To her immediate regret, there was a touch of old Cape Enid in her voice as she said that. Sarcasm was a staple at the club. She no longer wished to ever sound like that.

Mick was looking both apologetic and concerned.

"L-look—" he started, but she cut him off.

"But if it's important, of course I'll do it," she
said, in a completely different tone of voice. After
all, *she* hadn't thought of a plan; she'd been too
tired. She'd wanted *him* to. So now the least she
could do was to cooperate. Feeding Bubba wasn't all
that awful.

"Cherry won't have a problem with me hanging
out," she went on. "I'm pretty sure she likes me. She
really isn't a bad kid. You know—at heart. It's just
she'd been brought up a little . . . weirdly."

"I'll say," he agreed, and shook his head. He was
remembering how Cherry and her brother'd almost
hit him with a cannonball, and their uncle hadn't
minded in the least; you could say that was a little
"weird." She hadn't known that he was there, behind
the driftwood, but still. "So, anyway—I'll see you
here tonight. And getting back to 'fast.' I think we
could be out of here in . . . oh, forty-eight hours,
maybe. By day-after-tomorrow morning, say."

Tee got excited hearing that. Only two more
days? Two days to no more worries about any of the
pirates' plans for her, either short or long term? Two
more days until she got to be with Mick in—or on
the way to—a "normal" place and "normal" people?
Of course, if Maitland Crane had received Roger's

Express Mail, and had then gotten in touch with Mone (she was the only Talley in the Cape Enid phone book), they'd probably have to head back to Cape Enid and face the wrath and/or relief of their respective families. At first that might not be an entirely "normal" situation, though Tee had faith it could evolve into one. She didn't think that she'd be "made" to go to boarding school—not with *her* record.

But before she could put any of her excitement into words, Mick was out the door with a little wave. She giggled to herself. The hardworking man of the house was off to work before she'd even made it out of bed!

Terry did almost exactly what he'd asked her to that morning. She did look around the cottage after she'd brought his breakfast down, trying to see what "couple of things" he'd taken with him, but she couldn't notice what was missing. And then she scooted right back up and helped Cherry and Buddy and their mother with their enormous vegetable garden—pulling weeds and picking some disgusting blue-green worms off different plants.

For well over an hour, none of the Hollys acted in the least piratical—that was if you didn't count throwing squishy worms at one another. It was during that time Terry realized that by getting her to

227

spend the day with Cherry, Mick was making sure that she'd be safe from Short Bill Gold.

Before lunch she made a fourth for a game of croquet that they played on the lawn behind The Bucket O' Blood. It was Buddy and the Dragon Lady against Cherry and her (Cherry chose the sides), and the Dragon Lady cheated every chance she got, many times by nudging someone's ball into a better or worse position (depending) when she thought no one was looking. But she also made up new rules as she went along, like "First one through the middle wicket gets a bonus shot, you know," when such a rule would be to her or Bud's advantage. And she'd often sneeze, or cough, or slap a (supposed) mosquito just when one of her opponents was about to swing her mallet. At one critical point in the game, she pulled her pistol out and fired a shot into the tall grass right behind where Terry was crouching, lining up her shot.

"Snake," the D. L. said, by way of explanation. "I think I nicked the bastard." Not too many minutes later, it was, "Yay—the good guys won!"

That afternoon Tee was given the tour through Cherry's closet and bureau drawers, so she could pass judgment on the various items in the younger girl's wardrobe—what'd be considered "cool" in California and what wouldn't. After that, she did her second stint on the pet-feeding detail.

The smell in the carcass shack was just as bad as before, but this time she got even further into Cherry's good graces by saying it was "my turn" to carry the guts bucket. And she managed to do so without slopping any on her leg.

Shortly before supper, Cherry led her back to her room, where she pulled a package wrapped in tissue paper out from under the bed.

"Surprise!" she said. And "Go ahead, open it. I can't wait to see your face!"

What it turned out to be was more baggy clothing: a pair of Short Bill Gold's boxer shorts—white, but with many bright red Cupids scattered all over them, each as round and fat as the captain himself, and every one with an arrow at the ready.

Terry didn't disappoint. She let out a shriek of amazement and delight—and (unknown to Cherry) horror in that the naked cherubs did look an awful lot like the captain in the buff.

"Thanks," she said. "Great present! Even if I have to wear a belt with them! But have you got a paper bag or something? Just in case I run into him outside? I promise you, my friends back home will all turn *green* when they see these beauties!"

Terry thought that Cherry's grin lost a little of its width when she heard that last part. Maybe, for a moment, she'd forgotten Terry never *would* get home. Tee almost (but not quite) wanted to tell her not to worry—that she planned to be long gone before the older pirates got around to killing her.

And then she got what seemed to her to be a not-too-bad idea. For the sake of her safety tonight and tomorrow, she'd tell Cherry about the episode with her uncle on the beach. And she'd say she hadn't wanted to tell the Dragon Lady (of course, she'd say "your mom") because she didn't want her to have to kill her brother or anything. But that she sure hoped he wouldn't try something like that ever again.

As she put this idea into words, she could almost see Cherry's mind working. She was definitely planning to tell her mother, who in turn (so Terry, too, believed) would lay a warning on the captain that he wouldn't dare ignore. Cherry would want to do that for her big friend's sake. The little girl could accept that Terry would have to be killed, once the ransom money was collected, in order to keep her and her family from going to jail (instead of California). But there was no reason this fellow female had to be "ravished" by a pirate captain, especially if that captain was her uncle. In Cherry's young imagination, sex and somebody as old and fat as Short Bill Gold were simply not compatible.

Dinner and the cleanup after seemed to take forever that night. Terry couldn't wait to get down to the cottage, and have it be dark, and hear "the plan" in its entirety. Over twelve hours had passed since Mick had said they might be out of there in less than forty-eight. She was already getting butter-flies in her stomach. She was so excited she almost forgot to light the lantern.

By the time he got there, knocked, and was let in, she'd settled down somewhat. She kissed him just as he came through the door, which made her feel like the wife and mother in some ancient-history sitcom rerun on TV. She barely kept her-self from saying, "Dinner's ready, dear," and making a graceful gesture toward that evening's semi-all-American takeout: meat-loaf sandwiches with cold (by now) mashed potatoes, warm (by now) coleslaw (in separate paper cups), and some ketchup that she'd glopped into the plastic cap of a used-up container of laundry detergent.

But though his eyes were sparkling, that was not (she soon found out) solely at the sight of food (or her). Before he even sat down, he reached into his trouser pocket and produced . . . what seemed to be a paper napkin (and a used one, at that). Bizarre. But he held it out to her with what was clearly great delight.

"*Voilá*," the marquis said. "With this, The Plan begins. . . . "

# chapter 23

*It's an absolutely* brilliant *plan*, Terry kept telling herself as she went up the path to the Plantation House the next morning, a plan "of the greatest subtlety," as the marquis himself had put it the night before. It was attuned, he said, to *le profil psychologique* of the Dragon Lady's and the captain's personalities. Tee loved the way he used French terms in place of ordinary English words, like "nuttiness." It made what they were doing sound much classier and more grown-up, she thought.

The plan was also one, she'd realized right away, that could blow up in their (make that "her") face before it had even gotten off the ground. She'd been given not just the job but the responsibility to jump-start the entire thing that day, at breakfast.

What was sort of unfortunate, she felt, was that because he didn't exist in the minds of the pirates, the marquis couldn't be walking up the hill right then, instead of her. He could have done this easily, no sweat. Like many public officeholders, he could tell you things and you'd believe him, things that, if they came from someone else, would make you shout out, "Whadda buncha bullshit!" The marquis was convincing; she could vouch for that, all right.

They'd rehearsed the night before, of course. He'd worked out what she ought to say, and then she'd put it into her own words. And she'd felt herself becoming better, *real*-er, the more she practiced.

"I'm starting to believe this stuff I'm going to say is really *true*," she'd said to him at one point.

"I'm not surprised," he answered with a weary smile. "This same thing also happens in the minds of horny boys and used-car salesmen."

Terry'd had to smile at that, but to herself, invisibly. She wondered what the marquis thought *he* was.

She did what Mick had done the day before, hid and waited till she'd seen Roger, and then the Dragon Lady and the twins, go into breakfast. And then she'd waited a little longer to give everyone time to get what they wanted to eat and be settled at the table.

After that interval, she emerged from hiding, took two deep breaths, and hurried into the dining room herself, with her heart pounding. That was good, she thought: She wanted to sound excited. As soon as she stepped through the door, she started talking, fast.

"Wow! Hey, everybody—wait until you hear what I just found! Or what I think I found, anyway." Six heads (one of them a myna bird's) turned to look at her; she had her audience.

"Just now, when I was walking by the chicken coop, I was taking off the top of my water jug, so I could fill it when I came inside"—she held up the top, so everyone could see it—"and I dropped the stupid thing, and it rolled under the coop . . . "

The twins went back to spooning in their cereal, but the adults (including the winged black one) kept on listening as she stretched out her story, describing how she'd gotten down on hands and knees and then finally had to lie down on her stomach so as to reach way under there. The top, she told them, had come to rest against one of the big beams that supported the floor of the coop. And when her groping fingers touched it at last, they also came in contact with " . . . well, *this!*"

She'd taken the thing out of her pocket by then and was holding it and shaking it as she went on to say it wasn't until she had it out in the light that she realized "that it might be what the captain said blew off the table on the porch, whenever it was—the pirates' treasure map!"

At that point all hell broke loose in the dining room, and she shut up, fingers crossed behind her back. The fat little captain moved fast, rising to snatch the rumpled, dirty, folded paper napkin from her hand. Roger and the Dragon Lady leaped up too (as if the victims of an unexpected pair of geese) and ran around the table so as to peer over Bill Gold's shoulder. The twins stayed seated, but they, too, stopped eating and looked interested. Ishmael remained right where he was, holding tight to the captain's shoulder and muttering to himself.

Terry waited for reactions. This was the first test of the Plan. If they didn't bite on this, all the rest was chopped liver, and the Plan was as dead as at least half of last year's sitcoms.

"Well, boys and girls, the unbelieveable has happened!" Short Bill Gold exclaimed. "It's double-runner day in hell, I guess, 'cause this, by God, IS IT!" And Ishmael, by way of celebration or agreement, let out a piercing two-tone whistle.

Bill Gold had pushed his plate and coffee mug into the center of the table, and now he smoothed the map out on his place mat.

"Let's see . . . " He pointed with a stubby forefinger. "Too bad the map predates this house and all the other buildings, but we still can figure out . . . oh, sure, this'll be our harbor, right? Or part of it, at least. So that means this line here would be the brook that's right out back . . . and *this*"—he pointed at a little circle—"has to be the pond in Bubba's pen. Which means the X . . . "

His head snapped up and he was looking at his sister. "Jehosaphat!" he shouted. "Even as we speak, your goddamn largest living lizard may be pooping on the pirates' treasure!"

Roger, meanwhile, had bent way over to peer at the map more closely and draw his own conclusion.

"Let's have a look," he mumbled to himself. "Here's the bloody X, and . . . what's those squiggles there? Could be the number twenty: two, oh, and then a *P* . . . wouldn't that be twenty paces, more'n likely? So if the X is twenty paces due west of the brook . . . damn and blast! Bill *is* quite right. The bleedin' treasure's—"

"Inside Bubba's pen," the Dragon Lady finished for him, "fairly near one side of it, in fact."

By then the twins had made it to their feet and joined the other two behind the captain's chair. Buddy squeezed between his mother and his uncle's shoulder, so he could see the map.

"How d'ya know that's even a map?" said the young contrarian, scornfully. "It looks like a bunch of doodling to me. And even if it is a map, who knows if it's the one Uncle Bill looked at before? He never did study the other one, the old spaz. He said that himself."

"Nobody's making you believe it's anything, you little parrot's pizzle," Short Bill Gold informed him. "You don't have to join the expedition when we go to dig the treasure up. The fewer people help, the more there'll be for me when it comes time to divvy up."

"Divvy *this* up," Buddy told him, making a rude gesture at the back of his head. "I'm gonna find those two crossed palms you dreamed about. And when *I* dig up the treasure there, your share will amount to absolutely zippo."

To Terry's considerable relief, none of the adults paid any mind to Buddy's concerns about the map's authenticity. It had to be The Map, they clearly thought. How could there be another one? Roger and the Dragon Lady were buzzing about where the various buildings would be, if they were on the map, and how far Bubba's fenced-in pen extended.

"This is all your fault," Short Bill Gold said next, addressing his sister. "I never wanted the damn dragon living so near us. If you'd listened to me in the first place, his pen would have been up above the landing strip. And if it was, we could walk right out of here this morning and start getting fabulously wealthy. But no, you had to have your widdle baby right beside you. So now we have to take the time and trouble to organize a search-and-destroy mission against a bad-tempered three-hundred-pound killer before we can even get near the goodies. Cripes, I wish we had an antitank gun, Rog; that SOB is gonna take a lot of killing."

Terry shifted her eyes onto the Dragon Lady. According to the marquis's script, the next lines were all hers.

"The hell you say," she said, right on cue. "Nobody's touching Bubba. To get to him, you'll have to go through me. And me, I'll kill stone dead—with pleasure—anyone who even dirty-looks that lizard."

"What?" the captain shouted. "You put a higher value on that reptile than on the booty off a hundred Spanish galleons? Have the bats in your belfry gone flutt? Has your *comprenez-vous* rope been cut? Is there nobody home at the top of your dome, and your head's not a head but a *nut?* Listen, Hildy— here's a deal for you. We dispatch our Roger to the mainland, pronto. There he purchases a tranquilizer gun—you know, the kind they have on all the TV nature shows. Splat, a dart hits Bubba in the ass; minutes later he goes gaga and collapses. Wakes up after a few hours with a bit of a hangover while we're back here, looking at a prize that even Ed McMahon would envy."

238

But the Dragon Lady was shaking her head. "Unh-unh. No drugs go into Bubba's bloodstream, fat boy," she said firmly. "No way, nohow; I won't allow it. A Komodo dragon with a habit is one sorry lizard, Billy. What we have to do is dig when he's asleep. It'll be a breeze. Today we double-lunch the guy—give him twice his ordinary meal. Being a member of the clean-plate club"—she giggled—"he'll scarf it all down. And with that much food in his belly, he'll be konked for eighteen hours." She headed back to her place to finish her coffee.

"So you two great white hunters better get busy," she added. "Three little pigs should be about right, or two of these antelopey things."

"I suppose we *could* go in at night," the captain said, grudgingly. "If we set up a few lanterns, we'd be able to see what we're doing. And I'd bring my AK-47 along, in case the monster does wake up."

"Oh, no," the Dragon Lady said. "No guns. I know you, Billy-boy; if there's a toy around, you always want to play with it. I'm giving you boys a total body search before you set foot in that pen." She turned to Roger. "So don't wear anything you can't slip off real easy, handsome." And she laughed.

"Are you a myna bird?" asked Ishmael, to no one in particular.

Roger also laughed, but nervously, uncertainly,

it seemed to Tee. The captain was staring at the map again, nodding as he did so.

"Yep," he said, "this here's the very one I got from old Hugh Chew. It's got that self-same smudgy look about it. You know, I wouldn't be surprised if we find bodies buried in the same hole with the treasure. Many's the pirate captain who used a blunderbuss on all the lads that hid the loot for him. Dead men tell no tales, you know."

And then he turned partway toward Terry and added in a little whisper, out of the corner of his mouth, "And neither do dead tattletales."

She pretended that she hadn't heard. She was pretty sure he meant that as a threat, but heck, she knew already that he planned to kill her *sometime.* So all she had to do was make sure he couldn't do the job today and cause her to be part of Bubba's "double-lunch." She decided that she'd best stick close to Cherry, once again; she could show the little girl her clothes and jewelry—and makeup. And maybe even introduce her to aromatherapy, if there was time.

On their way down to the cottage, after she had finished cleaning up, she had a moment of panic when a thought popped into her head: Could Mick have left something of his lying out in plain sight that'd be a dead giveaway? She hadn't checked before she left. But then she called herself a silly goose: Mick *had* no things to leave around—he really had come with "the bare minimum" (as Mone described the way she traveled). And with no bathroom in the cottage, there wasn't even any toilet seat for him to—thoughtlessly—leave up.

When she'd finished laying out the contents of her duffel bag on the bed, Cherry spied the captain's boxers and said, "Did you try my uncle's shorts on yet? I bet they look fantastic on you—like, the baggiest! Maybe you could wear them over Roger's trousers, even. Let's see how that'd look."

Giggling, she looked around the room, expecting she would spot those multicolored items hanging up somewhere. But of course, they were below (also around) the waist of Mick J. Crane and therefore nowhere to be seen.

"Where are they, Terry, anyway?" she asked.

"Oh, gosh," said Tee. "I wasn't going to tell you. . . ."

*Damn!* She'd forgotten all about the purloined pantaloons. So now she had to stall, and think of something. She'd have to say she *lost* them somehow—but how do you lose a pair of trousers when there's no dry cleaner you can blame, and when the pants are so ugly no one would ever think of stealing them, even if the island were crawling with convicts, the way she'd read Australia was, once upon a time?

"The thing is . . . ," she began again, as a tiny shoot of an idea began to root itself in her imagination. "Early yesterday I thought I'd . . . wash them . . . them and the T-shirt, when I took my early morning dip." The idea grew larger, sent out branches, and began to flower. "And while I was at it, just for fun, I tied knots in the pants legs, down near the bottoms of them, and made them into a pair of water wings. You know how to do that, don't you? They teach it in lifesaving classes, back home."

Cherry'd never heard of such a thing, so Tee explained it in detail. The little girl loved the idea; she couldn't wait to try it herself.

"And so I swam way out, much farther from shore than usual. And then the scariest thing happened! It must have been the colors of the trousers that attracted it, because all of a sudden this *enormous* fish . . . "

Terry couldn't describe the fish too well, she said, except it had a mouth the size of an open suitcase, and it grabbed those water wings and just took off. So, totally freaked out, Tee dropped the T-shirt and started swimming for shore as fast as she could go.

Cherry bought the story, willingly.

"You're really lucky," she said solemnly. "It could have bit your leg off." Then, after a moment's reflection, she developed that idea.

"Personally, I'd hate to have a wooden leg," she said. "It'd probably be cool if I was going to be a pirate my whole life, but I can't imagine having one in California, could you? I mean, *surfing* and everything? And later on I'll probably be a doctor, or maybe a buyer for a big department store? Mom says they both makes lots of money. It'd look weird having a peg leg if you worked in a hospital or had a lot to do with ladies' fashions, don't you think?"

Terry decided she wouldn't get into explaining how much artificial limbs had been improved upon since Blackbeard's day, and pretty soon Cherry was trying on some of her jewelry and babbling about replacing the lost pants with other items from her uncle's wardrobe.

When they went up to lunch, Terry felt well prepared for Big Key Moment Number Two—to take place about midafternoon. If she could get through that . . . well, then the stage would be real close to being "set."

# chapter 24

Cleanup after lunch that day took a little longer than usual. The Dragon Lady had made an incredible multi-potted-and-applianced mess in the kitchen, in addition to the lunch itself. The meal was rich and filling, consisting of vichyssoise, open-faced ham and cheese sandwiches which the D. L. ran under the broiler to get the cheese melted and bubbly (and burned onto the cookie sheet), coleslaw, and éclairs for dessert. The idea, apparently, was both to reward the hunters for providing the fresh carcasses now hanging in the shack, and to serve a meal that would promote long naps for everyone. Supper, the D. L. said, would be light (though protein-rich), a pregame meal that would leave the future millionaires alert and hungry when they entered Bubba's pen.

Once Terry'd dropped off Mick's food and water at the usual place behind the outhouse, she thought she'd better hide somewhere (but stay awake!) till it was almost time to feed the pets. But when she swung around the Honeymoon Cottage, she noticed that its door was closed—and she was sure she'd left it open earlier, when she and Cherry had gone out. Was Mick in there? she wondered. Was he signaling a change of plans? She was sure the captain was asleep. She'd heard him snoring when she left Plantation House.

She crept to the window and looked in. The little house was empty. But in the center of the bed there was an envelope that hadn't been there earlier. A note from Mick, she thought, so she ran in and grabbed it. Then, wasting no time leaving the area, she darted halfway up the path that led to the compound and veered off into the thick vegetation that concealed that garden cart she'd hidden. Curled up inside it, she ripped open the envelope and pulled out the letter it contained.

*Yikes!* she thought. One look was all she needed to find out that it was not from Mick. The writing, though much neater, matched the writing in that other letter, the one she'd read two days before.

• • •

*My dear Terry,*

*A despicable crime has been agreed upon by Captain Gold and Mrs. Holly. To put it delicately, they plan to end your life, perhaps as early as tomorrow, surely before the passage of a fortnight.*

*I cannot, in good conscience, permit this. In the short while you've been with us, I've come to have fond feelings for you— and dare to hope they'll be reciprocated, once you've had the chance to know me better.*

*Yesterday the depth of my affection got quite clear to me when, from the hillside, I chanced to see you fruitlessly (thank God!) pursued along the beach by that cad, Gold. I realized then I had to help you, and this morning I conceived a foolproof plan by which to do so.*

*What I propose is this. Tonight, once the treasure has been found, I'll insist on taking my fair share up to the Crow's Nest with me. But instead, I'll hie me to the airstrip and our aircraft there, where, hopefully, you'll join me. By sunrise, then, we can be airborne, and winging our way toward an island where some chums of mine maintain a most delightful private club and cottage colony.*

*There, the two of us—now rich beyond*

*our wildest dreams—can spend a carefree*
*week, snorkeling and seeing the sights,*
*bowling on the green and frolicking in the*
*surf. I believe that as you come to know me,*
*you'll discover that, at heart, I'm not much*
*older than yourself!*

*What say you? It's only your sweet life I*
*want to save.*

*Always and affectionately,*
*Rog*

Terry read that through, and then she read it
once again. The second reading brought the same
reaction as the first. "Good grief!" she said (though
only to herself).

This had to be, she thought, the most bizarre
situation any female person her age had ever been
involved in. Roger, the latest seeker of her . . . company, was (as they say) "too much." He already had
a plan in place by which he'd double-cross the
Golds, but now, believing that another, even better
source of wealth was soon to be available, he was
ready to scrap plan A and substitute plan B, by
which he'd double-cross them in a different way.
(Of course, she had to admit, it wasn't all that un-
likely that when the Dragon Lady and her brother
woke up from their naps, *they'd* work out a scheme
to leave ol' Roger shareless, when it got to be cut-
up-the-treasure-time.)

Tee shook her head. She remembered the fantasy she'd had when she was talking to Connie about what'd happen to her when she reached "the islands," courtesy of Maitland Crane. Her imaginings had seemed pretty wild at the time, involving as they did a sunken wreck, a beautiful mute boy, and a job in retail sales with Banana Republic. But compared to what had actually happened—was happening—all that seemed about as exciting as a walk to the store in Cape Enid.

So far, she'd survived a monsoon and a shipwreck, lost and then recovered a young male companion who she surely had developed feelings for, been captured by a pirate crew who planned to kill her, been sexually pursued by one of them (and now lusted after by another), and was presently trying to implement a plan that would allow her (*and* her boyfriend) to escape. Eventually she might even get to a place where she could go to work for B. R.

But was that still an outcome she desired? A fashion job in an exotic setting? Possibly, but maybe not. Her earlier mind-set now seemed just a little . . . childish, maybe.

But on second thought, not totally so. Her wanting to spread her wings, to have her own life— that wasn't "childish." That was *good*! At her age, that was how she *should* feel. Stowing away on a stranger's boat . . . now, that had been a trifle foolish, not to mention dangerous—a bit of a mistake. But though she'd asked God to help her (when things seemed to be going seriously wrong), she'd never blamed her mother or her father, or felt sorry for herself, or tried to dodge responsibility for her decision. Even now, still very much in danger, she was managing to stay positive and hopeful (to "be herself," in other words) and to do whatever she could to make her situation better.

But not wanting to throw her shoulder out patting herself on the back, she asked herself this question: "So, hotshot, what else *could* you do?" And the answer to that was nothing, really, if she wanted to be sensible—which she very much did. The thing was, in the course of growing up, she'd discovered it made good sense to always try to do her best. Not to please other people, for her own sake. Because that way, however things turned out, there wouldn't be any reason to either beat her breast (in sadness and self-pity) or take bows (in triumph)—two things she disliked when she saw other people do them. She didn't expect to either win or lose 'em all; any life was bound to have its ups and downs. She'd hope, and sometimes pray, but she avoided expectations if she could.

The hardest—but also the best—thing about right now, she thought, was Mick, and this new relationship she seemed to have with him. And it wasn't just with him, she realized; it was a new relationship with Life: a recognition of a new and different "us."

When you are young (thought Terry), your family and you comprise your "us." But as you get into your teens, you see that, almost certainly, your life is heading for another stage. In it, the members of your family will still be very, very dear, but with any luck, another "us" will come to be, and grow, until *it* is the one you most depend upon, and think about, and cultivate.

This seemed to have happened now, to her, as a result of meeting/knowing Mick and the marquis. She couldn't think of herself apart from him. Not that they'd always be doing the same exact things or have identical interests. No, it was just that Happiness was him and her together. And she wanted Happiness, which seemed to mean she wanted, even needed, him. That was a little scary.

Lying curled up in her garden cart, she took refuge in the Psalm again—or at least a slightly altered version of it.

"The Lord is *our* Shepherd . . . ," Terry whispered to the lushness all around her.

Tee went the rest of the way up the hill well before the usual pet-feeding time; it was important that she *not* miss Cherry. She plumped herself down on the porch of The Bucket O' Blood to wait.

When she heard a lot of footsteps on the inside stairs, she guessed that Buddy'd joined his sister, coming down.

"Look," Cherry was saying, as the two of them came onto the porch, "I'll give you fifty bucks to help me. It'll only hold you up maybe fifteen minutes. And with both of us to look, you'll save a lot more time than that." Then, seeing Tee, "Hi, Terry."

"Hi," Tee said. "What's up?"

"I'm trying to get my darling brother to haul carcasses with me," she said. "You know—for Bubba's double lunch. But he just wants to go treasure hunting—look for Uncle Bill's crossed palms. He doesn't want to wait for me."

"I'll feed Bubba," Terry said. "You'll soon be doing me a real big favor, remember? A real big *baggy* favor?" And she gave the little girl one of those confidential winks she'd always hated when somebody gave her one. "I really wouldn't mind; I mean it. And I've got nothing else to do. I sort of doubt I'll leave the island with any part of the pirate treasure, no matter who finds it."

"You won't if Mom or Uncle Bill have anything to say," Buddy told her. "They're both greedy-guts."

"Well, you can't really blame them," Cherry said, practically. "We're the ones that own the island, so it really is our treasure."

"I know," said Bud. "But how about 'finders keepers'? Isn't that a *rule?* Suppose she found it—like with us. I wouldn't mind her having some."

"She isn't going to find it, 'cause she isn't going to look," Cherry said as Tee tried to make sense out of Buddy's unprecedented friendliness. "And she may not even want to." She turned to Terry. "You don't really want to take that stuff to Bubba, though—do you?"

"I absolutely do," said Tee. "It'll make me feel I'm doing something useful around here, and not just being a freeloader."

"Well, all right," said Cherry, "if you're sure you mean it." And then, to her twin, "Dibbies on the pickax, poop-for-brains; you can have the shovel."

And the two of them ran off.

Once she was sure they were well out of sight and earshot, Terry went and got the garden cart out of its hiding place and pulled it to the carcass shack. There she found two disemboweled pigs and one ditto "antelopey thing" awaiting her, along with three buckets of guts.

When she'd loaded all that into the cart, she started dragging it—but not around the pen to the gate on its far end. No, sweating and straining, she toiled up the path to the airstrip (the twins had disappeared *down*hill), and when she was about three quarters of the way there, she veered off into the jungle.

At that point the pulling became even harder, but the well-balanced, high-wheeled cart had enough clearance to move through and over the undergrowth. Veering around trees and bigger bushes, she kept on going until she reached one of those gravelike holes in the ground some unsuccessful treasure hunter'd dug a week or two before. Into it she dumped the contents of the cart, which she then covered with a thick layer of dirt (pushed in with her bare hands).

Still moving as quickly as she could, she rolled the cart back down the hill, returning it to its original hiding place. After that, she continued down to her cottage, badly in need of a bath and a change of clothes before dinner. For good luck, she put on the little flowered sundress she'd chosen at the time of her "rescue" by the pirates. If all went well, it'd be the first and last dress Captain Gold would ever see her in.

Now everything was set for that night, or as set as it could be, given what they knew and all they didn't know. It was fingers crossed on one thing, though. *Let's hope big Bubba doesn't make too big a racket when his lunch is late,* was the way that Mick had put it.

As of dinnertime, there were no unusual complaining noises from the pen. What Tee and Mick were counting on to happen was that the dragon would simply go to the far gate and wait there for his food to arrive. That seemed like a reasonable hope. Cherry'd said that on that other occasion when his meal had been greatly delayed, Roger had had to toss it over the fence because Bubba was right there by the gate with his bib on, so to speak. And she hadn't mentioned any sounds he'd made, up until the time he started eating. So it made sense to think he'd do the same this time. And with the pen being as huge as it was, and with Mick having put the X nearer the *near* end of the pen, the lizard probably wouldn't be aware of the hunters' presence in his domain until they started digging.

There was an air of excitement at the dining-room table, an eagerness, even an edginess, that Terry hadn't seen before. Part of that, she thought, could have been due to the one-night ban on booze the pirates had agreed to, but another part could probably be blamed on the Dragon Lady's high-energy menu: little bowls of trail mix for everyone, along with servings of cottage cheese with wheat germ, plus granola bars, all washed down by flagons of original-flavor Gatorade and cups of black coffee laced with honey.

In Roger's case, his excitement might also have had something to do with his hope to fly away with her at sunrise, Terry thought. If he paid as much attention to her clothes as how she looked without them, he would have known she'd changed for dinner, and so must have seen his letter. She played it cool, therefore, acting friendly enough so that he'd think she wasn't saying "no" to his . . . proposal, but not so friendly he'd be sure that it was "yes." She really hoped he wouldn't try to have a private chat with her and make her give an answer, while she was cleaning up, though. She'd always told the truth to boys back home who'd tried to hit on her, however unsubtly (in Cape Enid it was often, "Say, my folks are gonna be away this weekend, and we could have the whole place to ourselves, including the Jacuzzi."), and she didn't want to either give this older man "the wrong idea" or get his dander (whatever that was) up.

Luckily for her, the captain had plans for himself and Roger, as soon as they finished eating. He wanted the two of them to assemble what he called "the necessaries" for that evening's expedition, which was to begin a little after sundown. Short Bill Gold had been on a nonchemical high for most of the meal, it seemed to Terry, alternately rhapsodizing about the treasure he felt sure they'd find and twitting Buddy about the failure of "the crossed-palms party," as he called it.

"Ah, yes—methinks the only thing that crossed his palms this afternoon was blisters!" he announced after one big chaw of his granola bar. "My dream's become a nightmare for the little simp. The *map's* the thing, my boy. You'll see. You'll learn your dear old uncle knows a thing or three about treasure-hunting, after all. And for dinner tomorrow I'll make and serve your just dessert: a sour, skinny, little piece of humble pie!"

That made Buddy rise and leave the table in a seething rage, accompanied by his twin. But as he did, he managed—by pretending to reach down in order to pick up his napkin—to drop a tightly folded wad of paper into Terry's lap. Given his obvious desire for secrecy, Tee slipped the thing into the pocket of her sundress and didn't read it until just before she started down the hill. She assumed it was a note, but what, she wondered, could its contents be? Was it maybe even from his sister, not from him?

No such luck, she soon found out.

> *Dere Terry,* (she read)
> *If you wud be my girlfriend I wud give you my part of the trejer. I think yur the most beutiful girl ever. I saw you running on the beach with no close on, yeserday. I don wan anyone to kill you, I reely LOVE you and will save you frum them.*
> *Love +ooo+xxx,*
> *Bud*

*Good grief!* thought Tee again. And: *The way to even a very young man's heart is clearly through an organ other than his stomach.* It seemed that in the same five(?)-minute time span, every penis-bearing person on the island had garnered information she'd considered "classified," to wit: the color of her pubic hair.

Shaking her head (but fighting off a smile), she hurried down the slope, bearing food and drink for Mick. The next (and last) phase of The Plan was going to start soon after sundown.

⚓

# chapter 25

Terry figured Mick must have had the Honeymoon Cottage under close surveillance, because it was no more than two minutes after her arrival there that he came tapping at the door. And she could tell right away that he was suffering from what one of the Cape Enid baseball players once told her *he* had, "a bad case of the yips."

"Luh-let me eat real quick," he said, "s-so we can get right up there. I w-want to s-see what happens from the s-start." It was the first time he'd stuttered that much in days.

His request was fine with her. Their part of the plan, at first, was simply to position themselves outside the pen's high fence, but near the place the pirates would be digging. Mick had chosen the location for the X partly on the basis of there being a clear line of sight to that spot from a hiding place in the nearby jungle.

"They duh-didn't ask you to go on in with them, did they?" Mick asked her. "H-help with the digging or something?"

"Definitely not," Tee said. "The captain told me, 'Wish us luck, my dear' on his way out, and that was about all anybody said to me the whole meal. I'll tell you: You could almost *smell* the greed in that dining room."

Even though Mick was in a hurry, the two of them took the long way getting to their spot, staying well away from the compound. Sundown was late at that time of year, so they were able to get into position in plenty of time. In fact, they had a half hour's wait before the pirate crew showed up.

Terry was impressed by how quiet and businesslike they were, filing through the undergrowth in Bubba's pen. Ishmael, due to his habit of whistling loudly, had been left home in his cage, and she thought the Dragon Lady (who was wearing a black Oasis T-shirt, cutoff stretch blue jeans, and black Doc Martens) must have really read the riot act to the twins about loud talking and general jerking around. What she couldn't guess was that the D.L. had also personally seen to it that the captain and Roger had sprayed significant amounts of Right Guard on significant parts of their bodies. It so happened that Komodo dragons' world-class sense of smell is even better than their hearing.

The pirates' first piece of business was to try to find the exact spot marked by the X on the map. Apparently, Roger was the designated pacer, because it was he who took the twenty slow and measured steps due west from the brook, stopping a short distance from a large tree that had a big smooth trunk, many thick and well-spaced branches, and leaves that looked like the widespread fingers on a person's open hand.

Around "the spot" they arranged the five lighted lanterns they'd brought with them, and after much showy spitting on his hands and rubbing them together, Short Bill Gold hefted a pickax and prepared to "break ground." Just looking at his face, Terry could tell what he was thinking: It's final— You, Bill Gold, of Isla Muela Negra, are the latest countless million-dollar winner of the Pirate Treasure Sweepstakes. . . .

He never struck a blow, however. Before he'd even raised his tool up high, some heavy crashing sounds erupted from the thick growth to the right of him. And it was not the Prize Patrol the pirate crew heard coming.

No, even from the place where Mick and Terry

lay, safely on the other side of a sturdy chain-link fence, it seemed like the kind of noise a ten-foot-long, three-hundred-pound lizard would make, going hell-for-leather through a forest on a lovely island paradise.

It was about to be the moment Terry'd dreaded. The first time she'd heard The Plan, she realized it included the possibility she'd see five people (two of them children) torn apart before her very eyes and then devoured by a hungry reptile. Hopefully there aren't a lot of sixteen-year-old girls anywhere who'd enjoy a scene like that, and Terry Talley certainly wasn't such a person. Mone had brought her up to believe that human life was precious; she didn't even feel a state should be allowed to execute a criminal. "I'm part of my state," she told her friends whenever the subject came up, "and it's not fair to make me part of killing someone."

Mick (and the marquis), however, had insisted it was right to put the pirate crew in mortal danger. And anyway, Mick argued, if The Plan worked the way he thought it would, nobody would be killed or eaten. The Plan had everyone escaping the Komodo dragon by climbing the big tree that was "right there." According to the marquis's *profil psychologique,* all the pirates were "survivors" (as opposed to "victims"). The tree in question was an easy one to climb, even for a climber like the fat little captain—though it'd be impossible (Mick thought) for an enormous lizard. "Which is good," Mick said. "The last thing we want is to have big Bubba gobble up the key."

The marquis had a bit more of a fifteenth-century attitude, Terry thought. "Remember, *ma cherie*," he said, "all these people have agreed to kill you. We have here five who murder anyone in— how you say *sang froid?* cold blood? Let them take their chances."

When the moment came, and Bubba burst into the little clearing, Terry was glad to see she needn't have worried. Survivors all, the five went up the tree like so many gray squirrels, the captain actually pushing Buddy out of the way so as to be the first to scramble to a level he believed was safe.

Bubba was, indeed, a fearful sight (though hardly built, Tee saw, for climbing). He had a big wide head set on a thick muscular neck; when he opened his huge lizard mouth (which he was doing then, in anger and frustration), he made visible a lot of sizeable serrated teeth. His wide body looked a little flattened out—maybe in part by his enforced fast, Tee thought—and his limber tail was about as long as the rest of him. His skin, which seemed to be scaly, was a grayish brown color, and on the ends of all of his toes were long and scary-looking claws. Easily the size of a sumo wrestler, he could have weighed 350.

Terry breathed a long sigh of relief as she watched the pirates getting settled in the tree, now looking somewhat like a family of monkeys. They were not a happy family, though, going by the things they said to one another.

"What's he *doing* here?" the captain demanded to know. "How can this be *possible*? We *triple*-lunched the bastard! He should be too full to move!"

"You didn't forget to feed him, did you, Cherry dear?" her mother asked. "Could it have kind of 'slipped your mind,' sweetheart?" The tone she used made Terry feel that "yes" would be a stupid (and a very dangerous) answer.

"No, no. Of course not," Cherry said. "I did what I was told. And right on time. I swear I did."

"Oh, no you didn't," tattled her brother. "She got Terry to do it. I was there. I heard the whole thing. Terry said she would and Cherry let her."

"You *liar!*" Cherry cranked the volume way, way up. "How can you lie like that, you little jerk-off? He's lying, Mommy! Liar! Liar! Liar!"

"Am not! Am not! Am not!" Buddy matched her, decibel for decibel.

"Well, *some*body did *some*thing with the food," Roger announced, raising his own voice in order to gain attention. "The carcasses were gone when I passed by the shack at dinnertime. I rather doubt that anyone but Bubba would have eaten them. Or the various intestines, either," he added, dryly.

"Could Bubba just be having a bad dream?" suggested Cherry.

"Oh, sure," her brother said. "Just look at him. Does he look asleep to you, you moron? Hey, Mommy, I smell something. I betcha Cherry's pooped her pants."

Before his sister could reply, the Dragon Lady claimed the right to speak, in her usual understated style. "Look! The two of you! Just shut up!" she screamed. "We've heard enough from the peanut gallery. As a matter of fact, the only thing I want to hear from anyone is how the hell we end this little Tarzan episode without my boy there doing major organ transplants. Like, from us to inside him." She used her standard sneery tone, but you could tell she liked the way she'd put that last part.

"This may take a bit of patience, but—it stands to reason that the monster has to sleep e-*ven*-chally," Roger suggested, reasonably, "whether he's hungry or not. And once he does, I volunteer to scoot along and get—"

"That AK-47?" finished the captain. His tone then turned to devilish. "Or, if we don't want to wait that long, we could . . . distract him with a canapé or two. Someone young and tender would be best, I'd say." And he leered at Bud and Cherry.

"Oh, put a sock in it," the Dragon Lady told him. She placed the sole of one of her Doc Martens against his butt and gave it a couple of jabs. "I'd feed him chicken liver first."

"In the meantime, maybe we can summon help," said Roger, now sounding like an adult trying to change the subject. "I have my bos'n's pipe, and others here have healthy lungs, for sure. It's possible our young friend, Terry, should she be outside, would hear us. And she might feel it's in her own best interests to assist us."

"Not very damn likely—her hearing us, I mean," the Dragon Lady said, "but I suppose we might as well try. You blow your little whatsit, Rog, then I'll count to three and we'll all holler, 'Terry.' Ready? Blow!"

Roger sounded two high, piercing notes; the D.L. said, " . . . two, three," and everybody went, "Ter-ree!"

Silence.

"Again," the Dragon Lady said.

Under the cover of one of those calls for help, Terry leaned toward Mick and said, "How long d'you think I ought to wait?"

"Hours," he whispered back. "The more desperate they are, the better. The only thing that might make us want to start sooner is if it looks as if they're going to make a break. You know—have everyone jump down at once, figuring all but one'd probably make it out. We wouldn't want that to happen."

"*TER-REE!*" came the chorus from the big old tree.

Because of their naps, probably—and egged on by Roger—the pirates had the energy to keep calling for help off and on for most of the night. And because they did so, Bubba also stayed awake.

"You think it's time now?" Mick inquired. "You remember what you're going to say?"

"Yep—to both," Tee said. "I hardly have to act at all. Just a little bit."

"Don't forget your flashlight," Mick reminded her.

"Right," she said, and picked it up. Moving very quietly, she retreated through the jungle until she was a good hundred yards away from the pen. Then she turned her flashlight on and started back toward it, not worrying at all about making noise.

"Mrs. Holly?" she called out. "Captain Gold? Is that you, Roger? Cherry? Buddy?"

They heard her, of course, and started whooping and hollering. "Terry! Over here!"

"Are you all still in Bubba's pen?" she called, as she got closer. "Have you found the pirates' treasure?" By then, she was close enough so that her flashlight beam went through the fence.

"Wow!" she exclaimed. "Is that *Bubba?* He's enormous! Did he chase you up that tree? How come? You found the treasure, didn't you?"

A veritable chorus answered her, but not in any sort of harmony.

"No, you idiot!" "What does it look like?" "Help us, Terry!" "We've been up here all night!" "Good girl! I told them you'd help us, if we kept it up." And then, finally, from the Dragon Lady, "All *right!* Shut your holes, you simpletons!"

"Boy, you're really in a pickle," Terry said. "But maybe there's some way I could . . . whatchamacallit? *lure* Bubba away from you. Like if I could throw some food he likes into another part of the pen, maybe he'd go get it and—"

"Exactly," the Dragon Lady interrupted. "That's it exactly. Look, here's what you can do. . . . " You could tell from her tone of voice that her scheming mind had kicked into high gear, just the way the marquis'd said it would.

"Go back to the Plantation House," she ordered the girl, as usual omitting magic words like "please," "I beg of you," "you wonderful creature you," and the like. "In the freezer you'll find at least a dozen frozen steaks, big porterhouses. Pick out six of them and bring them to the front gate; unwrap them there and put them inside the pen. Bubba has a fabulous nose, so as soon as they start to thaw he'll know they're there and will run over to get them. And that'll give us time to leave this goddamn tree and escape out the back way."

"O-kay," said Terry, slowly. "I can do that. But—and please don't think me rude for saying this—what's in it for me? I *could* just leave you here, you know. I've gotten a little tired of being held for ransom and doing all your dirty dishes every day. So how about this? If I fetch the steaks and you get out of this predicament, you set me free, and we'll call the whole deal even." Tee didn't like having to act that dumb (this was her "little bit" of acting), but she could do it. The idea was to get the Dragon Lady overconfident.

"I guess that'd be fair," the D. L. said, keeping a straight face. "Tell you what—As soon as we're out of here, Roger will fly you anywhere you want to go—Miami, Lauderdale, Palm Beach, even Disney World—and let you go; he'll even give you money to call home. And that'll be that. All's well that ends well, all around."

"Is that a promise?" Terry asked.

"Cross my heart," the Dragon Lady said, and did so, twice.

"It's a deal, then," Terry said, and she started to turn away. But then she scratched her head (another bit of acting) and stopped.

"Wait," she said. "You said the steaks are in the freezer, but the freezer's always locked. I've never been allowed in there. Isn't it your strong room, too?"

The Dragon Lady snapped her fingers. "Of course," she said. "Good point. It *is* our strong room, but I trust you in there now; we have a deal. You'll need the key. Throw it to her, Billy-boy."

"*Throw* it to her?" the captain said. "Don't be ridiculous; I can't do that. That's much too far to throw a little key. I bet you nobody could throw a key that far, not even—" he groped for an athletic name—"that *Michael Jordan!*"

"Duh!" the Dragon Lady said. "You must have gotten every stupid DNA in both our parents' genes. You don't have to throw it by itself, dumbo. Take your stupid necklace off. Leave your key ring on it. Then twirl the whole deal around and give it a toss. When she has the keys, we can tell her which one works for the freezer."

"I guess that's right," the captain said. He sounded like a man in desperate need of a change of clothes and company, a big stiff drink, and Dreamland. He pulled his golden necklace over his head and started twirling it.

"Okay-dokey, everyone—here goes!" he shouted, as he slung it (with his ring of keys attached) into the fragrant early morning air.

# chapter 26

When she looked back at the next few moments, several days later, it seemed to Terry everything had happened in slow motion, beginning when the shiny keys and golden necklace started somersaulting through the air. But soon, and suddenly, this flight malfunctioned: It smacked into a little branchlet on the big tree nearest to the one the pirates perched in. Forward motion stopped; the necklace, crumpled now, collided with the ring of keys, and together they both dripped and dropped straight down, hitting the forest floor and going *clink*.

The captain's keys had traveled less than half the distance to their target. They were still a good ten yards inside the pen.

Imagine what would happen if, say, Michael Jordan were to have shot an air ball in the closing seconds of a play-off game against the Knicks (with the score tied 90-90). Chances are, he'd make some sort of comment, signifying disappointment or disgust.

Short Bill Gold did likewise, reacting to the failure of *his* shot.

"*Shit, Miss Mitchell,*" said the captain—this unusual locution being something he had often heard his father say. Who "Miss Mitchell" was, or might have been, was something that the captain always wished he knew. But the secret of her true identity, and why her name appeared in this expression, is buried (sad to say) with Daddy Gold.

"*Judas Priest,*" moaned Terry, not really sure who that was, either.

An instant later, the pirate tree became the recrimination center of the Western Hemisphere. Arrows of blame rained down on Short Bill Gold; "hopeless spaz" being much less sharp than many of the others.

There weren't any lines on Terry's cue card, and at first she simply stood there gaping at the fallen keys, her mind a blank. But then she shook herself and tried to think what she should say. Nothing too original, she figured—not coming from an airhead like the girl she'd been playing.

"So how about," she started, "if, seeing as I can't get steak, I go and get . . . um, like, a loaf of bread? And maybe cereal? You keep them in the pantry, so I wouldn't need the keys. Maybe you've got some stuff they eat in Indonesia, do you?" She pantomimed deep thought. "I could open a jar of salsa."

When the Dragon Lady answered, she sounded, for the first time, pretty beat, as if her speeding, scheming mind had started to run down.

"Sure, try some bread," she said. "And I think we've got potato chips left; he might like something greasy. But salsa? I don't think so. You decide. Whatever looks good."

"Okay," said Terry, brightly. "I'll see what I can find." What she really wanted to find was Mick or the marquis, so they could put their heads together. "It may take a little while," she added, as she turned away. "Just stay right there." She couldn't resist that last line, wrapped in an idiotic giggle.

Mick was where she'd left him, and although from that distance he hadn't been able to see the key ring's fatal flight, he'd guessed what had happened from hearing the ensuing dialogue. He shook his head as Tee came up to him, and together they eased their way through the jungle, not saying anything until they were a good ways from the pen.

"What stinking, rotten luck," he started. "The Plan was working perfectly. . . . "

"I know," she said, "but now what?" She wanted to get another plan in place real fast. This was like what she learned in history class, how when a British monarch dies, they say, "The king is dead; long live the king." At a time of crisis and despair, you had to keep going; it was important not to goop around, feeling sorry for yourself.

So, as they made their way toward the compound, they brought up—and then discarded—several ideas. He didn't know how to hot-wire a powerboat; trying to rig a mast and sail on any of the pirate's boats would have taken too much time; using a fishing rod to cast a lure with lots of hooks on it over the fence, hoping to snag the key ring that way—that'd take a lottery winner's luck.

"Well, maybe we should try that food idea," Terry finally said. "It wouldn't have to be just bread and cereal, or chips. There's leftover stuff in the fridge that Bubba might actually like: that curried tuna-and-potato salad, for instance, and I bet he could smell cold cuts from a mile away. What we could do is, one of us could toss the stuff over the fence while the other one snuck around into the pen"—she was making this up as she went along— "and as soon as Bubba went to check out the food, that one could run real fast and grab the keys. . . . "

Mick didn't react to that suggestion right away, but after a bit he started nodding to himself.

"I wuh-wonder where they keep their *guns*," he said. "If we had a gun, going in there wouldn't be so dangerous. Wuh-we could threaten them and even shoot old Bubba, if we had to."

As soon as he said that, one of those traditional lightbulbs went off, right over Terry's head.

"I'm pretty sure their guns are locked away," she said, excitedly, "but we've got something just about as good—that can of Mace, or whatever it is, of mine! You know—the stuff my mom got me to spray at muggers. Bubba'd be like a three-hundred-pound mugger! Why wouldn't it work on him? It wouldn't kill him, but it'd—whatchamacallit?—*incapacitate* him. That's what it says on the can."

Mick stopped dead while Tee was saying that. They were almost at the compound. She turned around to look at him.

"*Bien entendu*—your little can of Mace—or whatever it is!" The marquis slapped himself on the forehead. "I have forget about your spray! We toss food in, just as you say, and then with The Mace for my protection, I run in and seize the keys. If Monseiur Lizard comes for me, I squirt him—poof!—*comme ça*." He held up his hand, forefinger on an imaginary push button. "And the big *bébé* goes bye-bye!"

"Right," said Terry. "Or, still better, *I* run in, grab the keys, toss them over the fence to *you*, and then

274

Mace Bubba if I have to. When the pirates see *me* coming, they'll think I'm stupid enough to save them; they'll be cool. But if they saw you, no telling what they'd think or do. My way, you'd be able to get a head start down to the boat, maybe even get it started and bring it over to the pier—and we'd make a faster getaway."

The marquis was shaking his head at the start of that speech, but as she continued, the shakes turned into nods.

"Ah, *oui*," he said. "You make good points. That might be best. But now, right now"—he was beaming, clearly energized—"we have much things to do, as fast as possible. First we find a shovel; then you take us to your garden cart. . . . "

Terry saw what he was getting at, and plugged right in to it. That marquis! He had another plan in mind already! Clearly, its step one was digging up the pirates' treasure (she'd forgotten all about it), after which they'd cart it to the pier, put it in a dinghy, and row it right out to the *Kidd Me Not*. Why not? Then they'd pick up the Mace at the cottage, head up to the Plantation House (to pick up Bubba's food), and then on to the pen.

The one thing she was a hair disappointed about, at first, was that he hadn't given her any real argument about who'd be the one to run into the pen and (possibly) go one-on-one with the Komodo dragon. But, on reflection, she realized that *could* be seen as proof that, fifteenth-century guy or not, he wasn't any sexist. She'd had the Mace idea, so it was only right (he saw) that she'd be the one to say who played which part in it.

Also, this way she had the satisfaction of knowing that if she could get to the keys and throw them out to him, at least one of them would—for sure—be able to escape.

Not that Terry had thought the whole thing through and decided she would cheerfully give up her life for Mick (and the marquis). It wasn't quite like that. But the thing was, ever since they'd become an "us," she'd more or less thought of the two of them as one. So they were equally valuable and equally worth saving. But because he knew how to drive a boat like the *Kidd Me Not* and she didn't, he had a much better chance of escaping than she did, if only one of them could make it to the pirate craft.

Of course, the real truth of the matter was that Terry didn't think for a minute she was going to be killed by Bubba, or otherwise prevented from joining Mick in a mad, exulting dash down to the harbor. She believed this latest plan was going to work just fine. Bubba was big, all right, but he didn't look terribly fast or manueverable. And he probably had gotten pretty bored from lying there like a lump under that tree for all those hours; perhaps even one or more of his feet had gone to sleep, and he'd fall over if he tried to stand and run. Too, his little lizard mind could easily be thousands of miles away, like back in Indonesia where he could rustle up his own food and didn't have to wait for meals on wheels; he could even be feeling a little faint from hunger. Besides, Mone had given her that can of Mace (or whatever), so she believed (along with Mone) that it could keep her safe from anything (that walked or charged or slithered). And finally, she definitely doubted God had put her on this earth to be devoured by its largest living lizard.

Terry's lifelong tendency to see the glass as being half full had never come in handier.

They found a shovel lying in the garden, near the plants with all the blue-green worms on them; the cart was in the jungle where they'd left it.

Mick took them straight to the place where the treasure was, and after less than five minutes of digging, the chest was brought to light. It was about the size of one of those footlockers kids take to summer camp, but a little boxier and a lot heavier (in that gold doubloons do weigh a good deal more than baseball gloves and comic books, even when the latter two are plainly marked with owners' names). Terry thought the chest looked . . . well, *authentic,* with its big black iron lock in front. She grunted happily as she helped set it in the cart.

In another five minutes they had it in the dinghy and were rowing out to the *Kidd Me Not*. Once on board, Mick checked the fuel tank and was relieved to find it full—their craft was ready for a speedy getaway.

During the row out, and all the time they were on the powerboat, Mick went on and on, almost gloatingly, about how the next time they boarded it, they wouldn't be getting back in the dinghy and returning to the island. "Heck, no," he said, "the next time we'll just . . . " And he almost regressed into that repulsive "teaching personality" of his, telling her in detail how he'd get the cruiser off and running. Maybe he was babbling from nervousness, she thought, or possibly he was showing off a little. But at least he didn't ask her to repeat the stuff he said—although she thought she could've.

Their next step was the cottage, where, after scooping up the Mace can, Tee stuffed most of her personal possessions (plus, as mementos, the captain's underdrawers and that copy of *Moby Dick*) into her duffel bag. She left it on the path for them to pick up later, but the Mace stayed clutched in her right hand.

In the Plantation House pantry, they raided the refrigerator and the food cupboards, slopping a veritable all-you-can-eat buffet of stuff into a huge roasting pan. There was a big Tupperware container's worth of leftover tuna-and-potato salad, a chunk of Mother Goose brand liverwurst, a half dozen slices of meat loaf, four cans of pork and beans (decanned), a bag of barbecued potato chips, and (in case the dragon had a sweet tooth and was into heart-healthy) a box of Honey Nut Cheerios.

They lugged this fragrant, heavy meal around to the side of the pen—they could hear the twins and the captain and the Dragon Lady ragging on each other from a ways away—and Mick poured it over the fence, a little past the place where Tee'd been standing earlier, so that the pirates wouldn't be able to see him.

But they—and presumably Bubba, as well—did hear the sound the food made as it hit the ground.

"Terry? Is that you?" the Dragon Lady called. Then, more in character: "What the hell took you so long? And what sort of food was that, anyway? It didn't sound like bread and cereal to me."

"It sounded more like throw-up," Buddy opined.

"I b'lieve our Bubba smells it, whatever it may be," said Roger. "Cheers, old chap! Tallyho and all that rot! Go get it, sir!"

Mick and Terry, still out of the pirates' sight,

were moving rapidly through the jungle, heading for the spot where he'd been hiding at the time of the key tossing.

"Buh-before you go, guh-gimme a quick peek at that," said Mick, reaching for the can that Tee still held. "I wuh-want to see what's really in it—puh-pepper spray or what."

She handed it over, focused on what she planned to do next, not even noticing how much he'd stuttered. But as soon as it changed hands, he started running, much as if he'd grabbed a relay-race baton.

"I luh-luh-luh . . . ," was all she heard him say before he disappeared into the jungle, sprinting toward the gate.

⚓

# chapter 27

It never occurred to Terry to yell for him to stop, or to run after him. Days before, she'd sensed she ought to let him be the planner, and now she recognized that this was part of his new plan. He'd let her think that he agreed with her suggestion that she be the one to do that business with the keys, and to deal with Bubba, but that had been to shut her up and set her up for what he really planned to do. He'd even managed to give her a little class in powerboat operation without her understanding why.

But had he planned to say "I love you" just as he was leaving her? It didn't matter. Planned or not, she knew what he had tried to say was from his heart. And she was pretty sure he knew that her heart said it back to him, that she not only loved him but believed in him.

She got down on her hands and knees and crept a little closer to the fence; she didn't want the pirate crew to see her any sooner than they had to. What she'd realized—had Mick forgotten this?—was that he'd never seen the keys come down; he'd need her to direct him to the spot. And then she smiled: Of course he'd known she'd be there to do that. It was part of his plan to toss her the keys once he had them. He wanted to be sure she could start the *Kidd Me Not* and go—escape—if something went real wrong for him in there.

Peering through the jungle foliage, she saw that Bubba'd gotten up and moved a few steps toward the food they'd brought for him, the food they'd hoped would lure him farther from the keys. But then he'd stopped again. His head was up and his big mouth partly open. Tee was sure that he was checking out the bait with his outstanding sense of smell, and now was wondering what he should do about it.

She could imagine what was running through his lizard brain: *Yo—unfamiliar odors. Edible? Perhaps, but maybe underrotted. Go see? Or wait for live food here to fall from tree? Hungry. Better go.*

As Bubba started strolling once again, there was some movement up the tree, and Terry heard the

Dragon Lady hiss, "No you don't, young man."

Then, Buddy, in a sotto voce whisper, said, "Ow! Let me go! He's leaving; let me jump; we can escape. I'm sick of being up this tree."

To which his mother answered, fiercely, "Go ahead and jump, but if you do, before you hit the ground you'll be a *one*-eared jackass."

"All right, all right—let go. I swear I won't." Bud apparently knew better than to call his mother's bluff.

His surrender was hardly out of his mouth when Terry heard running footsteps coming, and an eye-blink later, Mick was on the scene, right there, his head on a swivel as his eyes went searching for the keys.

She jumped to her feet and pointed.

"Over this way more! Keep coming!" she cried out. "Look—*there!*"

His head came up and he grinned at her. Then, with one thumb up, he headed for the spot that she was pointing at.

Of course, the sight of him produced a wide range of reactions from the pirate crew.

"Who the frickety-frack is *that?*" asked Short Bill Gold.

"Dash it all!" cried Roger. "The bounder's got my patchwork bags on! I'd wondered where they'd gotten to!"

"But Terry said a shark or something ate them, if you mean your pants," said Cherry.

The Dragon Lady, typically, gave orders.

"Hey, you!" she screeched. "Come over here! You're trespassing on private property, you know." And then, when Mick paid no attention, "Bubba! Here, good boy! Sic him—yeah, look, look! Live lunch!"

Perhaps it was the nails-against-the-blackboard quality of her voice—who knows?—but something made the the giant lizard stop again, and turn his head. And Mick, at that same moment, using perfect jumpshot form, lofted the keys over the fence and into Terry's waiting hands.

That brought her to the pirate crew's attention.

"Thunder and lightening!" Short Bill Gold exploded. "The little tart's in league with him! Gad, sir—if I had my blunderbuss, I swear I'd blow the two of them to kingdom come! I'd shiver both their rotten timbers!"

"You shoulda let us make her walk the plank," cried Buddy. It seemed his affection for the girl he'd seen "with no close on" was short-lived. "She'd be fish poop if you hadn't stopped us, Uncle Bilges."

"Traitor!" screamed the Dragon Lady. "This is the thanks I get for agreeing to let you go? You conniving little bitch! I bet I know how you got *him* to help you."

Roger, though, still had his wardrobe on his mind.

"Bollocks!" he exclaimed. "If I'm not dreadfully mistaken, the bloody rascal's got my singlet on, as well." He pointed. "See? It's got that little pocket on the front."

"She said she dropped it when the fish attacked," wailed Cherry. "I can't believe she *lied* to me," complained one of the finest liars in her age group.

Meanwhile, Mick was yelling something too, to Terry. "Hurry up—get out of here! I'll meet you at the pier. But if I'm . . . delayed, don't wait. Fire up the *Kidd Me Not* and go—due east, remember!"

But she was not about to move, not yet. She flapped both hands at him in a gesture of dismissal.

"*You* go—quick!" she called. "Take off! I'll meet you at the gate."

He started to obey. The only trouble was, it seemed as if the dragon, too, had heard what Terry'd said—the first parts, anyway—and decided it was good advice. And so, if something more or less the size of a piano could be said to "scurry," Bubba scurried. Fast. And straight at Mick.

Mick didn't hang around and wait for him; he started motoring. And based on his initial acceleration (not to mention quick, responsive handling), most observers would have bet on him to leave the lizard in the dust (or jungle vegetation) somewhere between his starting point and the gate by which he planned to leave the pen.

But races are, by nature, unpredictable. An edge in form, equipment, or God-given ability can be canceled out by rotten racing luck. A hurdler can hit a hurdle. A basketball player on the way to an easy lay-in can have his final dribble carom off his foot. A speedy snatcher of gold chains or purses, pursued by the cop on the beat, might fail to notice icy patches on the sidewalk.

And a boy running through a stretch of unfamiliar jungle is pretty apt to be tripped up by either roots or vines, and to go flying through the air and end up stretched out on the ground.

That was what happened to Mick J. Crane. One minute he was showing his heels to every Komodo dragon on Muela Negra, and the next one he was prostrate on the forest floor, garnished with local greenery, and looking like something that the local lizard might have ordered from the luncheon menu.

Bubba kept on coming. And although still some fifteen yards away, he opened his great mouth, already drooling in anticipation of the meal he'd soon crouch down to. Very likely he was thinking, *I'm so hungry I could eat a horse.*

Mick was shaken by his fall, but the can in his left hand had also been well shaken: first in the course of his sprint to get to the keys, and then by his hard tumble. So when the boy rolled over onto his back, aimed his weapon at the dragon's open mouth, and fired, a good strong spray resulted.

The stuff in a can like the one he had is called oleoresin capsicum ("pepper spray" to friend and foe alike); it's an inflammatory agent derived from the cayenne pepper plant. Take it in the mouth and what you've got is sheer discomfort on a level you don't even want to think about. Pepper spray can burn the leather on an ancient weather-beaten western saddle, never mind the tender, moist interior of almost anybody's food hole.

Bubba *was* discomforted, at once. There's no point going into lots of ugly and unpleasant details; suffering is never nice to see, or even read about. Suffice it to say that after some preliminary . . . antics (accompanied by certain . . . audible complaints), he made tracks for the nearby brook. Once there, he got his head entirely underwater, opened wide, and let the cooling current try to stop the conflagration in his mouth.

Meanwhile, Mick, amazed and delighted by the potency of his weapon, picked himself up and headed for the gate; Terry, weak with feelings of relief, did likewise.

From the pirate tree there came a torrent of reactions to the boy's escape.

The Dragon Lady, almost automatically, chose a formulation used by villains for . . . well, centuries. "After him, you fools!" she cried.

But the captain, daunted by the firepower that the lad possessed, was not in any hurry to pursue him.

"Zounds! Young hooligan got pepper spray somewhere," he mused. "Looks like our fire-breathing dragon *in*haled. Betcha he won't order Mexican for months!"

"But how come the bleedin' bounder's got my *breeches* on?!" one-track Roger was still asking. "Confounded pantsnapper!"

"You think that's Terry's *boyfriend*, Mom?" asked Cherry, suddenly interested in the interpersonal possibilities of all this. "You think she *gave* him Roger's pants? Where d'you suppose his own are?"

"Now that Bubba won't bother me, I'm going to go ahead and dig up the treasure right now," said Buddy. "And you know what? I'm not going to share it with anyone. OOO-OW! Except you, Mom. Can't you take a joke?"

It seemed as if the Dragon Lady had her work cut out for her, if she hoped to muster up some "hot pursuit." Short Bill Gold was in no hurry whatsoever. He assumed that Tee and Mick would use the keys to open up the Plantation House strong room and take out his AK-47; that was what he'd have done in their shoes. And then the little floozy'd lie in wait somewhere and try to blow his brains out. The trouble with young girls these days, he thought, was that they didn't know their place and weren't any fun and couldn't recognize a compliment when they received one. In retrospect, he really *did* wish he'd let Buddy make her walk the plank.

He lagged behind his sister and the twins and Roger when they finally started from the pen.

## chapter 28

Both Mick and Terry were still in the grip of strong emotions when they were finally close enough to touch again, just outside the gate of Bubba's pen. Indeed, if a tall turbaned genie had suddenly appeared just then and told Tee she could have three wishes, she might very well have said she wanted (1.) to have him whisk them to a private club and cottage colony (yes, like the one that Roger's "chums" supposedly maintained), rent them (2.) a beachfront cottage far away from anybody else, and leave them (3.) the hell alone. She didn't have, like, an "agenda" for them; after all that they'd been through, she'd just wanted to relax a little while before they had to tackle still another scary thing, like talking to their parents.

And if Mick had dared to be so bold, he might have made the same three wishes; the marquis probably would have tried to get "a little glass of wine" in there, somehow.

But without a genie right on hand to take their order, and thinking that the pirates might be there at any moment, they settled for a heartfelt hug.

Mick also felt the situation called for him to say, "I thought I was a goner for a minute there," and Terry, staying with the script, came back with, "I was *sure* you were!"

Then, holding hands, they started jogging toward the path down to the harbor.

They never got to it, however. Since Terry'd left Cape Enid, she'd probably had a lifetime's worth of surprises—starting with that first immense one, when she'd come out of the yawl's companionway to find an undraped Mick J. Crane at the helm of the *Cormorant*. But the one that took place next had to be the biggest one of all.

At first they didn't know what name to give it. Like most Americans their age, they'd never been in—or expected to be anywhere near—an actual bombardment, and so had no idea that one was taking place.

"What's happening?" Tee asked. What she'd heard was the boom of four-inch guns, blended with the sounds of shells exploding in the harbor area below.

The two of them had stopped beside the Plantation House's big veranda, and they both were standing with their knees flexed, a little bit like surfboard riders. That was because the ground was shaking—not much, but a little. If it hadn't been for the noise, Terry would have thought this was an earthquake. Of course, they couldn't see a thing, uphill or down, because of all the trees.

"I can't imagine," Mick replied. "It sounds like something just blew up down there." He nodded toward the harbor. "You think they had explosives stored in one of those buildings? Or ammunition?" Naval ships, big guns, and shells never crossed his mind. "Maybe a fire started in one of the buildings where they kept that kind of stuff. Look—there's smoke." And there was a little then, visible above the treetops.

"It couldn't be, like, an *eruption*, could it?" Terry asked. "I know there *are* volcanic islands—but around here? And I didn't see a crater up where Roger's cabin is."

"Well, if we're in the Bermuda Triangle," said Mick, "it could be anything, I guess." He forced a little laugh. "Maybe some terrorist organization has a huge underground base down there, like in a James Bond movie. And a bunch of little guys in identical black jumpsuits and white turtlenecks are testing some new secret weapon that they're counting on to win them world dominion."

"Right," said Terry, mockingly—though at this point she was ready to believe almost anything about this island. "Maybe we should see if we can find the pirates' guns and strike a blow for freedom and the right to wear designer clothing."

But when the next series of shells crashed into the harbor area, she changed her tune and said, "I vote we go the other way." She gestured. "Up. It doesn't sound real safe down there, and besides, you can see much more from up by Roger's place."

He nodded. "Right," he said. "We can always go down later. To the boat, I mean. You've got the keys still, right?"

She pulled them out of her pocket and jingled them at him. "You don't suppose . . . , " she started. His saying "boat" had made her think that maybe . . . but that made no sense.

"What?" he asked.

"Nothing," she replied. "Let's go.

Glancing back in the direction the pirates might be coming from, they started up the hill.

There was another salvo just before they reached the top, while they were still in the wooded part of the slope. Ahead they could see bare ground—the side of the black molar's crown—and the silhouette of Roger's little house on it, his Crow's Nest.

But before they came out into the open, they heard the sound of planes approaching, fast.

The squadron didn't pass directly over them, but they saw it streak on by, going over Roger's place and heading to their right. And the planes had hardly passed before the ground shook, once again, and kept on shaking as some eight or ten explosions rent the air.

Terry turned toward Mick, eyes wide. "Those planes . . . , " she started.

"They had U.S. insignia on them," he said. "And it sounds as if they bombed the airstrip."

"How *come*, though?" Terry said. "What's going on?"

"It must be something like a navy weapons test," said Mick, "where they choose an uninhabited island and then just blast away at it."

"They can't test *nuclear* weapons, can they?" Terry asked. "Isn't there some treaty?"

"I think so," he replied. "But I also think we'd better get on top and out in the open, so maybe they'll see us and hold their fire." He grabbed her arm, excitedly. "Hey, wouldn't that be something? If they saw us and . . . well, *rescued* us? Maybe if we grab some more of Roger's clothes, we can lay them on the ground so they spell 'help' or 'SOS.' Then, if the planes fly over again . . . Come on!"

They ran out into the open and kept going until

they were on the knob by Roger's, on the island's highest point. For the moment, the pirates were forgotten.

Once there, they naturally looked down at the harbor and then past it at the ocean. Because they did, they saw a sight that no onshore Americans had seen since the medical students near St. George's had watched the invasion of the island of Grenada come toward them, back in 1983.

There were only three ships standing off Muela Negra on that early morning, but they seemed sufficient for the job at hand. One of them, with more of those fast fighter-bombers on its flight deck, was a "baby flattop," aka a compact aircraft carrier. Another—lower, sleeker—with its big guns pointed at the island still, was a destroyer. Its shells had "softened up" the harbor area, the place where the marines would have their "beachhead." And finally came the big wide troopship, from which a number of landing craft were already speeding toward this island that the navy oh-so-clearly planned to "liberate."

Terry turned to Mick. "You don't suppose," she said, "your father . . . ?"

He stared at her while that sank in. That possibility.

"I guess he would have gotten Roger's letter and the photo," he began.

"And because the *Cormorant*'s stern was in the picture," Tee went on, "and he knew you'd taken the *Cormorant,* the only way he could possibly find out what happened to *you* . . . "

"Even if he didn't care what happened, it'd look bad if he didn't at least *try* to find out," Mick continued.

"And if he got in touch with my mother," Terry said, "I'm pretty sure she'd put some pressure on."

"Well . . . " Mick smiled. "I know he made a huge—humongous, really—campaign contribution. Right before the last election. So if he wanted something badly . . . And there *are* American lives at stake."

But Terry had started shaking her head.

"All that adds up, but there's one big trouble," she said. "Roger's letter didn't tell him where we are. I don't think he even mentioned an island." She gestured at the fast-approaching landing craft. "So I doubt if they're coming for *us.*"

Just then they heard a low humming in the distant sky. They turned around and faced the east and saw more planes approaching. But these were neither sleek nor fast; they also were a good deal bigger than the flattop's planes, wide-bodied, slow. And when they reached the island, big doors opened in their sides, and out of them jumped men, members of a veteran elite division of the airborne infantry, whose parachutes soon filled the morning sky.

"I'll say this," said Terry. "Whoever organized all this has got real style."

Things were looking pretty good, she thought. Even if the rescuers had not been sent specifically for them, the odds now seemed very high they weren't going to be killed by the pirates or eaten by Bubba, and that they would be saved by about as neat a land-sea operation as anyone could possibly imagine. She saw no reason that they wouldn't be able to collect the treasure on their way off the island. And even if they decided to share some of it with the U.S. government—which seemed like the only fair thing to do—they'd still have plenty left to impress the home folks with.

Finally, given all that they'd been through, their parents couldn't get *too* mad at them for taking off the way they did. And though being kidnapped by pirates and rescued by a cool amphibious operation didn't exactly qualify as standard extracurricular activity, she was pretty sure that she could work them into her college application essays.

"Probably the smartest thing for us to do is stand here with our hands up," Terry said. "So they"—she tilted her head up toward the parachutists—"can see we aren't armed or hostile."

So they did that. As the jumpers floated closer,

Tee and Mick could see that they were all wearing camouflage gear and even had their faces striped with green-and-black (as well as some brown-and-orange) paint.

When one of them hit the ground a little ways from them, Terry called out, "Hi! We're both Americans, and really glad to see you!"

The trooper's first response was to extract a walkie-talkie from his pack and speak to it (instead of them): "Sir, I'm looking at a red-haired female here, who could be seventeen—and there's a boy about the same age with her." The radio squawked back at him.

He turned to her. "Is your name Terry Talley, miss?"

"Sure is," she said. "But how . . . ?"

The soldier had a hand up now, way high, and was waving it the way you do in class if you're really sure you know the answer. "Over here!" he yelled into his walkie-talkie. Further squawks came back. "Absolutely, sir. I've got her." He sounded quite delighted with himself.

Though Terry might have preferred "found" to "got" in his last sentence, she wasn't in the mood to quibble. Now three other men in camouflage were coming toward them, double time. The middle one, a stride or two ahead of the others, was sturdily built and ramrod-straight; he had two silver oak leaves on his collar tabs, and he started to hold out his hand to Tee.

But before he could speak, one of the troopers behind him (who wasn't much bigger than a jockey, surprisingly small for a soldier, Terry thought) started grinning broadly, saying, "How d'you like this outfit on me, girlfriend?"

It was a high, familiar voice, not soldierly at all.

"Connie!" Terry cried. "I don't believe it!"

And even as they started jumping up and down and hugging one another, the third guy pulled his helmet off. He had a rolled-up blue bandanna under it that kept his long (but neatly trimmed) blond hair in place.

"For God's sake, change your pants before they take a picture, son," said Maitland Crane, but he was smiling, too.

⚓

# epilogue

Terry was embarrassed she'd forgotten all about the note she'd put inside a bottle and sent to Connie, "mailing" it in waist-deep water. In that note she'd named the island she was on, and of course, the U.S. Navy knew exactly where it was.

Later on she thought up two good explanations for her absentmindedness. In the first place, she couldn't have expected that the Gulf Stream and Hurricane Jackson would combine to send her bottle shooting north (and slightly west) until it came to rest on a private beach just two estates up from the Cape Enid Club—where it was almost stepped on by a nerdy jogger (Reynolds Osborne IV) who had had a crush on Connie since fifth grade. And

secondly, so much had happened on the island between the time she'd sent the bottle on its way and
the invasion that the note had more or less gotten
buried in her mind.

"The thing is," Connie babbled in her rush to
tell Tee all about it, "the day after you left, I'm walking to the Club and who do I see on one of the tennis courts but Maitland Crane. Of course, I just
about flipped! What's going on? I think: Who's sailing *Cormorant*? But I don't say anything, partly on
account of how he looks—like, cool and calm, not
the least bit stressed—so I figured that he must have
lent it to some friend of his, which might be even
better for you, even though probably whoever it is
wouldn't be anywhere near as good-looking. But
when I got your letter I didn't know what to do, so I
took it to your mom and *she* said we ought to run it
up to Mr. Crane, who it turns out has just gotten
that Express Mail or whatever it was from the pirates with your photo in it—real nice picture, too,
didn't you think?"

She had to pause to take a breath.

"I guess he'd known all along it was his son
who'd taken the boat, hadn't he?" Terry managed to
get in.

"Yeah, he was pretty sure," said Connie, slowing
down a bit. "I guess his servants told him Mick disappeared the same time as the *Cormorant*. But when

he saw that photo, he figured you'd been in on it, too. He recognized you from the club, and I guess your name was in the ransom letter he got. So he realized you'd probably be able to tell him what the story was with Mick—was he alive or dead?—and what happened with his boat. When he saw *my* letter, which said exactly where you were, he got right on the phone. And bingo! Here we are!"

Once she heard the whole story, though, Terry discovered Connie'd oversimplified a little.

The biggest complication, right at first, had to do with the matter of the island's sovereignty. It turned out that this had been under discussion—and dispute—in a minor U.N. subcommittee ever since the international organization was founded in 1945 (and possibly even before that, in the League of Nations). At one time or another claims had been made that it was a candidate for membership in the British Commonwealth (by Great Britain), a Spanish colony (by Spain), a United States territory (by the U.S.), and an independent state (by a coalition of third-world countries).

But in the end it was decidedly unilaterally—at 1600 Pennsylvania Avenue—that regardless of the island's status, at least one American citizen was in mortal danger there, so intervention (and invasion) were completely justifiable.

With legalities thus taken care of, a "quick reaction force" was immediately mobilized, and the commander in chief personally authorized that it be augmented by two civilians: Maitland Crane (a world-famous mountain climber, auto racer, single-handed sailor, and campaign contributor) and his "personal assistant," Connie Slavin (a recreational hang-gliding enthusiast, bungee jumper, and para-chutist whose indulgent father had paid for more jumps than any person her age had ever taken).

It turned out that Maitland Crane had rather liked the idea of his son commandeering the *Cormorant* (at least at first). In fact, the marquis had come close to hitting his attitude right on the button: Maitland Crane had always hoped that Mick would do the kinds of things he did—including backing winners in elections.

"A little single-handed sail will help to make a man of the boy," he'd opined to his butler when he first learned that boat and boy were "missing." "And it could do more for that damn stutter of his than five years of therapy."

"Yes, sir. Will that be all, sir?" said the butler, who had applied for his seventy-five-thousand-dollar-a-year job under the name of "Jarvis," but whose wife and friends all know him as Sharif Muhammad.

So, for Mick, one of the outcomes of this big adventure was a much better relationship with his father, who, though still a self-centered jerk, was at least newly respectful of him. Mick's mother never had a moment's worry because, all the time that he was missing, she had "known" that he was staying with his father—and Maitland Crane had never bothered to tell her otherwise.

Both Terry's parents, though, had a couple of weeks of being worried sick.

"Imagining you hitchhiking all the way to the West Coast was even worse than imagining you stowed away aboard the *Cormorant* would have been," Mone told her daughter. "I'm not that wild about Maitland Crane, but I'm pretty sure he's not some kind of dangerous lunatic. But tell me the truth, now. What prompted you to fly the coop— really? Did you hate the whole idea of boarding school that much?"

"No, it wasn't that," Tee answered. "Although the possibility of being pressured into choosing to go away did bug me. What really spooked me was that maybe you and Daddy still saw me as a little kid. So I talked myself into thinking it'd be good for me to get off on my own and prove to you I wasn't." She laughed. "What you said about it being time for me to 'spread my wings'—that really stuck in my mind. Why not *really* do that? I asked myself. And—though this is pretty dopey— I didn't see stowing away on *Cormorant* as being at all dangerous. I'm really sorry, Mom, for what I put you through—you and Daddy both."

"I blamed myself *and* your father *and* you," her mother said, "depending on which day of the week it was. I warmed a lot of lavender oil, I'll tell you that. And I'll tell you something else."

"What's that?" asked Terry.

"You're different now," said Mone, "aren't you? I wouldn't think of even *saying* 'boarding school' to you now—not anymore. You seem like someone who could . . . I don't know, become an astronaut, or run for Congress—really, I'm not kidding!"

There wasn't any talk of Terry being "punished." As a matter of fact, from that time on, her only contact with the word *ground* was when she saw it in a recipe between *freshly* and *black pepper*.

She did initiate a talk with Mone about Mick, a little while after she got home. She told her mother she believed they loved each other—although they have to see how that held up in "ordinary life."

The difference in their ages—he turned out to be fifteen and two years behind her in school—didn't bother her, she said (no matter what other kids thought), and would matter less and less as years went by. She wanted to spend a lot of time with him during the rest of the summer, while his father still "had" him, doing things like hiking part of the Appalachian Trail, taking a cruise with his father, and maybe flying out West to see her dad. Given the existing custody agreement, Mick would be back in his old school, and living with his mother, come the start of the school year.

"I don't intend to make love with him," she told Mone. "Not because I don't want to, but because I think if we did, it'd put a weird kind of pressure on him, and I don't want that. I mean, he really hasn't known too many girls, and I'd like him to date when he's back in school without feeling . . . I don't know, bound, or *beholden* to me. Do you know what I mean? I'm sure you would if you knew *him* a little better."

Mone said she thought she understood—marveling once again at her dear daughter's wisdom.

"Of course, if I change my mind about the sex thing, I may have to marry him before school starts," Terry went on, with a straight face. But she couldn't keep from cracking up at how Mone looked before she realized her daughter still was quite the kidder.

The pirates were captured by the marines. They were all in the Plantation House, conducting a systematic search of the captain's bedroom, the living room, and the kitchen, looking for his extra set of keys. They'd wanted to unlock the strong room and get out the guns they had in there. These they as Malibu, with much less famous neighbors.

It was "reasonable doubt" that saved the D. L., up and down the line. The prosecution couldn't prove she lied when she maintained the *Kidd Me Not* was on the fritz; in the course of the bombardment, it—indeed, everything that floated in the harbor—had been hit and sunk.

The pirates' treasure never got a mention at the trial. In fact, it was only talked about by Terry and Mick when they could be sure they were alone and out of anybody's earshot. At the moment shortly before their "liberation" when they learned the *Kidd Me Not* had become a sunken wreck, they exchanged a look and a nod, and that was it.

They both (of course) realized that only the two of them knew the treasure chest had been discovered, and dug up, and put aboard the *Kidd Me Not*.

So it is fitting, they believe, that only they—the two of them—now know exactly where it lies.

The Newbery Medal is awarded each year to the most distinguished
contribution to literature for children published in the U.S.
How many of these Newbery winners, available from
Aladdin Paperbacks, have you read?

## Newbery Medal Winners

❑ *Caddie Woodlawn*
by Carol Ryrie Brink
0-689-81521-2

❑ *Hitty: Her First
Hundred Years*
by Rachel Field
0-689-82284-7

❑ *The Grey King*
by Susan Cooper
0-689-71089-5

❑ *Mrs. Frisby and the
Rats of NIMH* by
Robert C. O'Brien
0-689-71068-2

❑ *Call It Courage*
by Armstrong Sperry
0-02-045270-5

❑ *From the Mixed-up
Files of Mrs. Basil E.
Frankweiler*
by E. L. Konigsburg
0-689-71181-6

❑ *King of the Wind*
by Marguerite Henry
0-689-71486-6

❑ *Shadow of a Bull* by
Maia Wojciechowska
0-689-71567-6

❑ *The Cat Who Went
to Heaven* by
Elizabeth Coatsworth
0-698-71433-5

❑ *A Gathering of Days*
by Joan W. Blos
0-689-71419-X

❑ *M.C. Higgins,
the Great*
by Virginia Hamilton
0-02-043490-1

❑ *Smoky the Cow Horse*
by Eric P. Kelly
0-689-71682-6
$5.50 US / $8.99
Canadian

❑ *The View from Saturday*
by E. L. Konigsburg
0-689-81721-5

## Newbery Honor Books

❑ *The Bears on
Hemlock Mountain*
by Alice Dalgliesh
0-689-71604-4

❑ *The Jazz Man*
by Mary Hays Weik
0-689-71767-9
$3.95 US / $4.95
Canadian

❑ *The Planet of Junior
Brown*
by Virginia Hamilton
0-689-71721-0

❑ *Misty of Chincoteague*
by Marguerite Henry
0-689-71492-0
*The Moorchild*
by Eloise McGraw
0-689-82033-X

❑ *Calico Bush*
by Rachel Field
0-689-82285-5

❑ *The Dark Is Rising*
by Susan Cooper
0-689-71087-9

❑ *Dogsong*
by Gary Paulsen
0-689-80409-1

❑ *The Courage of
Sarah Noble*
by Alice Dalgliesh
0-689-71540-4

❑ *A String in the Harp*
by Nancy Bond
0-689-80445-8
$5.99 US / $8.50
Canadian

❑ *Hatchet*
by Gary Paulsen
0-689-80882-8

❑ *Sugaring Time*
by Kathryn Lasky
0-689-71081-X
$5.99 US / $8.50
Canadian

❑ *Volcano*
by Patricia Lauber
0-689-71679-6
$8.99 US / $12.50
Canadian

❑ *The Golden Fleece*
by Padraic Colum
0-02-042260-1
$9.95 US / $13.50
Canadian

❑ *Justin Morgan
Had a Horse*
by Marguerite Henry
0-689-71534-X

❑ *Yolonda's Genius* by
Carol Fenner
0-689-81327-9
$5.50 US / $8.99
Canadian

All titles $4.99 US / $6.99 Canadian unless otherwise noted

Aladdin Paperbacks
Simon & Schuster Children's Publishing
www.SimonSaysKids.com